Catherine forced herself to enter her trailer.

Everything looked the way it should. Curtains stirred restlessly in the breeze. The old refrigerator was chugging as though getting ready to draw its last breath, but that was normal, too.

She looked the other way, at the bed. Something dark sat on the woven blanket. Some sort of animal. She wanted to run. Then, preposterously, Jericho leapt to her mind. That was exactly what he would expect her to do. She forced herself to cross to the bed instead.

It was a small owl. It had been shot. Her hand went to the bullet scar at her own side. The wounds were in the same place. There was a piece of cloth wrapped around the owl's beak. Catherine's mouth went dry. *Someone knew.*

It seemed incredible, impossible, but the message was unmistakable. *If you talk, Catherine, you will die.*

Dear Reader,

Many of you love the miniseries that we do in Intimate Moments, and this month we've got three of them for you. First up is *Duncan's Lady*, by Emilie Richards. Duncan is the first of "The Men of Midnight," and his story will leave you hungering to meet the other two. Another first is *A Man Without Love*, one of the "Wounded Warriors" created by Beverly Bird. Beverly was one of the line's debut authors, and we're thrilled to have her back. Then there's a goodbye, because in *A Man Like Smith*, bestselling author Marilyn Pappano has come to the end of her "Southern Knights" trilogy. But what a fantastic farewell—and, of course, Marilyn herself will be back soon!

You won't want to miss the month's other offerings, either. In *His Best Friend's Wife*, Catherine Palmer has created a level of emotion and tension that will have you turning pages as fast as you can. In *Dillon's Reckoning*, award-winner Dee Holmes sends her hero and heroine on the trail of a missing baby, while Cathryn Clare's *Gunslinger's Child* features one of romance's most popular storylines, the "secret baby" plot.

Enjoy them all—and come back next month for more top-notch romantic reading…only from Silhouette Intimate Moments.

Yours,
Leslie Wainger
Senior Editor and Editorial Coordinator

Please address questions and book requests to:
Silhouette Reader Service
U.S.: 3010 Walden Ave., P.O. Box 1325, Buffalo, NY 14269
Canadian: P.O. Box 609, Fort Erie, Ont. L2A 5X3

A MAN
WITHOUT
LOVE

BEVERLY
BIRD

Silhouette®

INTIMATE™MOMENTS®

Published by Silhouette Books

America's Publisher of Contemporary Romance

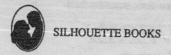

SILHOUETTE BOOKS

ISBN 0-373-07630-4

A MAN WITHOUT LOVE

Copyright © 1995 by Beverly Bird

This edition published by arrangement with Harlequin Enterprises B.V.

® and TM are trademarks of Harlequin Enterprises B.V., used under
license. Trademarks indicated with ® are registered in the United States
Patent and Trademark Office, the Canadian Trade Marks Office and in
other countries.

Printed in U.S.A.

Books by Beverly Bird

Silhouette Intimate Moments

Emeralds in the Dark #3
The Fires of Winter #23
Ride the Wind #139
A Solitary Man #172
*A Man Without Love #630

**Wounded Warriors

Silhouette Desire

The Best Reasons #190
Fool's Gold #209
All the Marbles #227
To Love A Stranger #411

BEVERLY BIRD

has lived in several places in the United States, but she is currently back where her roots began—on an island in New Jersey. Her time is devoted to her family and her writing. She is the author of numerous novels, both contemporary and historical romance.

To Mom and Dad—for the kid, the cat, the dog,
the smoke and the missing glassware

Chapter 1

Catherine Landano was scared. Her instincts told her to keep moving, yet she hesitated near a telephone kiosk in the airport and wondered if she dared call her father.

But what could she possibly say to him? *Hi, Paddy. I'm going to New Mexico to finish what I started. Oh, and by the way, Victor tried to kill me, so I'm calling myself Lanie McDaniel now.*

She choked back a wild laugh. Paddy would just say, *It's a good name, Cat, but this time we'll wait and see about your doctorin'.* Paddy Callahan was a simple, no-nonsense man. He had never understood why she had quit her last year of medical school to marry Victor Landano, and he wouldn't understand why she was running from him now.

A Callahan never ran. But then again, to her knowledge, a Callahan had never been shot at before either.

She backed away from the kiosk, combing her fingers self-consciously through her black hair. It was shoulder length now because Victor had always liked it long. It was a tangle of corkscrews too, because it had always been water-fall straight. She had paused in her flight across Connecticut to get a spiral perm and to cover its deep auburn with some dye, but hints of red glinted stubbornly through the black. She prayed it would be enough, because her eyes had proven too sensitive to tolerate the contact lenses that would have changed their vivid green to brown.

Victor would recognize her anyway, but she didn't think it would be Victor who came looking for her. He would send someone else, someone who had her picture, someone who had memorized her features.

She fought the urge to look around the crowded gateway to see if anyone suspicious was watching her and fumbled in her purse for her ticket instead. Moments later, a flat, mechanical voice intoned a call for her row. She made her way down the long boarding tube, her skin itching as though a million eyes were upon her. She squeezed her way into a window seat beside a young man with a round face, her spine feeling unnaturally stiff.

Finally the plane taxied and its nose lifted. Catherine felt a familiar sinking sensation in her tummy as they left the ground. She had never liked flying. Now she craved each breathless moment of ascension. It carried her closer and closer to safety.

She wished again that she could have called Paddy, and regret lingered like a bad toothache. But in the end, she knew it was best if no one knew where she had gone.

The plane reached full altitude. Though she would have thought it impossible, she put her head back against the seat and slept.

They hit turbulence somewhere over the Midwest. It jarred Catherine awake, and she was embarrassed to realize that her head had dropped onto the shoulder of the passenger beside her.

"Sorry," she murmured, shifting her weight to the other side of her seat.

"My pleasure," the man answered. "Sincerely."

Her gaze snapped to him. The round-faced young man was gone. Her heart chugged in alarm, then she realized that man must have deplaned in Atlanta. This one was not the least bit threatening. She wasn't sure what Victor's thugs might look like, but she was pretty sure it wouldn't be like that man. He was wholesome, in his mid-thirties, with friendly gray eyes and shaggy, vaguely brown hair.

"Twilight Zone." He laughed at her expression.

"Something like that." *If only he knew.*

"You slept right through the layover and dinner, too. I hope you don't mind, but I told them you didn't want anything."

Catherine shrugged. Food was not one of her priorities at the moment.

"So what takes you to Albuquerque?" the stranger persisted. "Do you live there, are you just visiting, or would you rather not get into a mindless conversation with someone you don't know?"

Catherine smiled in spite of herself, then she stiffened. She was going to have to learn to lie, she thought, then she realized it wasn't necessary, at least not yet. This was a question she could answer honestly.

"I've gotten an externship there."

"University Hospital, by any chance?"

She was startled. She hadn't thought he would even know what an externship was. Most people didn't. During their third year, medical students chose an elective so they could study something that particularly interested them. It was a good system for both the facilities that offered the posts and the students. The facilities got inexpensive manpower and the students got experience in their area of interest. Med-school rotation was a sampling of every field. It didn't necessarily provide in-depth experience in one's specialty.

Catherine cleared her throat and nodded. "I hope to be working with some of the staff there."

"Me, I hope." He extended his hand awkwardly in their cramped space. "I'm Richard Moss. I'm a doctor at University, as well."

He waited for her to introduce herself. Catherine opened her mouth, then snapped it shut again. Now it was time to lie, and her mind went blank.

"Lanie," she gasped finally. *Her grandmother's name.* "McDaniel." *Her mother's maiden name.* She had deliberately chosen ones that would be easy to remember, and she had almost forgotten them anyway.

Still, he was looking at her oddly. She rushed to get him to talk about himself. "What do you do there?"

"Epidemiology. Technically, I'm with the CDC, the Center for Disease Control in Atlanta. They've established a temporary post at University."

Her pulse quickened. "You're there because of the Mystery Disease?" Catherine had read about it in the papers and had immediately made a few phone calls. Four years ago, epidemiology had been her chosen specialty. The Mystery Disease provided probably the only externship in her field that would accept her.

Richard was nodding. "So we're colleagues, after a fashion."

Not quite, Catherine thought. "Actually, I'm at a clinic on the Indian reservation."

"The Navajo Res? The clinic outside Shiprock?"

She nodded cautiously.

"I'd heard they had a hard time filling that post."

They did. "I guess you heard wrong."

His eyes measured her. It irked her to realize that he probably thought her grades were below average, which they hadn't been. Or that her back was to the wall...which it was. Richard looked away first.

"So what do you think of our Mystery Disease?" he asked finally.

She didn't know enough about it yet, only what she had read in the papers. The disease had surfaced in the spring among young, healthy people in the Four Corners area of New Mexico. Most had died within hours. The newspaper articles had been written for laymen and sensationalism; what specific physiological data Catherine needed she was going to have to gather by the seat of her pants.

No time like the present, she decided.

"Another immunity virus?" she suggested, fishing.

"I don't think so. I don't think it's transmissible via human contact."

"What then?"

"The Navajo will tell you it's a wolfman."

"A *what?*"

"A witch. They think someone got ticked off and put a hex on his enemies. Personally, I'm more inclined to go with an environmental factor. Have you ever been out here before, to the Res?"

She shook her head.

"Then you're in for a shock. Poverty and squalor are rampant."

She was surprised. She'd done what homework she could since securing the post, since deciding she was going to have to disappear for a while. "I thought the Navajo were the wealthiest tribe in the country," she ventured.

Richard was full of information. "The tribal entity, maybe," he explained. "But not many of the individuals are. Truth to tell, I try to avoid working in the field as much as possible. The people live in trailers in the best areas, in hogans in the more traditional conclaves."

"Hogans," she repeated slowly.

"Mud houses."

"*Mud?*"

He had the grace to look abashed at his harsh analysis. "Well, logs and some sort of adobe. Thatched roofs, round, one room. Just like the last two hundred years never happened. The sheep and the goats and the chickens wander wherever they please, often right indoors. It's no wonder disease runs amok."

"Does it?" she asked curiously.

Again, he flushed. He had the kind of complexion that made it easy. "Alcoholism does. STDs are healthy. And now this."

"Alcoholism is a problem on a lot of reservations." She remembered that from med school.

"But only the Navajo seem to have respiratory bugs that kill them."

Catherine nodded slowly. Suddenly, she was tired of Richard Moss's cheerfully dismal opinions. He seemed so... disdainful of the people he had been sent to help. She

turned to the window and looked out into the pitch darkness of night at thirty-thousand feet.

"We're almost there," he persisted. "That should be
Santa Fe right over there. Albuquerque can't be far behind."

There was a very distant, very faint glow far off the right
wing. The rest of the ground was as black as the sky.

What had she let herself in for?

She reminded herself that she hadn't had much in the way
of choices. All of the best externships would go to this year's
graduating classes. Only the most desolate, desperate posts
were interested in a woman who had quit one elective away
from her degree, four years ago at that.

Besides, even the wind could get lost in all that darkness,
she thought. Surely she would be safe here.

Richard kept on, and Catherine dragged her attention
back to him. "We should be landing at about nine-thirty,"
he said. "Can I interest you in a drink or something to replace the dinner you missed? I can fill you in on the rest of
what you'll be facing out here."

She wasn't sure she wanted to tarnish her own impres-
sions with any more of his opinions, but she was very sure
she didn't want him to buy her anything. She shook her head
politely.

It was going to be a long time before she would trust anyone to buy her anything again. But that was okay because
this time she fully intended to take care of herself on her
own terms.

Catherine drove as far as Gallup despite the lateness of the
hour. She was curious to see the reservation in spite of—or
maybe because of—Richard Moss's warnings. She spent the
night in a cheap motel and was up at dawn to pull on jeans
and a T-shirt and strap sandals onto her feet. If what Richard had said was accurate, she wasn't going to be over-
dressed.

She stopped for take-out coffee at a diner, then she spread
her map and her contact's directions on the hood of the
rental car. The Indian Health Service hadn't been able to

offer much in the way of amenities, but they had supplied the car. She had not checked in at the car rental counter in the airport, but at the booth in the parking lot. The man there had a set of keys waiting for her, and the tired brown Ford had been parked away from the others, behind a chain-link fence, like an outcast.

There was no breeze. The sky was still and gray blue, the sun only just beginning to nudge gentle warmth into the day. In a moment, Catherine forgot the map and gazed out at the desert beyond the highway.

It was scrubby and endless. The spare grass grew in patches, red sand showing between the clumps. She sorted through her memory for details of what she had read about this country and decided the larger bushes were mesquite and greasewood. The smaller, pale green, spiky plants were probably rabbitbrush. She looked down at the map again, but something drew her gaze back.

It was the immensity, she realized. Even here, on the out-skirts of a city, there was such a feeling of space and sky. It should have made her feel vulnerable and exposed, but it didn't. She felt as small and insignificant as a needle in a haystack.

She swiped the map up again and got into the car. She left the interstate and turned north on U.S. Route 666, following her contact's directions. Then some clouds started coming in, appearing first over a butte that jutted up starkly from the horizon. She had read that in this region they often hovered over the peaks, then dissipated without moving on. She kept an eye on them, curious, and they moved.

So much for that theory.

They were blue black and ominous looking, and just before she reached the road where she was supposed to turn off they opened up on her. The downpour was sudden and without apology. Rain drummed against metal and sheeted down the windows, and the wipers groaned.

The scar at her side began to put up a mild ache, as though even from this distance Victor was mocking her efforts. Catherine pulled over, pressed a hand against it, and looked at the map again. She thought she should have kept going straight to get to Shiprock, but Shadow—her contact—had told her to come this way.

She took her foot off the brake and coasted forward again. She went only a couple of miles before the asphalt gave way and the car lurched down onto a slick unpaved road. The back end slewed dangerously, and she fought with the wheel.

No, this couldn't be right.

She hit the brakes again. Her scar throbbed badly now, responding to the dampness. She bit her lip and decided to go on another four or five miles. If she didn't find some sort of town by then, she would turn around and go the other way.

She put her foot to the gas again. The wheels beneath her spun and whined.

"No. Oh, no."

She pushed against the door and scrambled out into the downpour. The tires of the Ford were mired inches deep in red mud.

What now? Push it? Impossible. Even if she somehow possessed the strength to do it, there was no one to guide the wheel and nowhere to go.

The rain kept coming down hard. Catherine was beginning to feel overwhelmed.

Suddenly the drone of another engine came to her. She whipped around to look up the road. A four-wheel-drive of unknown vintage bucked through the mud coming toward her. She waved it down, pushing away the sudden, absurd thought that Victor had followed her, that he had somehow lured her down this isolated road to finish the job.

The vehicle—a Land Rover, she saw when it got closer—slid to a stop. A man got out and came toward her, seemingly impervious to the rain.

"Help you?" he asked laconically.

"Uh...yes. I'm looking for Shadow Bedonie. Do you know her?" What were the odds of that? she wondered. She felt foolish, but to her amazement he nodded.

She waited expectantly for him to go on, but he only studied her, then her car, with a look of critical impatience.

"Can you tell me how to find her?" she asked.

"Not in that."

"How, then?"

"Guess you'd have to slog through the mud on foot."

Frustration made her head pound. "Can't you please give me a straight answer?"

"Thought I had."

He stepped back toward the Land Rover.

"Wait!"

He didn't look back at her, but he stopped. Her frustration nose-dived, trembling on the edge of panic. If he left her here, what would she do? She looked around at the barren country through the rain. It could be days before another vehicle came along.

"Please," she tried again. "I have to find Shadow Bedonie."

Her voice sounded strangled and pitiful, even to her own ears. The man seemed to consider her desperation, then he turned back to her and waved a hand toward his truck.

"I can give you a lift across the wash, but your car's not going anywhere until tomorrow."

She couldn't imagine why she would want to go over a wash, or even what one was, but she opted to trust him. She wasn't sure she had a choice.

Catherine pushed through the mud to the Rover. It took her two hard tries to get into the passenger seat while he stood behind her and watched. Her sandals slipped wetly off the panel and she dropped down into the muck again, red ooze welling up over her ankles.

"This going to take long?"

She heaved herself up one more time. *Sarcastic, arrogant bastard,* she thought. "Thank you," she snapped. Sarcastic or not, he was her only hope at the moment.

He went around and got behind the wheel, turning it. The Rover careened neatly around. He had not been long on conversation in the rain; now his silence seemed deafening. She looked across at him out of the corner of her eye.

In the downpour, he had seemed of indiscriminate age. Now she put him at about thirty-five. Sun wrinkles touched the corners of his eyes. His hair was long enough to cover his collar, curly and black as midnight water. Navajo? she wondered. One of her would-be patients? He needed a shave and he smelled of smoke and the wet leather of a comfortable, well-worn jacket. But other than that he was... attractive.

His eyes—what she could see of them—were dark, as well. He would have been handsome, if his jaw weren't so hard. Yet his mouth looked soft enough to nuzzle babies.

She ran her eyes down his body and put him at about six foot two. He was solid, yet he gave the impression of being lightning fast.

And she was out of her mind.

"You said it would be possible for me to move my car tomorrow?" She wasn't sure why she was so concerned. It wasn't hers. Still, it belonged to someone, and she felt responsible for it.

"The sun'll bake the mud hard by then."

"Is this storm supposed to clear?" She leaned forward to look up at the sky.

"Always does, way too soon."

"Will the car be safe if I just leave it?"

"Probably won't be just where you left it."

"I beg your pardon?"

The Rover lurched to a stop in front of one of the mud houses Richard had mentioned. She stared at it, then wrenched her gaze back to the stranger.

"You're here," he said.

"This can't be Shiprock. It isn't a...a town."

"Not hardly." When she continued to looked at him blankly, he added, "Shadow Bedonie lives here. That's who you said you were looking for."

Catherine twisted to look back down the road they had traveled. "What about my car?" she demanded.

"It's late in the season. It shouldn't go far."

Suddenly she gaped at him. "You're doing this on purpose," she realized. "You're giving me a runaround. Why?"

He glanced down at her muddy sandals as though they somehow said it all. "I brought you up here to help out Shadow."

"And any friend of hers is a friend of yours?" she snapped.

"Not really."

She fell silent, stupefied at his antagonism.

She looked back at the hogan and pushed open the truck door. As soon as her feet sank into the mud again, she cried out in alarm and pressed back. Just to the right of the dwelling, the desert dipped into a chiseled culvert. A rush of water came along it, foaming and strong.

A moment later it had surged past, leaving a roiling stream in its wake. Catherine's jaw dropped. Now she understood. She had parked in the same sort of depression, only it had been deeper, wider—a wash. The one she had left her car in would carry a lot more water.

She gasped, looking back at him. He almost smiled, but it was anything but a pleasant expression.

"Too late now," he drawled.

Chapter 2

Catherine wanted badly to choke him. Because she didn't trust herself not to, she turned away from him abruptly and went to the hogan.

She had nearly reached the dwelling when a flock of sheep and a scattering of goats came bleating and trotting around the far side. She dodged through them determinedly, but the sound of the Rover door opening behind her finally made her steps falter.

She knew beyond a doubt that he wasn't escorting her to the door out of courtesy. And she had been right—he was fast. Almost before she spun about to look back, he was beside her.

"You got a hell of a dander up for a city girl who doesn't even know where she's going."

The rain had flattened her hair against her forehead. Catherine pushed it back. "I'm trying to find Shadow."

"She's not here."

"What?" Why had he brought her here, then? Dear God, was he working for Victor?

Her terror must have shown on her face. He studied it for a moment, narrow eyed, then he waved a hand at a corral behind the hogan.

"Her horse is gone."

His tone was like a slap in the face—as though any imbecile would know that Shadow Bedonie owned a horse. And suddenly her dander *was* up—but it had nothing to do with living in Boston these past several years. She came by it more honestly than that. She was a Callahan. Before Victor had found it necessary to polish her up to suit his monied image, she had been born the daughter of Irish immigrants.

He turned away from her and looked out at the desert. She followed his gaze. A woman cantered toward them on horseback, as impervious to the downpour as the man was.

"Hey," he said when she reached them.

Catherine scowled. In that one syllable, his voice held more warmth than in any of the sentences he had spoken to her. Apparently, he didn't hate everybody.

The woman swung her leg over the horse and dropped to the ground. Her face split into a grin. "Jericho! You stay away too long."

To Catherine's amazement, the woman hugged him hard and he allowed it. Her hair was pulled back in a severe ponytail and it glistened wetly, like a black waterfall to her waist. Her features were perfect enough that they didn't need anything to flatter or soften them.

"Zuni," he said. His cryptic response obviously meant something to her, because the woman nodded. "The pottery wasn't ours."

"That's a relief." Finally, her gaze moved to Catherine. She looked confused for a moment, then she smiled again. "You must be Lanie McDaniel. I'm Shadow Bedonie."

Before Catherine could take her outstretched hand, Jericho interjected. "I found her down in Chaco Wash. Figured she was one of yours."

His voice had hardened abruptly. His animosity was truly beginning to sting, though Catherine couldn't fathom why it should. With any luck, this reservation was so big she would never see him again. He didn't matter. Victor mattered—Victor and his gun and his friends. Standing here in this downpour mattered; she was beginning to shiver. But a cold, handsome stranger was the least of her worries.

Yet she heard herself demand, "Why?"

His dark gaze passed over her in a dismissive look. He didn't answer.

"One of her *what?*" she persisted.

"Broken doves."

The woman laughed nervously and intervened. "Jericho thinks I have a problem taking in lost souls and championing lost causes. Mostly I just try to preserve our heritage and occasionally I take in stray animals." She looked at him again. "Lanie has two feet, not four, and she's with the health service. Jack Keller asked me as a favor to help her get settled and I said I didn't mind."

Jericho lifted one shoulder. "I rest my case. It's not even your job. You work for the museum, not for Jack."

"It's something I care about. Ellen and Kolkline need help."

"Not this bad."

He turned away. Before Catherine knew she was going to, she stepped in front of him to block his way.

"Have I done something to offend you?"

"*Offend?*" He repeated the word in a mocking tone, and she flushed.

"Couldn't you have just told me my car was going to get washed away?"

"What would you have done about it?" His gaze said she clearly wasn't capable of much.

"You could have helped me push it to higher ground!"

He looked at her sandals again and she fought the urge to curl her toes. His eyes were so hard, so black and unfathomable, yet they burned.

"Thought I'd let you see for yourself."

"See *what?*" Then, suddenly, she figured it out.

He didn't think she belonged here. Were the Navajo that clannish, that defensive against outsiders? She looked back at Shadow with her clear eyes and her easy smile. No, she decided. With this man, it was something personal.

She took an instinctive step away from him. He strode past her without another look, his broad-shouldered silhouette becoming more and more obscured by the rain.

"Thanks for going to Zuni!" Shadow called after him as he reached the Rover.

Jericho didn't answer.

The hogan was rustic and cozy in a rough-hewn way. Catherine looked about and decided Richard's description had been decidedly uncharitable.

It wasn't actually round, but six sided, built of logs that drew in above the walls so that a sort of beehive roof was achieved. The only mud in evidence was an adobelike substance packed between the logs. Though the rain continued to drum down outside, the dwelling was dry and comfortable. It was complete without being cluttered. A single bed was pressed against one side, covered with a beautifully woven Native blanket. A wood-burning stove sat in the center and teal blue wildflowers dripped from planters hung about the walls.

Catherine found herself wishing that Shadow would invite her to sit by the stove to rest awhile and warm herself. She knew somehow that she *would* be warm here, inside and out.

Instead, the woman handed her a towel to dry off. She followed Catherine's gaze as she looked back at the open doorway.

"The Holy People—our gods—prescribe that all openings should face east to let in the sun. Spiritually, it's a place of birth and beginnings. There's the added advantage that almost all of our storms come down from the Chuska Mountains, and they're west of here. So with the doors facing east, we stay relatively dry."

"What about at night?" Catherine asked. "Don't animals come wandering in?" She was remembering what Richard had said about the sheep and the goats.

Shadow shrugged. "Not usually."

"Doesn't it get cold in the winter?"

"The stove throws off a lot of heat, and the place isn't that big. It's easy to warm it. In the worst weather, I hang a blanket over the door." She paused. "I'm not as traditional as some of our people, but I was raised in a place like this and old habits are hard to break."

"And Jericho?" Catherine heard herself ask. "Is he traditional?" *Who cared?*

She did. Catherine could not figure why, but she was curious.

Shadow shrugged again. "It depends on the issue. In some ways yes, in others, no." Suddenly, her expression turned apologetic. "I know my brother seems...rude sometimes. He's a private person, slow to take to strangers."

"Your *brother?*"

Shadow laughed.

"You're as different as night and day," Catherine blurted. "You're warm. He's so brusque and remote."

As soon as the words were out, she was appalled at herself. For someone who desperately needed to hide here, she was not doing much to endear herself. This was just the sort of impulsiveness that Victor had always tried to drum out of her.

But Shadow was unoffended. "It seems that way until you get to know him," she allowed. She took the towel back. "Come on, I'll show you the clinic and where you'll be staying."

Jericho shifted the Rover into gear, but he didn't let up the clutch. He waited, watching until his sister and the Anglo woman came back out of the hogan and headed around to Shadow's truck in the rear.

There was something about this stranger, something that irritated the hell out of him even as it tried to wrap hot, treacherous fingers about his gut.

Maybe it was the hair, he thought, that cascade of wild black curls that beckoned for a man's fingers to tangle in them. Or the eyes—she had the wide, wary eyes of a cat looking out from the mountain at night. She had legs up to her neck, but although she was tall there was nothing big about her. She was fine boned and slender with ivory skin and classic Anglo features.

And one or two spattered freckles on the bridge of her nose.

She was a wounded bird, all right. He would have known it even if she hadn't asked for Shadow. It was there in the desperate pitch of her voice. She was shaky, frightened of her own shadow... but she did have a temper.

Once or twice, he had thought she would come at him like a little, wet terrier, her teeth bared.

He grinned and almost choked when he realized he was doing it. He wished like hell his sister would stick to dogs and mules and questionable archaeological finds.

It didn't matter. This dove was not only vulnerable, but he smelled a faint aura of money and culture on her, as well. Jericho knew from firsthand experience that this unforgiving Navajo land would quickly send such a woman packing. She'd run home, muddy sandals, big green eyes and all. And if she didn't run, she would crumble, just as Anelle had done.

The pain of that memory was old but it made him flinch anyway. He took his foot off the clutch abruptly and the Land Rover shot forward.

No, he thought, Lanie McDaniel wouldn't be underfoot for long.

Catherine's eyes widened and she gave a little gasp as the truck bounced wildly. Her head nearly hit the roof, and she wrapped her fingers tightly around the arm rest.

Shadow spared her a quick glance as she swung away from the road and headed out onto open desert. "You okay? Just hang on and lock the door."

Catherine pried her fingers loose to do as she was told.

"This reservation is huge. You'll find it's a lot easier to travel this way, as the crow flies. Otherwise, you'll be driving all day to get from Point *A* to Point *B*." She paused to wrestle with the wheel as they hit a particularly rough stretch, then she added, "Also, they excavated the top layer of soil to make the roads. Without that, all you've got is mud when it rains. Only a few of the main arteries are paved."

Catherine noticed that the unmolested desert did indeed give better traction. The tires of the four-by-four truck were able to grip rather than slide.

Suddenly their way was blocked by a herd of sheep, too big to be driven around. Shadow slowed down to nose the vehicle gently through the animals.

"Don't they wander away?" Catherine asked. Richard had been right. She saw no fences to contain them.

Shadow let go of the wheel long enough to point to a large cluster of brush shelters farther out on the horizon. "They'll roam, but their owners will follow them. That's a sheep camp. This would be the . . ." she paused to think " . . . probably the Yellowhorse outfit."

"What's an outfit?"

"Sort of a group of extended relatives, smaller than a clan but larger than a family. Clans are a bloodline sort of thing—we're all born to the ones our mothers belong to. That makes for hundreds upon hundreds of clan members, and we don't even know most of who we're related to that way. Outfits are made up more of second and third cousins, aunts and uncles by marriage, that sort of thing. There's usually a matriarch holding it all together. These Yellowhorses are a traditional people. Most everybody living out here, south of Beautiful Mountain, is traditional."

They climbed out of a wide culvert, and suddenly the mountain itself lunged up from the horizon like a mighty sentinel standing guard over the craggy land. Catherine's head began to spin. Between the camp and the wandering sheep, it *did* feel as though the last two hundred years had never happened.

Women moved around the brush shelters in long tiered skirts of vibrant hues—mostly royal blue. Catherine caught sight of a man riding a horse at a distant edge of the flock. He wore a bandanna across his forehead. His hair was long and sleek and black, and his muscled chest was bare. She wouldn't have been surprised to see a quiver of arrows hanging over his shoulder.

A quick laugh sneaked up on her. Victor would never think to look for her here. It was as far removed from his world of dark, crowded restaurants as the moon was from the sun.

Shadow looked at her curiously.

"It's wonderful," Catherine said, and realized she meant it.

They approached the mountain and came to another road. This time Shadow turned onto it. The tires threw mud up behind them and wings of water spewed up on either side of them as they passed through places that were awash. Finally, Shadow turned onto a smaller side road and two trailers appeared on the desert before them.

Catherine jolted. They looked incongruous—a flash of modern America in the midst of stark, endless land. Well, maybe not *modern*, she allowed. The first trailer was gleaming silver metal, but the one that sat behind it was painted a white color that had long since gone to gray brown.

A rust-ravaged Toyota sat nearby between a huge metal barrel and a growling generator in the parking area, a space of raw sand where the grass and the brush had been stripped away. Shadow stopped behind the Toyota. They got out and slogged through the mud toward the silver trailer.

"You don't have to worry about water here," Shadow told her, waving at the barrel. "That tank is filled twice a week by a truck that comes down from Shiprock."

"Where's that?" Catherine had gotten the distinct impression from the health service that the clinic was *in* Shiprock.

Apparently not so. Shadow motioned at the road. "A hundred miles or so."

They went up three wooden steps into the clinic. Catherine's jaw dropped. Given the sheep camp and Shadow's quaint hogan, she had expected primitive conditions. The place *was* small, but most of the equipment looked brand-new, scarcely used. Everything was immaculate.

A nurse came out of one of the back rooms at the sound of their footsteps. At first impression she was stunningly beautiful, but as soon as she saw them her face hardened. Her eyes turned hostile as they moved from Shadow to her, then back again.

Catherine felt her heart sink fast. Apparently the nurse didn't want her here any more than Jericho did. She'd been on the reservation less than a day, and already she'd made two enemies through no legitimate reason she could figure.

"Lanie McDaniel, Ellen Lonetree." Shadow made the introductions brightly, but Ellen did not respond.

The silence lengthened. Shadow cleared her throat. "Well," she said finally. "Dr. Kolkline isn't around?"

Ellen's face finally changed expression. She looked incredulous. "Are you kidding?"

"I'm supposed to be working under him," Catherine ventured.

Her contribution earned a glare from Ellen, and the nurse turned abruptly and went back to the other room. Shadow shrugged apologetically.

"Well, you'll meet him sooner or later. He spends most of his time at University Hospital." She hesitated, then apparently decided to be frank. In many ways, she reminded Catherine of her father, preferring honesty, however brutal, to polite evasions that would only make things messy later on.

"Abe Kolkline is sort of a society dropout," she explained. "He shows up occasionally, but not many of our people feel a need for his Anglo medicine. The Mystery Disease has changed things some, but there still isn't much of a demand for his services. He usually hangs out in Albuquerque unless Ellen calls him to come here."

Something in Shadow's eyes told her Ellen didn't do that often.

Shadow motioned to the door and Catherine followed her outside again. "She's a respected healer in her own right," Shadow went on as they crossed to the other trailer. "She's very good with herbal cures, with more traditional, holistic approaches. But she went to nursing school because it was the only way the health service would allow her to officially work the clinic. I guess she has reason to resent Anglo medicine. The doctors they've sent us either don't care or don't understand the People's spiritual needs, and they're very intertwined with their health according to Navajo doctrine. As for the externs..." She shrugged as she worked a key in the trailer door. "Well, let's just say they put in their time and they're all the service can afford by way of assistants. They leave again as soon as their elective is up, and some of them don't even stay that long."

They stepped inside, and Shadow turned to her abruptly. Suddenly, her black eyes were as hot as her brother's. "I hope you're not like that," she said bluntly. "We need someone to stay, someone good who cares, even if many of us don't realize it."

Catherine felt herself flush. For the first time she found it difficult to meet Shadow's gaze. Once Victor was behind bars, if he was convicted only of her attempted murder and not of what she had overheard, if neither the FBI nor Victor's friends found her, then eventually she would be able to return to Boston.

She swallowed dryly. That was a whole lot of ifs.

"I'm not sure your brother shares your opinion," she answered, then she flinched inwardly. She reminded herself again that Jericho Bedonie was the least of her problems.

To put him out of her mind, she looked around the trailer. It was bleak and nearly empty, a single room with a bathroom tacked on at one side. A narrow bunk sat at that end and there was an old Formica table at the other. The table leaned precariously on a bent leg.

"It's not much, is it?" Shadow sighed.

No, but it was safe. Catherine smiled, and Shadow seemed to know that her response wasn't forced this time.

The woman rushed on in her dauntless, efficient way. "I've got to go into Shiprock this afternoon. While I'm there, I'll find someone to go look at your car."

Suddenly, Catherine grimaced. "My suitcases are still in the trunk."

Shadow chewed her lip. "Can you get by overnight? I think there's toothpaste and stuff in the bathroom." She went to look and came back, nodding. "It's all still there."

Then her gaze slid down to Catherine's feet, as well. Catherine was beginning to wish she had never heard of sandals.

"Did you bring boots?"

"I don't even own a pair."

"Well, you'll need them. What size do you wear? Seven? I can get them in Shiprock. Is there anything else you think you'll want?"

Catherine looked about the trailer again and almost laughed at the question. It was, for all intents and purposes, empty.

"A coffeepot?" she asked.

Shadow gave a sly grin. "If you'll stay long enough to drink it, I'll even bring you a month's worth of coffee."

"If I ever get my suitcases back, I've *got* coffee." Her favorite was french-vanilla roast, and she hadn't thought much of her chances of finding it on an Indian reservation. "But I'll promise anyway," she added. It would take at least that long for the problem with Victor to be resolved. And if she didn't finish the externship she didn't have a career, didn't have any way to pick up the pieces of her shattered life and go on.

Shadow turned for the door, then looked back at her one last time. "Give it a solid chance, Lanie. That's all I ask."

Catherine flinched again at the sound of the assumed name. Suddenly something rebelled in her to tell Shadow the truth, to be as forthright as she had been. It would be such a relief to share the burden, but Catherine didn't dare. One man with the health service knew who she really was, and she had only told him to get her credentials straight. Victor was smart. That was all she could risk.

She finally nodded noncommittally and Shadow darted out the door. Catherine moved to the window to watch her go. The trailer was starkly silent without her chatter.

"Get a grip, Lanie," she said aloud. "It could be worse. You could be dead."

Instead, she was going to have to relearn epidemiology by the seat of her pants, evidently without even a doctor to guide her. She was going to have to do it with a nurse who apparently hated everything she stood for, and somewhere in this empty land there was a tall, hard man with simmering eyes who didn't think too much of her, either.

But at least she had a job and a solid roof over her head.

She heard a plopping sound and her brows knit. She went to the bed and found a puddle beside it. She groaned and looked up.

Scratch the part about the roof. It was leaking.

She dropped down onto the bed, and one of its slats gave way beneath her with a splintering sound. She slid down onto the floor, into the puddle, and laughed for the first time in weeks, harder and harder until she cried.

Jericho watched his sister's truck turn north toward Shiprock and he fell in behind her. When she finally stopped at the hardware store, he followed her inside.

He caught up with her at a display of coffeepots and stood next to her silently. She ignored him. She was angry. He was thirty-five years old, and his little sister's disapproval still brought him to his knees.

"So what'd she think of her new home sweet home?" he asked finally.

Shadow raised a brow in direct imitation of one of his more favored expressions. "You followed me all this way to ask me that? Awfully curious, aren't you?"

Jericho shrugged.

"She *is* your type, isn't she? Soulful eyes and all those legs."

It had been the wrong thing to say. His face closed down, and for a minute she thought he would leave again without another word. But he hesitated long enough for her to judiciously change the subject.

"Who took everything out of the trailer?" she asked. "You or Ellen?"

Both of his brows shot up. "Good idea, but you had me busy down in Zuni."

"That lopsided table used to be in Uncle Ernie's cabin up on the mountain," she said accusingly.

"Could be, but I haven't been near the place in months."

"Honest?"

She watched him closely. He gave a genuine grin and it transformed his hard face.

"Honest, but I wish I had thought of it."

Shadow took a coffeepot and carried it to the cash register. "I'm going to do everything I can to make her feel welcome," she warned him.

"Never doubted it."

The total price with tax came to a little over twenty dollars. Shadow had eighteen. She looked at him pointedly, and Jericho fished three more bills out of his pocket.

"I give her two weeks," he said, "even with the coffeepot."

"She's promised me a month."

"City girls don't have the grit to keep promises."

Shadow sighed. "Oh, Jericho, they're not all the same. They're not all like Anelle. That's like saying all sheep are white."

"Most of them are."

He carried the box to her truck for her. "Still mad at me?"

"I won't be if you talk to Ellen and ask her to back off."

"Won't do any good if little Lanie can't hold her own anyway. Ellen's a kitten on a Res full of tigers. The isolation alone'll get her."

Shadow sighed. She couldn't argue that.

She hoisted herself behind the wheel. "Tell you what. If she doesn't make the month, I'll give you your three bucks back."

"You're on."

"Hope you don't need the money."

She said it with more conviction than she felt. She liked Lanie McDaniel, she really did, but something in Lanie's eyes spoke of secrets and that troubled her.

Chapter 3

A coyote greeted Catherine's first dawn on the reservation with a mournful song.

The sound insinuated itself into her dreams, turning them into familiar nightmares. She jerked awake, her throat closing over a scream. Then the bed creaked beneath her and she remembered where she was.

She had propped the bed back up with some cinder blocks she had found outside. Now she reached down and ran her fingers over them as though to reassure herself.

"No, Toto," she murmured, "we're definitely not in Kansas anymore."

She padded barefoot to the window, hugging herself. The sun wasn't quite up yet. A sliver of moon still showed on the horizon. Other than the deserted clinic trailer, no other sign of civilization was in sight.

Catherine shuddered. She had never been this alone in her life.

She squared her shoulders. If she went next door now, she thought, then she should be able to get something done before Ellen arrived to scatter her concentration. She went back to the bathroom to get the clothes she had washed by hand the night before. She pulled her jeans off the shower rod and groaned. They were still damp.

She had noticed a blow dryer beneath the sink. She plugged it in and aimed the nozzle at the denim. By the time they were dry, the sun was up.

She stepped outside to find her sandals where she had left them on the tiny porch. She knocked the crust off them and looked around again. It was a glorious sun-swept day. The sky was the most cloudless blue she had ever seen. The mud had already baked dry in air that was thin and arid again.

She hurried back to the bathroom to brush her teeth, then she stiffened at the sound of a car door slamming outside. She went to the window again.

Not a car. A Land Rover. *Jericho.* Her stomach clenched. What was *he* doing here?

He had probably brought a shotgun to drive her off, she thought bitterly. She pulled the door open and hurried across to the clinic. It didn't matter. She had been shot at before by the best of them and she was up to anything this man might throw at her.

She skidded to a stop in the open clinic doorway. It wasn't just Jericho, she realized. They were *both* here, he and Ellen, their dark heads close together as they leaned over something on the desk. His leather jacket was tossed over the chair. He wore a blue chambray shirt, his hair hiding the collar, and his jeans were just tight enough to make her swallow dryly.

"Hello," she ventured.

Jericho looked up. His gaze swept over her without emotion, then he turned back to whatever they were looking at. Neither he nor the nurse said a word.

The smell of coffee hit Catherine hard. She finally moved inside, looking for it. She thought she felt his gaze at the back of her neck, hot and probing, but when she turned around he was still looking down at the desk.

"May I have some coffee?" she asked with forced politeness.

It didn't appear as though he would answer, but then he shrugged. "Help yourself."

"I would, except I can't find it."

He lifted a thermos that had been sitting on the desk, showing it to her without looking at her. One of them had brought it, then. It occurred to her that she would rather die of caffeine withdrawal than drink it, but Paddy had always said that pride went before a fall. Catherine crossed and took the Thermos from him.

"Thank you," she said deliberately.

"There are some paper cups beneath the sink. No cream or sugar."

"I'll take it black." She got a cup and sipped as she tried to see what they were looking at. The coffee shot through her sinuses and made her sputter.

Jericho glanced at her, less curious than satisfied. "A little too much for you? Don't they make it that strong back in the city?"

She gritted her teeth. "It's fine."

She forced some more down to prove it, then she looked over his shoulder. "What's that?"

Ellen promptly pulled the paper off the desk. But Catherine had seen what it was—a map, with little red dots sprinkled over it. Pinpoints of the Mystery Disease outbreak? If so, why in the world wouldn't they want her to see it? Were they so determined to exclude her that they would keep data from someone who could possibly help them? And what was Jericho's role in the investigation?

He was watching her with narrow eyes. She licked her lips. "You know, this isn't my first rotation in epidemiology," she told him. "I managed to get two others in med school."

"Good for you."

"No, good for *you,*" she snapped. "It sounds to me like you need all the expertise you can get in solving this thing."

"We have the expertise of every medicine man on the Res," Ellen said.

And what if it's not Indian hocus-pocus? Catherine caught herself before she blurted it out. She didn't need to antagonize them more than she already was just by being here.

"What if its root is more organic than mystical?" she asked carefully instead. Jericho's gaze grew sharp enough to cut her anyway. "I mean—"

"Oh, don't worry, Cat Eyes, I get your drift."

Cat Eyes? She flinched. This was getting personal. But then, she supposed it had been from the start.

She took a deep breath, pressing on doggedly. "There's a chance that—"

"You're way out of your element here. There's a chance that maybe you shouldn't tangle with things you don't understand, with things that are tougher and meaner than you are."

Something shivered oddly inside her. She got the sudden impression that he wasn't talking about the disease.

Her throat went unaccountably dry, but she was saved from a response when Shadow appeared in the doorway.

"Now, now, children," she scolded. "Be nice."

"And things were just getting interesting," Ellen mused.

Shadow shot her a warning look. The one she sent her brother was even more scathing. "I'd hoped you'd at least play fair."

"You know what they say about love and war." He took the paper from Ellen, folded it up, and slid it into his shirt pocket.

"Yeah," Shadow said, watching him with a knowing look. "So I do."

"Watch your tongue."

"I've got some stuff for Lanie in the back of my truck. Will you help me with it?"

Catherine fully expected him to refuse. Her jaw dropped when he nodded curtly.

They went outside. Catherine hesitated a moment, then she hurried after them. She leaned against the side of the truck to peer into its bed and her eyes widened.

Not only had Shadow brought her suitcases, but there was a threadbare sofa, as well, a portable television and an old compact refrigerator. She pried the top off a box and found boots, curtains, a beautiful blanket like the one on Shadow's bed and a brand new coffeepot.

"Going a little overboard, aren't you?" Jericho asked.

"All's fair," Shadow drawled.

Catherine was moved beyond reason. It was such a simple gesture, and not entirely altruistic—she knew Shadow wanted her to settle in and stay. But she had been struggling on her own for a good many weeks now and it was the nicest thing anyone had done for her in a very long time.

"Thank you," she said.

"Jericho will set everything up for you. Just show him where you want it."

His expression turned incredulous. "You're pushing your luck."

"That's okay," Catherine said quickly. "If you could just dump the heavy stuff inside the door, I can take care of everything else and straighten it out tonight."

She reached for one of her suitcases. As soon as she pulled it over the side an odor hit her, musty and fetid. She wrinkled her nose.

"That's the bad news." Shadow sighed. "Your car got tumbled."

"Tumbled?" Catherine pulled the other one out. It smelled the same way.

"The water rolled it over. Everything inside got soaked and it's not going anywhere for a while. The good news is that I know a boy from up near Shiprock—Eddie Begay— who works in the garage there and he takes some jobs on the side. He said he'd go out to the wash and see if he can get it running again for you."

"What'd you use to twist Eddie's arm?" Jericho asked dryly.

Shadow gave him a withering look. "Not every arm needs to be twisted."

"You couldn't prove it by me."

Catherine hadn't been able to catch herself this time before the words came blurting out. Two pairs of startled black eyes came around to her. Shadow laughed, and for a wild moment Catherine actually thought Jericho would do so, as well. Something moved at the corner of his mouth as he watched her, then he yanked his gaze away and moved toward the house trailer.

"Bring the truck over here," he snapped. "I'm not carrying that sofa on my back."

Shadow made a move toward the cab.

"The car's not even mine," Catherine objected.

"No, but you'll need it to get around while you're here. Your rotation is what—six weeks?"

Catherine nodded.

"Long enough that being stuck in these trailers will make you crazy. You'll need to get into the city now and again to keep sane."

She probably would, but she didn't dare. She had the sure sense that if she went where people were, Victor would find her.

"In the meantime," Shadow went on, "if you want to go through your suitcases, I'll take whatever needs to be washed up to the Laundromat in Shiprock."

Catherine's gaze snapped back to her. Shadow was watching her curiously and something uncomfortable moved in her stomach again. "I'm sorry—what?"

"Your soggy clothes," Shadow repeated patiently, "need to go to the Laundromat."

"Oh—right."

She kneeled and opened her suitcases. She was particularly pleased to see that her coffee had come through unscathed in its metal tin.

The bite of Jericho's brew still lingered on her tongue.

She wanted to take an inventory of the equipment and the supplies. From everything Shadow had said, she wasn't hopeful that Dr. Kolkline had kept up on the task and she doubted if Ellen cared enough about the entrapments of Anglo medicine to keep stock. She was finally able to get to it early in the afternoon when Jericho left to take Ellen into Albuquerque. Apparently, the old Toyota was hers and it didn't run too reliably.

Catherine took a deep, steadying breath when they left. Finally, she could move about without his dark, measuring eyes watching her. She couldn't actually catch him looking her way, but his gaze had weight and it rattled her.

She pulled the desk chair over to the shelves and set to work. But before an hour had passed, a dull, throbbing headache started behind her eyes. She didn't know what half this stuff was.

She recognized the equipment and all of the drugs. But next to the suture material was a little unlabeled box of some powdery substance. In between some clamps and scalpels was a jar of dried weeds. She climbed up onto the chair to explore the top shelf. *Nothing* up there was identifiable.

She opened a small cardboard box and gasped, pulling her hand back. It was full of dead birds. "Yuck."

"I warned you against things you don't understand."

She wheeled around and nearly fell off the chair. Its seat swiveled dangerously. Jericho had come back. She looked past his shoulder. At least he was alone this time.

"Why do you keep coming here?" she demanded. "Shadow didn't say you worked for the service."

"I don't. Get down from there before you break your neck."

"I'm fine."

"Then get down before you stick your nose into something that's none of your damned business."

That made her all the more determined to stay put. She forced herself to pick up the box of birds again. "What are these doing here?"

"For Enemy Ways when the soul has been stricken by a wolfman's spell. Or Ghost Ways when the spirit has been tainted by contact with the dead."

The dead? In spite of her best intentions, a cold shiver puckered her skin into gooseflesh.

"That's not . . . medicine," she managed.

"It is here."

His hand flashed out like a snake. Before she could even react, he snatched the box away from her. He grabbed her around the waist with his other arm, lifting her bodily off the chair.

Fear made her heart cram its way into her throat. For a wild moment she was sure he would hurt her, but he only shoved at the chair with his boot.

It careened toward the desk on its little wheels and cracked solidly into it. Catherine's heart slid back to where it belonged, but then it began beating wildly. He did not let her go.

She slid down his body until she was standing once more. Her first impression yesterday had been that he was cold and remote, but now she was aware of the heat of him. It touched her as palpably as the hard strength of his hand at her back, as the solid fit of his body against hers. It was angry and dangerous, passionate and strong—all of those things, and no single one of them.

The fluorescent light over their heads turned his hair blue black; she found herself staring at a curl that brushed against his neck. More dark hair showed at the open collar of his shirt. He smelled of wood smoke and the outdoors, of something indescribably male.

Her breath fell short. She took a quick, choppy step away, putting space between them.

"You didn't answer my question," she challenged.

"What else do you want to know?" His voice was too quiet, as simmering as his eyes suddenly were. Had he spoken provocatively on purpose, or was that just his way?

"What are you doing here?" she breathed.

"People can find me here."

"Oh, of course."

He raised a brow at her sarcasm, even as he tried to keep his expression neutral. He didn't want to wonder about her, but she made it impossible not to. He didn't want to get lost in those wide, green eyes, and they were luring him in. He had known women with those fine, classic features before and he had long since curbed his taste for them. Yes, she had great legs, but so did hundreds of women who could embrace this land—his land—and thrive on it. He was damned if he was going to get sucked in by her type again.

But even as he girded himself against it, Catherine shivered at his perusal. He saw it and bit back a curse. It had been one single shudder, nothing more, but he knew instinctively that it was not fear that sent it through her. It was expectancy, as though every muscle in her body was poised for him to reach out and touch her again.

Arousal shot through him, hot and alive in spite of all his better judgment. *Damn her.*

He turned away from her abruptly, even as a car door banged outside. Then she was back in his line of vision again, darting in front of him to look out the door, standing there in those snug-fitting jeans, her hands on her hips. Jericho kept a careful distance and looked over her shoulder.

"It's a patient," she said, her voice faintly excited. Then she groaned. "Oh, God. We don't have a doctor. I'm just an extern—I can't do anything without a doctor. I can't dispense medication without Kolkline's approval, I can't—"

"Doesn't matter," he said flatly. "She's looking for me."

Catherine spun back to him. *"Why?"* What in the world was going on here?

He ignored her, stepping around her to greet the woman as she climbed laboriously up the steps. He helped her to the chair and Catherine backed away to give them room to maneuver. The woman looked older than the mountain, but although she leaned heavily on a cane she wasn't frail at all. Her substantial girth spread the gathers of her voluminous traditional skirt. She wore a blue velveteen blouse and enough turquoise and silver to double her weight.

"Grandmother Yellowhorse," Jericho said warmly. Catherine's jaw dropped at his tone.

The woman was followed by a tall, lanky boy—apparently her driver, because he jangled a set of keys in his hand. He looked her way and Catherine smiled at him, but his gaze skipped over her.

His eyes went to a point over her head, then slid to a place beyond her shoulder until he finally solved the problem of her presence by simply putting his back to her, shutting her out. Catherine felt temper and frustration build heat into the headache that lingered behind her eyes.

"It's Tommy." The old woman sighed heavily. "He got into it with a stranger over Two Gray Hills way. Now he has dreams."

Jericho settled one hip on the desk beside her. "What kind?"

"There are *chindis* in them."

"Just in his dreams?" Jericho asked. "He hasn't seen any for real?"

Grandmother Yellowhorse shook her head.

"Were the *chindis* anyone he recognized? Kin or a stranger?"

The old woman grunted. "If it was a stranger, I could maybe help him myself. No, it was his father. Kin is worse, isn't it?"

Jericho nodded thoughtfully.

"Will it take a long sing to fix him?" she asked.

"Three days, Grandmother. You know that."

"I'm a poor woman," she grumbled.

Suddenly Jericho grinned, and Catherine caught her breath. The smile transformed him. His face was no longer hard and angry, but strong and devastatingly handsome. He straightened away from the desk and Catherine's eyes followed him, rapt.

"And I," he answered slowly, "am the president."

The boy laughed loudly. The old woman glared at him, then she looked accusingly at Jericho.

"Now see what you do. You make my own nephew think I am foolish."

"Grandmother, I charge everybody the same thing. If they can pay me, they do. If they can't, they do it later. You, on the other hand, are well known never to have given more than a dollar fifty for two buck's worth of gasoline in your life. You have so many sheep you must worry that people talk about you."

"You show me no respect. I should tell this to your uncle."

"How is Uncle Ernie?"

"Someone stole the table out of his hunting shed."

He laughed again. "I heard that."

He turned his back to her and winked at the boy. "I will sing for your son, Grandmother, for twenty-five of your sheep and seven hundred dollars. I think his father's *chindi* might have been trying to warn him of something. Maybe the stranger at Two Gray Hills was a wolfman. I think we should do an Enemy Way to counteract any spells that might have been put upon him."

She grunted and heaved herself up from the chair. "You must think you're as good as your uncle."

"I am, and Uncle Ernie doesn't sing anymore."

"He'll do it for me, for my Tommy."

"Maybe, but he'll want the sheep, too. We want to send twenty of them to Angie Two Sons. Her husband died last year. You know she's hungry. She has nothing."

Grandmother Yellowhorse scowled. "Okay. I'll send Angie the sheep, but I'll give *you* only three hundred dollars."

"Five."

Her mouth opened in a wide, nearly toothless grin. "You work too cheap, but it's a deal."

She went back outside, cackling all the way. The boy looked at Jericho, shaking his head.

"Why did you let her do that? You know she could have given you seven."

"But the standard rate for an Enemy Way is five."

The boy looked confused, then he laughed again. Catherine felt a strange hot-cold feeling work its way down her spine. She had to pull her own jaw shut deliberately.

He had treated his sister with a certain warmth, but this was different, yet a new side of him. Among his own people he was still undeniably arrogant and very much in control. But he was kind, too. Whoever Angie Two Sons was, she had a staunch friend. And Jericho had taken care of her without once truly insulting the old woman whose reputation for thrift obviously preceded her. She watched him as he shrugged into the leather jacket he didn't really need—it was still early autumn, and the day was dry and warm. But the garment seemed to be a part of him.

"You can tell everybody I'll be there Friday, early," he told the boy. "I want to see Tommy first before we start."

"Okay." The car horn began bleating repeatedly outside. "Gotta go."

He left, and Jericho started to follow him.

"What's a *chindi?*" Catherine asked.

He turned back to her with a long, slow look. "What difference does it make? It's not something you can fix, Cat Eyes."

"And you can? By singing some songs for him?"

His eyes narrowed. "More or less."

"What kind of songs?"

"Chants from our Origin Myth. We use different ones for different problems."

He closed the distance between them again slowly, almost lazily, except everything about him was too intense to be called lazy. His eyes bored down into hers, depthlessly black, steady enough to bring gooseflesh to her skin.

"A *chindi* is a ghost," he said. "The dead get up and go about their affairs at night. Sometimes they bother people, get into their dreams. Sometimes they go to their kin, trying to warn them of sickness, of their own imminent deaths. Or a wolfman can raise them and send them after someone he's angry at, as a prelude to killing them, as a warning."

Catherine swallowed dryly, unable to look away from him. He was trying to spook her, and she was damned if she was going to let him succeed.

"So Tommy is going to die," she said nonchalantly.

"Not if I have anything to say about it."

He was serious. Or was he? Did he honestly believe in all this *chindi* stuff? She couldn't be sure.

"How can you stop it?"

"By healing his spirit, where all illness starts. Did they teach you that in medical school?"

"I . . . no."

"Of course not. That's why the People don't need you, Cat Eyes. That's why they don't look at you, why they don't want you or Kolkline. They want their shamen, they want the chants and sings that are more ancient than the sky, the cures that have been healing the Navajo for centuries.''

His voice was silky, his anger quietly volatile. It made something inside her tremble, and she knew it was best to just let him leave. Yet something in her persisted.

"Are you one of those shamen?"

His gaze moved over her face, and he nodded.

Catherine felt her head swim. She had said it without really believing it. The term brought to mind a gnarly old man with wild gray hair and mystical eyes. It didn't suit him at all . . . and yet it did.

Looking at him, she realized that he certainly had the eyes.

"Ellen, too?" she asked.

He looked startled, and it broke the spell of the moment. He finally stepped back, away from her.

"No," he said, his voice flat now. "She's a healer. She can treat various ailments with herbs. Medicine men are schooled by the elders in whatever sings they're worthy of learning, and only sings can cure the spirit."

He was nearly to the door again. "How many are there?" she asked quickly. "Sings, I mean?"

He answered without looking back at her. "Over fifty. Some are so ancient they died with our ancestors when the old ones found no one to pass them on to. Others are remembered by only one or two elders on the whole reservation. No shaman knows more than half a dozen of them."

"How many do you do?"

"Three."

He picked up the box of birds. She understood now. They were his. She felt a silly, almost superstitious dread at having tampered with them.

She opened her mouth to apologize, but he had already left. He slammed the door hard behind him.

Chapter 4

Dr. Kolkline did not make an appearance the next day, nor the day after that. Three patients came in, all of them looking for Ellen. The nurse sold them an odd collection of herbs from an odd collection of jars. Catherine wondered a little giddily what her professors would have thought of such methods of treatments.

She had never felt so useless in her life.

She sat behind the desk and tried to rub the ever-present headache out from behind her eyes. Not only wasn't she learning anything here, she thought, but she wasn't earning her keep either. Granted, the post didn't pay anything, but her room and board were free and she felt as if she ought to do something to deserve them. She tried to tell herself that it was enough that she was safe... but it wasn't. She was frustrated, angry and bored to tears.

She was also spoiling for a fight.

She watched Ellen lock up a jar of brittle dried leaves in a glass case that held some of the more dangerous drugs.

"What's that?" she asked, knowing she was not going to get an answer. "You know—" she continued on in the silence, "—there's probably some legal ramifications to dispensing that stuff from what's essentially a government facility."

That got a reaction. Ellen paused as she unzipped her white jacket and hung it neatly on the coat tree.

"It's *essentially* a legal substance," she snapped. "It grows all over the desert. I just cure it and tell people what to do with it."

"Then why won't you tell me what it is?"

"Because I don't need your medical opinions. I had my fill of them in nursing school."

Her color was high as she left, stomping heavily down the steps. Catherine sighed and leaned back in her chair. She wasn't going to be able to stand six weeks of this.

She pushed to her feet as footsteps sounded outside again. She looked up, expecting that Ellen had forgotten something, or maybe she just wanted to remind her again how unwanted and unnecessary she was here. Instead, she found herself looking into Jericho's dark, watchful eyes.

He hesitated, almost as though he was startled to see her. "Thought you'd be heading home by now."

"Sure. I have such a long commute."

The corner of his mouth moved again in that reflex that almost wanted to curl into a smile. Then he turned away from her as another man shuffled in behind him. The man moved slowly, his head down, moaning quietly to himself.

"Sit yourself down, Lance, and I'll fix you up."

He went to the shelves, spilling a couple of pills into his left hand. He took a jar of dried leaves with the other and Catherine's heart punched hard against her ribs.

"You can't do that," she blurted.

He stopped cold to look at her. "Come again?"

"I said...you can't do that." Everything about him warned her to back off. But she couldn't. What he was obviously going to do was morally, legally wrong. Ellen, at least, had a nursing degree, but suddenly Catherine couldn't watch any more of this slaphappy disregard for the rules that governed medicine and protected patients.

"Look," she said carefully, "I understand that you're a . . . a shaman, and I'm sure you're very good at what you do. And I don't mean to interfere, but—"

"Then don't."

"You have no license to give medication to anyone!"

His anger came off him in waves. Once again, she could physically *feel* the heat of him. He closed the distance between them and she stepped back warily, but he only responded in short, clipped tones.

"This—" he held up his left hand "—is aspirin. And this—" he held up the jar "—is prairie clover root."

"I . . . oh." She flushed.

"Guess I don't need much of a license to give him either one, do I?"

He turned back to Lance, pouring a little of the root into the man's waiting palm. "You know the routine, old friend. Boil the root and drink down the aspirin with it."

"What's wrong with him?" Catherine ventured.

"Headache," the man groaned. He wasn't actually answering her; it was more like a general complaint. He got up again and shuffled off toward the door, clutching the weed.

"Wait!" Catherine cried.

His feet went still. Jericho's gaze came around to her again warningly.

"At least let me take his vital signs. My God, you didn't even examine him! Any number of things could cause head pain, especially if it's recurring. Are his eyes dilated? Are there any other symptoms?" She yanked open a desk drawer and grabbed a stethoscope. "It could even be that Mystery Disease," she went on, "and you're going to send him away with aspirin and some dried grass!"

"It's not *Tah honeesgai,*" Jericho said flatly.

Catherine scowled. "Tah-what?"

"*Tah honeesgai.* What the Navajo call your Mystery Disease. It means 'illness that our medicine cannot cure'. And Lance doesn't have it."

"But you can't know that!"

"I know." He looked at the man. "Go home, Lance. It's okay."

"No!" Catherine protested.

"Leave him alone."

Catherine tried to block the man's way. In the next moment Jericho had her wrist in his hand, stopping her.

She felt the blood drain from her face at the suppressed fury in his grip. He didn't tell her to sit down, didn't waste the words. He pushed her implacably backward until she felt the chair bump up against her legs. She dropped hard and looked wildly at Lance again.

He was gone.

Anger pounded hard at her own temples. "That was irresponsible."

"No, it wasn't. And I'll be damned if I'll let you embarrass him further."

He let go of her wrist, moving around the desk so that he was facing her. He leaned forward, his palms flat against the wood.

For the life of him, he didn't know why he was going to bother explaining to her. She would give up and leave in another week, and he would have three extra bucks from Shadow. She was a stuck-up, bleeding-heart princess, tiptoeing down from her ivory tower to mingle with the savages. They all started out that way, and they all ran. One way or another, they all ran.

The old pain came back, strangling him.

"Lance drinks," he growled.

His hands, Catherine thought. She stared at them.

They were strong and calloused, and suddenly she remembered the way they had felt when he had lifted her off the chair three days ago, hard and hot at her waist. When he had pushed her to sit down, his grip had been like iron...but he had not hurt her. Velvet and steel, she thought, and swallowed hard. She wondered what they would feel like against a woman's sensitive skin, without cotton or denim to dull the sensation of them.

Why was she thinking this?

She looked slowly, dazedly into his face again. "I...beg your pardon?"

Jericho felt an invisible fist ram into his gut. *Don't do this to me, Cat Eyes. Damn you, don't do it.*

She squirmed a little in the chair, a breathless little hitching of her weight, and hot need sluiced through him. She was so damned readable, so open in her awareness of him. No woman could be that guileless, that innocent.

He straightened away from the desk hard and fast, turning his back to her. "Lance drinks," he said again. His voice sounded strained, even to his own ears. "His habit," he began, biting out the words, "is to do it near an old abandoned windmill not far from my place. *My* habit is to swing by there on my way home. I sober him up and send him back to a harping, dissatisfied wife who can't keep her mouth shut about the kids who've left the Res and never come home. There's not a damned thing wrong with his head except a woman named Ida and a jug bottle of Thunderbird."

He picked up the jar of prairie clover again and slammed it back on the shelf. Before Catherine could respond, he was gone.

She sat very still in the sudden quiet of the clinic. Outside, she heard the engine of the Rover roar to life.

She felt stupid, useless . . . shaken. She couldn't have known that. She couldn't have known because she didn't know the people here, and it was doubtful they were ever going to allow her to.

Suddenly she wanted to go home so badly she ached with it. She wanted to go back to Boston, where people didn't mock her and look through her. But more than anything, she wanted to run from this man with his burning eyes and strong hands, this man who was making her feel things she didn't dare feel again.

Again? No. This was like nothing that had ever happened to her before.

She stood shakily and scrubbed at the hot tears that had somehow escaped her eyes. She took the jar of prairie clover root and turned out the lights, locking the door carefully behind her.

If no one would tell her what medicinal properties these weeds had, then she would just have to find out for herself.

No one at all came to the clinic the next day—not Jericho or Ellen, not Shadow or Dr. Kolkline. By mid-morning Catherine felt wild with isolation. Energy made her skin itch. She couldn't say she missed Jericho or the nurse, but she needed to do something before she went crazy.

She found the keys Ellen sometimes dropped absently into her jacket pocket before she left at night. She wasn't interested in the locked glass cabinet. Except for the herbs, everything in it was stuff she had seen before and was familiar with. She was more curious about the two bottom desk drawers that were always kept locked. She sifted through the keys until she found one that fit.

Patient files. She wasn't sure what she'd expected—more dead voodoo birds?—but she felt deflated. There were precious few of them; she had noticed that Ellen did not keep records of her own treatments. These files were all on the rare patients Dr. Kolkline had treated, and a few apparently went back even before *his* time. Those were signed by a Dr. Medford.

She counted all of them. Forty-two files for what—seven years? No wonder Dr. Kolkline could get away with never showing up. No one ever needed—or wanted—his services. She put the old ones back and piled Dr. Kolkline's in front of her. At least they might tell her a little bit about the man.

She opened them and noticed immediately that the five on top were victims of the Mystery Disease—what had Jericho called it? *Tah honeesgai.* That was even better. She had been here nearly a week now and still didn't know anything about the ailment other than what she had read in the eastern newspapers. She poured herself a cup of coffee and settled down to study them.

The first thing that struck her was the sudden, fierce onset of the illness. She could understand why a superstitious people would think it to be some sort of spell or curse. She read further, taking notes. Apparently it was characterized by a high fever, muscular cramps, and respiratory problems. Many of the patients had been fine in the morning, and dead by the afternoon.

Catherine shuddered unconsciously. Until the CDC learned what was causing it, they could only treat the patient's symptoms. There was, at present, no known cure.

She was thoroughly engrossed when she heard the arrival of a vehicle outside. She jumped to her feet, startled to realize that the morning had somehow passed without her being aware of it. When she reached the open doorway and looked up, she saw that the sun was high overhead.

A big, ponderous truck was parked beside the water barrel. It was the water delivery from Shiprock that Shadow had mentioned. A muscular young man worked to unravel an immense hose from the back of it. Catherine said a little prayer that he wouldn't ignore her like everyone else did around here and hurried over to him.

"Hi," she said, planting herself beside him. "Can I help you with that?"

A feeling of relief swam through her when he smiled at her. His hair was black like everyone else's, and it fell into eyes that were a startling blue.

"Left you here all by yourself, did they?"

"It seems that way." She hesitated. "Do you know where everyone is?"

"Sure, and I'm headed there myself soon as I finish here. Jericho Bedonie is doing an Enemy Way sing over at Old Lady Yellowhorse's place."

Of course. She had forgotten that it was Friday. It was frighteningly easy to lose track of time in this ageless land where the mountains and the desert never changed.

"How long do these things take?" she asked. "I thought I heard Jericho say something about three days."

"That's about right." He threw a lever to send water hurtling through the hose. "An Enemy Way is one of our three-day sings. 'Course, people usually stay for a while after it's over. You got to understand, this Res is huge and there are only a few hundred thousand of us living here. So anytime we get a chance to meet, it's a big deal. Anyone even remotely related to Tommy's or Jericho's clans will show up. There'll be dancing and all the old women will get together to gossip. They'll throw a few sheep on the coals and we'll all eat until we burst.''

Absurdly, Catherine felt slighted that she hadn't been invited, not even by Shadow. She was also a little put off that no one had checked to make sure she didn't mind manning the clinic while they were gone. But by the same token, she was hardly surprised.

She sighed as he wound up the hose again.

''That oughta hold you till Wednesday or so,'' he told her. ''In the meantime, hang in there. Everybody'll be back by Monday.''

Monday. He drove off to the ceremonial festivities, and Catherine hugged herself as she watched him go.

It seemed a lifetime away.

On Sunday she scrubbed the clinic floor for lack of anything better to do. Her own place was as clean as it was going to get, and she'd long since memorized the patient files.

She was up to her elbows in suds when she heard a vehicle outside again. She wondered without much hope if the sing had ended early, then she knew that that wasn't the case. This car was moving fast. Its brakes screamed and gravel spattered as it came to an abrupt stop.

Catherine ran to the door. A boy leaped out from behind the wheel, and her heart staggered.

''You the doc?'' he demanded.

Oh, my God. Panic closed her throat and for a moment she couldn't answer. She nodded mutely. She knew beyond a doubt that only one thing would bring this boy looking for her instead of Ellen or Jericho. If it were something they could handle, he would certainly have gone to the sing to find them.

He had come here instead because he was scared, because *Tah honeesgai* had claimed another victim.

She hurried to meet him. On closer inspection, his face was flushed and sweaty, but other than that he seemed fine and she almost breathed again. Then he motioned toward the back of the old, dilapidated Dodge.

"It's my sister. She's in there."

Catherine pulled open the door. The girl was young, sixteen or so, and she lay prone across the back seat. Her face and eyes were bright with fever, just as the *Tah honeesgai* files had indicated the other patients had had. She half wheezed, trying to get air; half groaned as she hugged herself against muscular cramps.

"Help me get her inside."

They dragged her out between them, draping each of her arms over their shoulders to carry her into the clinic. Catherine's heart pounded and her head hurt as she tried frantically to remember what she had read in those files.

Damn Kolkline. Damn him a million ways to hell for not being here, for not caring! It had been four long years since she'd had any hands-on practice with medicine. She wasn't even legally a doctor yet. She wasn't equipped to deal with this.

But she had to be. In that moment, technicalities didn't matter much after all.

They laid the girl on a table in one of the examining rooms and the boy looked at her with frightened, pleading eyes. "Is she going to die?"

Catherine closed her eyes, thinking hard. For once, for this one time, the people here needed her. She had to do something. She had to try.

She took the girl's temperature. Her fever was at a hundred and four—dangerous, but not in itself a bad thing. Her body was just speeding up its metabolism to conquer the invasion of infecting microbes. Unfortunately, none of the files had told her what those microbes might be. Even the CDC didn't know yet.

Some germs died when the body temperature was raised above normal; others did not. If she brought the girl's fever down, the Mystery Disease might run rampant through her system, killing her. On the other hand, if she didn't bring it down, maintaining such a fever could eat up her body's stores of protein, thereby debilitating her strength.

Catherine grabbed the IV equipment and started her on an intravenous saline solution to combat her cramps and dehydration. "When did it start?" she asked the boy.

"Just a little while ago. We were up Two Gray Hills way. I took her to see her boyfriend. Then we heard about Jericho's sing down here and we decided to come back. We were halfway home when she started getting sick."

Two Gray Hills way. Where had she heard that before? But there was no time to think about it now.

"You've got to go to the sing," she told him. "Bring back Jericho and—and Ellen Lonetree." It was no time to stand on principle, she decided. She needed all the help she could get. In the meantime she had to find Kolkline, had to notify the CDC.

"But the sing—" the boy began.

She didn't care how sacred the damned thing was. "This is more important. *Go!*"

He fled as she attacked the shelves, looking for antipyretic drugs that would bring the girl's fever down. She still wasn't sure it was the right thing to do, but the only one she was legally able to administer was aspirin anyway. She found the bottle and took it back to her, helping her to swallow down the pills.

The girl's cramps were subsiding, but she was having an even more difficult time breathing.

As the car shrieked away outside, Catherine left to get the mobile phone in the front room. She carried it to a list of emergency numbers tacked on the wall and punched in the one for University Hospital.

"Dr. Kolkline," she demanded breathlessly when a woman's nasal voice answered.

"One moment please."

She held on for what seemed like an eternity before the operator came back. "I'm sorry, he doesn't answer his page."

He didn't even hang around University with any regularity, Catherine thought wildly. But, of course, it was Sunday.

"Dr. Moss, then," she tried remembering her chance meeting on the plane. "Richard Moss. He's with the CDC."

"I don't have individual extensions for those doctors. They're set up on the sixth floor."

"Isn't there a phone there?"

"Of course."

"Then ring it! It's an emergency!"

A moment later, a man picked up that line. He identified himself, and his name slid in and out of her mind. It wasn't Richard, but then, she supposed it didn't have to be.

She told him hurriedly who she was and what was happening. He promised to send a helicopter out for the girl immediately.

"What do I do until then?"

"We can't cure the thing, so we can only treat the symptoms. Use antipyretics, fluids, oxygen when she can no longer breathe on her own."

Catherine's heart staggered. "Will it come to that?"

He hesitated. "Undoubtedly."

She went back to the other room to check on her. The girl was struggling. Catherine rigged up an oxygen mask, and then she prayed.

She was so young. The compassion and sensitivity that had dogged her through medical school tore through Catherine anew. She found the girl's hand and held onto it tightly, using her free one to monitor the oxygen and the IV. She leaned closer to her head and coached her.

"Breathe in, come on, pull. There, good girl. Out...good, that's good. Now in. You've got to help the mask as long as you can."

The girl's wild eyes found hers and clung. Catherine kept talking senselessly even after she closed her eyes, exhausted from the effort.

Finally, blessedly, she heard the *chut-chut-chut* of the chopper blades outside. Hot tears of relief burned Catherine's eyes.

"Just a little bit longer," she whispered. "They're here now. You're going to be just fine."

She stood shakily, gently disengaging her hand from the girl's. Then she turned for the door and moved squarely into Jericho.

She gasped, backing up, startled. "How long have you been here?"

"Long enough."

"Then why didn't you do something? Your songs, your birds—" She was grasping at straws, at things she didn't even believe in, and they both knew it. His face twisted.

"There's nothing I can do. It's too late."

She didn't understand, didn't *want* to understand. She whipped back to look at the girl again.

Her chest was no longer rising and falling with each labored breath. But she still wore the mask. Surely as long as she wore the mask...

Catherine moved back to her and groped blindly for her wrist, feeling for her pulse. It was gone.

"No," she breathed. Then she said it louder, not believing it, not able to accept it. *"No!"*

Someone caught her from behind, pulling her toward the door. It was Shadow. They dodged the paramedics and the CDC doctors coming in. Shadow led her outside. Night was falling, a million shades of blue and purple tracing across the sky.

It was too beautiful a night for dying.

Catherine cried. The tears came silently at first, then sobs took her. She sat down hard in the dirt where she stood.

"You tried," Shadow murmured.

"Kolkline should have been here. A doctor—someone who *knew*, who could have done more!"

"There's nothing anyone can do once it starts."

Catherine shook her head. "At least Kolkline could have given her something stronger than aspirin. The CDC doctor told me to give her antipyretics, but all the others are prescriptive drugs!"

Shadow shrugged helplessly, but Catherine looked up and saw her jaw harden in fury.

"Who was she?" she whispered. "I need to know her name." Somehow it seemed important, even as it didn't matter anymore now at all.

Shadow hugged herself hard. "Lisa Littlehorn. She is...was...Uncle Ernie's blood granddaughter."

Catherine gasped. "Kin to you?"

But Shadow shook her head. "Not the way you mean it. Uncle Ernie is everyone's uncle. He's the grandfather of the Towering Rock clan." Suddenly, something seemed to occur to her. "Oh, God. Jericho."

He had come out of the clinic behind the stretcher that carried Lisa Littlehorn. "What?" Catherine asked. "What's wrong now?"

"Uncle Ernie taught him all his sings. They're close. He's going to take this hard." She backed away. "I'm sorry, Lanie, I have to go to him. He needs me more."

Shadow ran to meet her brother at the Rover even as someone switched on the lights in the helicopter. Catherine watched them miserably in the brilliant, artificial light, then a deep pain speared all the way into her soul and she groaned.

She grieved for Lisa Littlehorn, but worse than that was seeing Jericho's face. The strong, arrogant man was crying unabashedly.

She pushed to her feet, her fists clenching. She took two steps toward them even as she knew she had to leave them alone.

She was an outsider. He hated her. She couldn't comfort him, shouldn't even try. And yet something drew her inexorably, keeping her moving until she stood by his side.

He looked down at her, and at first she would have sworn he didn't even see her. But then he touched her hair, one finger winding into a flyaway curl.

"I'm so sorry," she said faintly. "I did everything I could think of, everything I knew how to do."

His hand slid behind her neck, pulling her forward. At first she resisted, startled and wary. But he only leaned his forehead against hers and closed his eyes.

"I know, Cat Eyes. I saw."

Chapter 5

Nothing changed between them after Lisa died, and everything changed. Jericho's demeanor was as arrogant and forbidding as ever, but suddenly Catherine began catching his gaze when it rested upon her. It was always narrow, searching. It made something roll over in her stomach, made each nerve ending feel exquisitely raw and exposed. She couldn't concentrate when he was doing it.

A little more than a week after the latest *Tah honeesgai* incident, he arrived at the clinic with Shadow. They stood together just inside the door and Shadow was grinning.

Jericho dropped his jacket on the chair. "You going home today?" he asked shortly.

Catherine blinked. "Who? Me?"

Jericho shrugged and Shadow grinned even wider. She patted her jeans pocket and went to sit down in the desk chair.

"It's a pleasure doing business with you, brother."

"Don't spend it all in one place."

Catherine wasn't sure she understood what was going on, and it was apparent that Ellen didn't, either. The nurse's gaze moved suspiciously from brother to sister before she snapped, "Well, *we* have business to attend to."

"Where's the map?" Shadow asked. "Give it to Lanie. We've all looked at it a hundred times. Maybe a fresh perspective will help."

Jericho snorted rudely. "That's like asking a bird to find something in the deep blue sea," he muttered.

"Maybe," Shadow said. "But have you got any other ideas?"

Catherine felt Jericho's gaze come around to her again. She fought the urge to shiver and forced herself to meet his eyes.

Oh, those eyes.

She jumped when he thrust the folded map at her, the one she had seen them looking at on the day she had arrived. Her gaze moved to each of them uncertainly and she opened it on the desk.

"Is this where the Mystery Disease has broken out?" she asked.

Jericho moved up beside her, close enough that she was aware of the smoky scent of him again. She closed her eyes briefly and tried not to think about it.

"No. It's where all the victims spent their time in the days before they came down with it."

"Two Gray Hills," she said suddenly. She remembered now.

His eyes narrowed on her. "Come again?"

"Lisa's brother said they were on their way back from there when she got sick. And didn't Grandmother Yellowhorse say her son had been up there as well?"

Ellen made a deprecating sound. "Tommy and Lisa have nothing in common."

"No, wait," Jericho said. "Look, three others were in the vicinity of that clan, too."

"But three out of how many?" Ellen demanded.

"What is it now—twenty-six cases including Lisa?" Shadow asked.

"No, there's no thread." Jericho scowled. "Five doesn't make a heavy percentage."

"And Tommy was ghost-witched," Ellen persisted. "He wasn't even a victim of the disease. That leaves four. Only fifteen percent."

"Who's new up there?" Shadow asked Jericho. "Anybody?"

Jericho moved away. Catherine breathed again.

"Only one guy that I know of," he said finally. "Becenti, he calls himself. Can't remember his first name. He say's he's from L.A., that his father was a Navajo. Who knows?"

"The tribal council wouldn't let him settle here if he wasn't," Shadow observed.

Jericho lifted one shoulder. "There've been questionable people hiding out here before. Takes a while for the council to catch up with them. I know those guys. They don't send anybody packing until they're sure."

Catherine felt a dull, warm flush creep up her neck. *Questionable people.* She supposed, in a manner of speaking, that that was what she was . . . a wolf in sheep's clothing, masquerading, pretending to be someone she wasn't.

No. She *was* a qualified extern. She had done three years of med school. If she was hiding here, then at least she was trying to do what she'd been assigned to do in the meantime.

Then she realized what they were getting at, and all thoughts of her own dubious role here vanished.

"You think this stranger is . . . is hexing people?" she asked disbelievingly. Did they actually think that was what was causing the ailment? This was the twentieth century!

Shadow sighed, rubbing her eyes. "It comes on so quickly," she said. "And it's just happening here, on the Res. What else could it be?"

Viral, carried by a contaminant unique to the region . . . Catherine grimly kept her mouth shut.

"I need a cup of coffee," Jericho snapped suddenly.

He went to her new pot and poured himself a cup. He took a hefty mouthful then he coughed, looking down at it incredulously. "What's this?"

Catherine felt herself flushing. "Coffee."

"The hell it is."

He looked back at the pot, then he grabbed her tin, prying the lid off. He pulled out the bag inside.

"French vanilla?" He slammed the lid back disgustedly. "Pretty little coffee for a pretty little city girl."

Catherine stiffened. She didn't know if she ought to be insulted or flattered. "Then don't drink it."

"I won't." He pushed the cup at her. "Here. You finish it."

She had an absurdly hard time putting her mouth where his lips had just touched. It seemed so intimate—like if she closed her eyes she could feel the warmth of them there. She looked up to see him watching her closely again. Suddenly she was sure he knew what she was thinking.

Awareness prickled over her skin. She found herself trapped in his eyes again and she wrenched her own away. But then her gaze fell right back to his mouth.

"Hello?" Shadow said quietly. They both turned to her sharply.

Shadow brought her feet down off the desk and rested her elbows there instead. "I'd like to point out that while it's vitally important to find out where this disease is coming from, it's equally important to consider where the People *think* it's coming from. We've virtually got a panic on our hands here."

Catherine managed to nod, keeping her eyes carefully averted from Jericho. People had been in and out of the clinic all week, whispering rampant tales of shadowy forms running as fast as cars, transforming themselves into coyotes or wolves as they went. Wolfmen.

"We must have had twenty people in here this week, looking for something to ward off the threat," she mused aloud.

"Emetics," Jericho said shortly. His voice sounded strangely absent, as though he was thinking of something else.

"Purgatives? Why?" She couldn't help it; she looked at him again, but he did not glance her way.

"They think that if any of the wolfman's evil is inside them, they can get rid of it by throwing up."

"That could be dangerous! If they do it often enough, it could open them up to all sorts of problems."

"We need to do something," Shadow agreed. "I think you should do a sort of communal sing, Jericho, something to throw blanket protection over everybody in this region."

Catherine chewed her lip. She couldn't argue with the sense of that. If the people thought they were safe, they would stop weakening themselves with forced vomiting and that certainly wasn't a bad thing.

She saw a fleeting spasm of grief cross Jericho's face. "I'd have to talk to Uncle Ernie," he said. "I'm not sure it's possible to alter the rites. They're all designed for one individual patient. I'm not sure if they can be adjusted to protect the People as a whole."

"Can you find out?" his sister asked.

He hesitated, then went to look out the door. "He's not himself these days, but he'll want to help," he said to the sky.

"Lanie, I think you better come to this one, too."

"Me? Why?"

Jericho's tone suddenly sharpened. "Why?" he echoed, looking back at them.

"Why?" Ellen demanded.

Shadow studied them all as though they were addled. "*Tah honeesgai* doesn't just affect people of Navajo blood. It hit the Ganado Trading Post, too—remember? And personally I think it's cruelly unfair to leave Lanie vulnerable and unprotected against this wolfman's evil."

Catherine felt her head begin to spin. Sound medical reasoning was getting all tangled up with superstition again. She thought the sing was a good idea to placate the People's fears, but now they were talking of hobgoblins again, as succinctly and reasonably as though one might walk in the door at any time.

"I'll . . . uh, I'll take the risk," she decided.

"I don't think that's a good idea," Shadow persisted. "You treated Lisa. Of all of us, you've been the most exposed."

Medically that was true, assuming the ailment was communicable. But Catherine doubted if a sing would help matters if it was.

Incredibly, Shadow kept on. "What if the wolfman blew corpse poison all over Lisa? You would have come in contact with it while you were helping her."

"Corpse poison," Catherine repeated slowly. In spite of herself, her skin crawled. "May I ask what that is?"

Suddenly she felt Jericho come up behind her again. His hands closed over her hips and he turned her to face him. Neither of them saw Shadow's brows shoot up. Neither of them heard Ellen gasp.

"You may," he said quietly.

He was out of his mind, and he knew it. He was playing with fire, but curiosity got the best of his reason. He had to see if she would react to his touch again, if it was real or contrived, her awareness of the simplest things such as drinking from the same coffee cup. He felt something tremble through her again as he held her, and he knew he was damned. There was no more potent lure than her awareness of him, whether she was a fragile, Anglo city girl or not.

"It's the ground-up dust of a dead man's flesh. Wolfmen sprinkle it on their victims. It carries their evil."

Catherine nodded, barely willing to move. He could have told her that the United States was on the brink of World War III. She wouldn't have cared.

"Wouldn't that victim know if he was...ah, being sprinkled upon?" she whispered.

"Not if he was sleeping. Not if he was dreaming."

"Oh." Her own dreams were going to be interesting tonight.

She needed to move away from him. This was insane. They didn't even like each other. She thought he was arrogant and rude. He seemed to think she was some kind of fragile hothouse flower. Yet the warmth of his hands seeped through her jeans, and she was acutely aware of his nearness, so male, so volatile. No matter what they felt about each other, her physical attraction to him was undeniably real and it left her shaken this time as it never had before.

Jericho moved away first. Cold air rushed at her when he was gone.

"Leave Lanie out of this. She'd be a distraction."

"For who?" Shadow wondered dryly. "You or the people?"

Both. "The people. They need to lose themselves in the chants. Can't do that when someone's watching them like she's waiting for them to grow horns."

He was talking too much, an impulse he rarely succumbed to. But he had the distinct feeling that he had just stepped into a gilded cage, closing the door behind him. And now his sister was trying to throw away the key.

He did not want Lanie McDaniel at the sing.

He needed to scorn her, to dislike her. She took everything so seriously to heart, and that irritated the hell out of him. But there was something genuine about it too, an intense, fierce caring. He remembered watching her with Lisa Littlehorn, thought of the way she shivered beneath his hands and how she had stared at his hands when he had told her about Lance.

Yes, there was something intense about her. Something uninhibited and hot just underneath the surface. And she was, impossibly, still here. Despite the isolation, despite losing a patient, she hadn't run ... yet.

Anelle had been ready to go with the first lonely moan of Navajo wind.

He was beginning to think there was an outside chance she wasn't a fragile broken dove at all. In any case, he definitely didn't want her watching with those wide green eyes while he was trying to perform an important rite. Watching him, speculating about him ...

No.

He grabbed his jacket off the chair, suddenly in a hurry to be gone from here. "I've got to talk to Uncle Ernie.

Might not even be a sing if he doesn't know a way to adapt it."

His boots thumped heavily on the stairs outside. Ellen bolted after him. Catherine's breath left her in a long, uneven rush.

It was probably best if she didn't go. It would only irritate him, and she certainly didn't need to solicit any more of his rancor. Nor did she need to see any more of him than his constant appearances in the clinic demanded. Subconsciously, she scrubbed her hands over her hips where he had touched her.

"Someone really ought to remain here at the clinic," she told Shadow. "Look what happened the last time you all took off for a sing."

But Shadow shook her head. "If anyone's going to get sick, they're going to do it right there. I have a feeling that once word of this ceremony gets out, everyone within two hundred miles will come. They're all frightened badly." She stood and moved for the door as well. "Just think about it, Lanie. I really don't like the thought of leaving you unprotected."

When she was alone again, Catherine thought of very little else. Unfortunately, all the pros and cons were caught up with images of Jericho.

She was just about to lock the door and go back to her own trailer when another car pulled up. This one definitely did not look as though it belonged on the reservation. It was a shiny if nondescript rental car, bearing none of the ravages of sudden desert rains or the brutal New Mexico sun.

Her heart slammed up into her throat. She had not given serious thought to Victor for days, had truly started to believe that he would never find her here. Now she realized this barren, arid land left her nowhere to hide, and there was certainly no one to hear her scream.

She backed up hard, her heels stumbling against the door frame. Then the car door opened and Richard Moss emerged.

"Oh!" Relief made her legs wobbly. She held on to the knob and laughed breathlessly.

Richard eyed her curiously as he approached. "You look like you just saw a ghost."

"No, but I've spent the afternoon talking about them." She led the way back inside.

"I warned you these people were different."

"I'd call them superstitious and scared. Would you like a cup of coffee? I just turned the pot off. It should still be warm."

He agreed and she poured a cup for each of them. He took the chair and Catherine sat on the desk, her legs swinging.

She looked at him for a moment, with his easy, open features. Now that her panic was past, she wasn't sure when she had ever been so glad to see anyone in her life. Richard was a friendly face, a rush of reality, a piece of the world she had known for twenty-nine years before coming to this rugged, unwelcoming land.

"You're a little far from Albuquerque," she mentioned finally. "I thought you said you avoided the field."

"I usually do, but now the field has something going for it." He eyed her appreciatively. Odd, Catherine thought, but for all his easygoing charm, his perusal was somehow even less comfortable than Jericho's. Jericho's gaze was certainly breathtaking, but Richard's was...awkward.

He noticed her hesitation and moved over it smoothly.

"I volunteered to be the one to interview you regarding the Littlehorn case. You handled it, didn't you?"

"Had to. Kolkline was nowhere to be found."

Suddenly, she straightened. Good Lord, she was even starting to *talk* like Jericho—short, clipped sentences that were fast, unpretentious and to the point. Or maybe it was just life on the Res wearing off on her. Living here, being alone so often with death creeping up on her cruelly seemed to reduce feelings and issues to their bare, vital essentials.

She dragged her attention back to Richard.

"I need you to tell me everything that transpired," he was saying, "from the time the girl got here to the time she died."

Catherine slid off the desk and moved around beside him to unlock the bottom drawer. "That's easy enough. It's all in the file. I wrote everything down. Believe me when I tell you there's been ample time to keep records."

He glanced over them. "Good. Can I take this?"

"I don't see why not, as long as you return a copy to me."

"It would be my pleasure." He flashed a grin at her then read for a moment. "Well, you did everything you could do."

It was a comfort, yet Catherine flinched. "The last voice she heard was mine, telling her everything was going to be fine."

Richard shrugged. She was a little startled at his coldness. Of course, she had seen it in other doctors as well. When one was surrounded by death, one tended to distance himself from the emotion of it. But it was something she had never really learned to do.

"We're groping for ways to treat this thing," Richard said. "If she had made it into University we would have done what you did, only a little more of it. Of course, we could have drawn blood for tests. Posthumously, our hands are tied. These folks don't believe in autopsies. It's infuriating, really. We need information if we're ever going to beat this bug."

Catherine nodded slowly. "Well, they're pretty determined in their beliefs. The current feeling is that we're all beating our heads against the wall for nothing. There's no organic root to this Mystery Disease at all. It's the work of a wolfman."

His mouth twisted into something that was almost a smile. "I warned you about that, too."

"They're going to have a big sing—a ceremony—to offer everyone some sort of mystical communal protection against the witch. I don't think it's going to stop any of them from being stricken, but it'll be good for their morale."

She was startled to see that he was truly aghast. "You can't possibly support such an idea."

"It has some psychological value. You don't know what they're doing to themselves—"

"I know what they're *going* to do," he interrupted harshly. "They're going to breed twenty-six new cases through person-to-person contact, if they all gather together."

Catherine felt herself getting angry, though she had no idea why she should. He had a point.

"I thought you felt that the source was environmental," she remarked stiffly.

He had the grace to look momentarily nonplussed. "Theories are abundant at the moment. Until we learn more, theories are all they are and we can't take chances. Nonsense like this is risky. These pagan rites should be strictly prohibited."

Prohibited? "I'm not sure we have the right or responsibility to prohibit something that's essentially their religion. You know, that's the problem around here, why so many people with possibly serious illnesses are being treated with weeds and dead birds. As long as our doctors disregard their beliefs and their fears, they'll never use us, they'll never cooperate. And an explanation or cure for this thing will never be found."

Richard stood slowly. "Are you trying to tell me you actually *believe* what the Navajo are saying? That it's a wolfman?"

"*They* believe it, Richard. They believe it, and that's all that matters."

"And you'd entertain such hocus-pocus? Are you going to go to this thing?"

Catherine hesitated. "Yes." *Yes,* she thought, *and Jericho be damned.*

She wanted to see what happened there. She wanted to understand and know what she was up against. Otherwise she would spend the rest of her externship groping around in the dark, an ignorant outsider.

Chapter 6

Shadow provided her with a hand-drawn map showing the location of the sing. Catherine was startled when she handed her the keys to a Jeep, as well.

"Whose is it?" she asked. "Won't they need it?"

"Not until Monday. It's Eddie Begay's—the boy who's trying to fix your car. He'll be at the sing all weekend. He'll go with his parents."

"I . . . oh." Catherine was dazed. For a people who were so intent upon shutting her out, a few were certainly hospitable enough. She thought of her Camaro back in Boston and couldn't honestly say she'd lend it to someone she'd never laid eyes on.

"Of course, you could always come now, with me," Shadow mentioned. "I'm not sure how much protection you'll get out of this if you just show up on the last day."

"None," Jericho said flatly. He was sifting corn pollen from one of the jars into tiny doeskin sacks. "Doesn't matter. The chants don't help people who don't believe."

"The Holy People aid anyone who seeks their help," Shadow argued.

"She doesn't want help. She's collecting souvenirs to take back to the big city."

Catherine flinched. Is that what he thought? He gathered up the little pouches and made for the door.

"I don't understand him," Shadow muttered. "I really thought he was warming up to you."

So did I, Catherine thought. But she sensed instinctively that that was why he was being hostile again. Somehow, for some absurd reason, she threatened him as much as he unnerved her.

"You really should come with me," Shadow tried again.

Catherine hugged herself and shook her head. "No. I don't want to leave the clinic deserted for three days. That's not what the service hired me for."

Shadow shrugged. "It doesn't bother Kolkline, and the service never checks. But suit yourself. I'm just glad you've decided to come at all."

She followed her brother out. Silence, thick and heavy, filled the clinic in her wake.

Catherine sighed. She was alone again.

She closed the clinic relatively early on Sunday and went outside to the Jeep. She had memorized the map by now. Jericho had chosen a site just outside the village of Toadlena, accessible to nearly everyone in this region of the reservation. She had a choice. She could either drive all the way out to U.S. Route 666 and loop back on another dirt road to get there, a distance of some thirty miles, or she could simply go south across the desert, a direct ride of perhaps ten.

When in Rome, she thought.

Still, she felt foolish as she guided the Jeep across the terrain, and more than a little shaky without the guidelines she was so accustomed to—most notably a road that led where she was going. The vehicle bounced and lurched, and she realized she might not even be heading south any longer. For all she knew, she had looped around in a big circle. The rabbitbrush and the greasewood were not trustworthy landmarks. There was simply too much of both.

She panicked when she passed a rocky chasm that looked familiar, but then she noticed something dark on the far horizon. She pointed the Jeep that way, and as she drew closer she saw that it was a gathering of people.

She parked and got out. Pickup trucks and a scattering of cars formed a long line along a wash. Dusk was gathering fast, but she could see still other vehicles drawn up close to some leaping orange campfires. There were even horse-drawn wagons, she realized, and she felt the same strange, disassociated feeling she had experienced when Shadow had first taken her to the clinic.

In many ways, it seemed as if she had stepped back two hundred years. The horses snorted and stomped as they munched at the gnarly grass. People moved in and out of the shadows cast by the fires, rugged male silhouettes in cowboy hats and jeans, younger women in jeans and others in the long, traditional skirts. The smell of roasting mutton filled the air, as well as the sweet, mouthwatering aroma of some sort of cake. It was an intriguing scene, but she felt immediately like an outsider.

Suddenly, she wished she hadn't come. No one had looked up when she had arrived, so she was sure they wouldn't notice if she left either. She eased the door of the Jeep open again, then she hesitated at the sound of Shadow's voice.

"You made it!"

Catherine looked back to see her hurrying toward her. She wasn't sure if she was disappointed or relieved.

"Come on, I'll show you where we're sitting."

Shadow took her arm and began dragging her into the throng. Suddenly, Catherine was struck by the utter lack of solemnity. Children raced about, barefoot in the dirt and grass, and the adults were laughing and talking animatedly. She had suspected that there would be festivities after the rite was over—the water-truck driver had told her as much. But there was still one last night to go and such frivolity now surprised her.

"Not what you expected?" Shadow asked.

"I thought it would be...I don't know, more like the Catholic masses I went to as a child. Grave and ceremonial."

"That part'll come in due time," she assured her. "Uncle Ernie said we should do an Enemy Way to counteract the wolfman's spell, but those rites have to take place at night. We're waiting for full dark." She guided her past campfires and through shrieking, giggling knots of children. "Wolfmen masquerade as ordinary people during the day," she explained, "so it's difficult to fight them directly. We cast magic upon them instead. With the help of the Holy People, an Enemy Way can turn their own evil back upon them. In the old days, this same sing was used against mortal enemies—the Utes, the Mexicans and the white men who invaded our land. In those cases, the Enemy Way turned their own power back against them."

"Now *that* makes me feel more comfortable," Catherine muttered dryly.

Shadow looked at her, startled, then she laughed. "As long as you're not the wolfman, you're safe. These days a full half of us have some Anglo or Spanish blood."

Suddenly, the gathering did indeed quiet down. Catherine looked and saw a sliver of moon inching up on the horizon. The children were called back to their families' fires, and a hushed, tense expectancy replaced the laughter and the shouting.

She sat beside Shadow at one of the fires, looking circumspectly at the others gathered there. Of all the people in this camp, she recognized only Ellen. That startled her. Was she a guest of Shadow's or Jericho's? Why wasn't she with her own family?

There was no time to wonder about it, even if she *could* think of one good reason why she should care.

A hogan sat at the center of the gathering, and she saw Jericho there. She watched him and something fluttered in the pit of her stomach. He was the same as always...and he wasn't. His eyes seemed darker, more fierce. His body seemed harder, more tensed. When he began singing, she gave a quiet gasp.

It was not a song, not as she had expected. It was a rhythmic, almost monotonous cadence in a language she didn't understand. His voice was deep, strong, powerful. It reached inside her and stroked a place that had never been touched by another human soul.

He began dancing around the hogan and her eyes followed him, rapt. His feet moved with the same hard, thumping urgency as his voice, and his body swayed slowly and provocatively with the rhythm. Catherine felt her mouth go dry. He chanted in English this time, turning the magic of the wolfman back upon him in an angry song.

"The dart of the enemy's ghost, its filth, has turned away from me! Upon him it has turned, far away it has returned! It has changed into water, it has changed into dew, while I should go about in peace...."

His voice faded out, bringing to mind the quiet he sang of. She heard soft murmurs of relief from some of those gathered.

Suddenly a horrible scream shrieked out from behind her. Catherine jumped, scrambling halfway to her feet before Shadow caught her arm.

"It's okay," she whispered. "It's part of it."

Catherine felt her heart sink slowly again as she turned to look. Six men galloped toward them on horseback, coming across the open desert.

As they drew closer, she saw that one of them carried a pouch on the end of a stick, slightly larger than the ones she had seen Jericho wrapping on Friday. Shadow leaned close to her again.

"It contains the fur of the wolfman. Someone found a swatch of it snagged in a mesquite bush not far from here."

Catherine's head spun. *There is no such thing. Wolfmen do not exist.* All her educated intelligence told her that the swatch was undoubtedly from some unfortunate dog who had gotten snarled there. If she could somehow get hold of it and look inside, she knew that was what she would find—just plain, ordinary mongrel hair. But suddenly, she had a hard time believing it.

More riders came from the other side of the gathering behind the hogan. When the two groups met, they engaged in a mock battle. Her heart started pounding. The night had fallen black and hard now, and it reverberated with the sharp, cracking sounds of their lances coming together. Woven into it all were their war cries, shrill and terrifying, making her blood curdle.

"If a wolfman's prey is too strong and well protected, his evil spell almost always bounces back to him," Shadow explained in an undertone. "Jericho and the warriors are proving to the Holy People that these eastern clans are still strong and worthy of their help."

Catherine nodded slowly, feeling herself drawn almost hypnotically into this mysterious and sacred culture not her own.

When the fighting stopped, Jericho began moving among the people. He carried the pouches he had wrapped, and one by one he opened them, sprinkling the pollen over the various campfires.

"You are protected," he said quietly. "You are protected."

Women wept, and men nodded reverently. Catherine shivered.

Finally, he went back to obliterate a sand painting in front of the hogan.

"The artwork is sacred," Shadow said. "It should never be left on display after the rite is over."

Catherine cleared her throat carefully. "*Is* it over?"

Shadow nodded.

The "warriors" began returning to their kins' camps, and Catherine felt herself stiffening. Jericho followed them and sat down on the opposite side of the Bedonie fire.

She watched him warily, knowing he did not want her here, waiting for more of his scorn. But his gaze only moved idly to Ellen as that woman jumped to her feet.

"There's meat and roasted potatoes and fry bread," she told him.

"I'll have some of the bread. Thanks."

"I brought those beans you like, the ones with the peppers."

"That'll be good." But he was no longer looking at her. His gaze had finally come around to Catherine.

"Enjoy yourself?" he asked flatly.

"Very much."

He lifted a brow at her.

Ellen brought the bread. It was a round, flat pancake, heaped with spicy refried beans, lettuce and chunks of tomato. Catherine's mouth watered.

"Would you like some?" Shadow offered.

"I . . . yes, sure."

Her first impulse had been to leave when Jericho came back here, to excuse herself politely and go. Now that the rites were over, the spell they had woven had released her. She felt awkward again, uncomfortable, but Jericho chewed steadily with his gaze hard upon her. If she left now, it would be as good as admitting that his disapproval intimidated her, that she felt like an outcast here. She stood stiffly instead.

"Personally," Shadow said, "I like mine with honey, but it's your choice." They went to a big vat where the bread was deep-frying and she plucked out two pancakes with a pair of tongs. An old woman with a threadbare blanket around her shoulders was rolling wads of dough in her hands, smacking them flat, then dropping them into the sizzling fat.

Catherine shuddered at the thought of all that cholesterol, then she shrugged. In for a penny, she thought, in for a pound. "I think I'd like the beans."

Shadow showed her where they were, and Catherine heaped them upon the fry bread, adding a dash of taco sauce for good measure. They went back to the campfire again, but Shadow gulped her food and stood again almost immediately.

"I'll be right back," she said suddenly. "I want to find the Two Gray Hills fire and see if Casey Red Shirt knows anything about that Becenti guy."

Catherine fought the urge to grab her wrist and detain her. She didn't want to be left alone here, but Shadow was gone almost before she finished speaking.

Catherine looked down at her food, grimly ignoring the sharp, hot feeling of Jericho's eyes upon her.

"Roll it up," he said.

"I beg your pardon?"

"Roll the bread up," he said impatiently. "Like a taco."

She tried it, and the beans squished out, plopping down on the leg of her jeans. "Damn it."

She heard Ellen snort and she looked up again. The nurse was sitting close beside Jericho. One corner of his mouth moved again in that almost-smile, but it wasn't entirely pleasant this time.

"Guess you got your souvenir."

"Aren't there any knives and forks around here?" she asked exasperatedly.

"Sorry, Cat Eyes. This isn't the Ritz. You're dining among savages."

Suddenly she'd had enough. She stood, clutching the fry bread. She didn't care if he knew he was intimidating her, didn't care what he thought, because he clearly didn't have a high opinion of her to start with. She looked wildly for Shadow, to thank her for inviting her, but she was nowhere to be seen. And Catherine didn't relish the thought of wandering around like a lost soul, looking for her.

"I'm leaving," she blurted rudely, then she flushed. She looked at the woman at the frying vat again. "Thank you."

The woman gave a toothless grin and nodded. Catherine fled, hurling the soggy bread into a big rubber trash can as she passed it.

She reached the Jeep before she realized that Jericho was behind her. She spun back to him, as angry as she had ever been.

"Coming to get in one more barb?" she snapped, then her heart skipped a beat.

There was something about him in the moonlight. It threw shadows over his hard face, accentuating the planes and angles of it. He was so ruggedly attractive and she felt the heat coming off him again, felt his intrusive eyes this time as if they were touching her very soul. There was a certain intensity about him now that made her breath fall short.

"Why'd you change your mind?" he asked. "Why'd you come here?" He genuinely seemed to want to know; he spoke as though it was very important.

"Because Richard Moss thought it was a bunch of hogwash," she blurted.

His eyes narrowed. "Who?"

"One of the CDC doctors. He came out on Wednesday."

"And what do you think?"

"I think..." What *did* she think? At times his performance had made her believe there truly was a wolfman. It had certainly made her believe in a sacred spirituality not her own. But now she thought the people were as exposed to the Mystery Disease as they ever were.

She swallowed carefully. "It doesn't matter, does it? I wanted to learn more about Navajo beliefs. I wanted to learn if such an event could compromise containment of the disease if it turns out to be communicable."

He gave a dark curse, and she flinched.

"You've got to at least believe that's a possibility!" she protested.

"What I believe, Lanie McDaniel, is that you damned well ought to go home."

He started to turn away from her. Impulsively, she shouted after him.

"Why? What have I done here that's so wrong?"

He moved back to her and came close, too close. Catherine fought to hold her ground.

"It's not what you've done. It's what you are."

"You don't know what I am," she retorted. "You can't get to know someone by sniping at them all the time."

"Is that what you think I do?" he asked quietly. "Then how should I go about it?"

Touch me again.

The thought leaped crazily into her head. She backed away from him, shaken by it, and came up hard against the Jeep. She was trapped.

He watched all this with his sharp shaman's eyes, then he followed her.

"I think," he said silkily, "you can tell a good bit about someone from the way they fight back."

"So how do I fight?" she managed, struggling for flippancy.

"Not like I thought you would." She fought with treacherous things such as shivers and sighs and wide, cat eyes, he thought. She fought with the tenacity of a pit bull and the urgency of a summer storm.

His mouth was inches from hers, and she couldn't back up any more. She looked wildly for his eyes, to see if he was really going to do what she thought he was going to do. He was studying her lips. Her heart slammed.

"Do you want me to kiss you, Cat Eyes?"

She tried to shake her head and couldn't do it.

"Is that what all the shudders and the wide-eyed stares have been about?"

"I don't . . . shudder."

"No? Then it shouldn't matter, should it? But you've got me damned curious. Let's give it a shot. We'll find out you don't shiver and that will be that."

"You are so insufferably arrogant—" She broke off as his mouth closed over hers.

Her breath plummeted, leaving a painful hole inside her. And then she trembled. He felt it, and they both groaned at the same time.

He didn't touch her with anything but his mouth. He braced his hands against the Jeep on either side of her and his tongue dove past her lips, her teeth, intrusive and demanding, proving something. He was not gentle, but after a moment his mouth softened, turning provocative.

Daring her to respond.

He moved his head slowly, slanting first one way then the other, making her body change with nothing but the kiss. Something hot and weakening slid through her, taking her strength. Still his tongue glided—slowly, then with more force—until she found herself kissing him back, moving her tongue over his, trying to taste him.

She groaned again and dug her fingers into his waist, hanging on as sensation spun through her. He tasted of hot winds and dark secrets. *This is insane,* she thought again, and found herself moving into him, away from the Jeep, wanting to feel him, wanting the intimacy of his hard body against hers. Something coiled inside her, something painful and tight, something treacherous that wanted more.

Jericho felt her inching closer and didn't dare allow their bodies to meet. He needed to keep control over this. But at some point he stopped taunting her, and she drove him past memory. He forgot what she was, who she was, and that he needed to keep her at arm's length.

He felt the heat flare inside her, the heat he had sensed but now knew was real. As long as he kept his hands on the Jeep it wouldn't burn him, he thought again. It was a kiss, only a kiss...but he felt himself getting hard and hot and suddenly he realized that his hands were buried deep in the thick, wild curls of her hair. He was falling into her like a man drowning.

His mouth moved to her cheek, to her ear, to her neck, hot and wet. She tilted her head back and groaned, then she turned her face into his again, seeking his lips with her own. They met, slid away, came back, and he covered her mouth again.

"Oh, God," she moaned.

Then something about her changed. It took him a heartbeat to realize that she was fighting him now, struggling. He stepped back, his own heart pounding hard.

She literally reeled away from him, turning back toward the Jeep. She leaned against it for support and looked over her shoulder at him wildly.

"Why?" she breathed. "Why did you have to do that?"

It seemed an odd thing to ask, then Jericho understood. He recognized her fear because he knew it so intimately himself.

It shook him. "Just testing," he bit out.

"Testing *what?*"

"Life in this country is like that kiss, Cat Eyes—hard and hot and dangerous. Just wanted to see if you have what it takes to handle it."

"And do I?" she said tightly.

Yes, oh yes. "We'll see."

He moved away, back toward the fires, before she could realize that his own voice wasn't quite steady, before he could ask who the man had been who'd left her scarred and scared. He didn't want to care.

Catherine watched him go, but it was a long time before she trusted her legs enough to let go of the Jeep door.

Chapter 7

Catherine used the roads to get home. It was no time to try to navigate the desert.

Her hands shook and she still felt dizzy. But even though her head spun, her thoughts veered stubbornly, again and again, to the same tormenting question. She had been so wretchedly wrong about Victor's character. How could she even begin to trust her responses to a man such as Jericho Bedonie?

She couldn't. She shouldn't. And yet she had never been kissed like that before.

He was hard, uncompromising, openly angry, and he left her no defenses at all. Yet all her instincts told her he was a good man. She trusted him intuitively—she knew that if he ever truly hurt her it would only be because *she* had hurt or damaged something dear to him.

But she had once thought the same thing about Victor. She had seen in him a man of charm and wit and sophistication, a man who could not possibly stoop to crass and vicious cruelties. Then he had shot her—and God only knew how many others.

She groaned aloud as she found the short side road to the trailers. She turned onto it hard and came to a skidding stop in a shower of spattering gravel. It had been foolish of her to go to the sing, she thought. There was a certain safety to their encounters in the clinic; even if he was only a shaman, there was a sense of professionalism about working together within those four walls. She had known better than to risk meeting up with him in moonlight, but she had done it anyway. She had played with fire, and she had gotten burned.

But oh, she thought, what glorious flames.

She sighed and made her way toward her trailer. Then she came up short, staring. Even in the darkness, she could see that her door was open.

She closed her eyes, trying to think. She had left for the sing directly from the clinic. Had she locked her own door when she had left her trailer that morning?

She couldn't be sure. Though autumn was half over, this torrid land was still warm at midday. She had gotten into the habit of leaving the place open to catch whatever freshening breezes there might be.

She backed up, away from the trailer, inching quietly up the clinic steps instead. She tried that door and found it tightly locked. She was just spooked then, her nerves unraveled by the events of the evening. If anyone was going to break in anywhere, she reasoned, then it would be the clinic, with its plethora of drugs and expensive equipment.

Unless it wasn't your average burglar. *Victor?*

But no, that made no sense. He wouldn't leave the door open, warning her away, nor would any of his goons. They would close it and hide inside in the darkness, waiting for her to stumble into their deadly arms.

Catherine forced herself to go back to her own trailer. She stepped carefully inside, hitting the light switch, looking around. The generator growled into life, and it was a comforting sound.

Everything looked the way it should. Shadow's curtains stirred restlessly in the thin breeze that came inside. Beside the crooked table, the old refrigerator chugged as though getting ready to draw its last breath, but that was normal, too.

She looked the other way, at the bed, then she scowled.

Something dark sat on the woven blanket she used for a spread. Some sort of animal. Her nape prickled and she wanted to run. Then, preposterously, Jericho leaped into her mind again. That was exactly the sort of thing he would expect her to do. She forced herself to cross to the bed instead.

It was a bird, a small owl. When it didn't move, she picked it up by the wing with her fingertips, then a thin, mewling sound escaped her throat. It had been shot. Her free hand went unconsciously to the bullet scar at her own side.

The wounds were in the same place, she realized, but the one in the owl still bled.

No. From deep within the recesses of her mind, logic reared up through her panic. The substance seeping from the wound was bright red, but the bird was cold. If it were blood, it would be brown and oxidized by now. The red stain was only paint.

There was a tiny piece of cloth wrapped around its beak, tying it shut. Catherine's mouth went dry and she dropped it again. *Someone knew.*

It seemed incredible, impossible, but the message of the bullet hole, and especially the cloth, was unmistakable. *If you talk, Catherine, you will die.* Either someone on the Res knew what she had run from and was taunting her, or Victor had found her and was warning her.

Who on the reservation hated her enough to do this, to try to make her cower and run and leave? She laughed a little wildly. Ellen, of course. And though she was suddenly loathe to admit it, Jericho.

No. She shook her head unconsciously and pressed her fingers to her temples. Jericho had been at the sing. Her lips still felt tender from his sweet assault. And he tackled things head on. He wouldn't stoop to such childish, evil pranks.

Would he?

Catherine stumbled backward, for the door, then she hesitated. She didn't want to go outside. The night held too many shadows. On the other hand, she couldn't stay in here either. That bird... She shuddered and wondered if she would ever be able to sleep in that bed again.

She went outside. She stood for a moment, poised, her heart thumping, but nothing happened. No one shot at her, and no one stormed at her out of the night.

She scurried down the steps and saw a stick lying half under the trailer. She grabbed it and went back to the porch, sitting carefully with her back to the door. Shaking, feeling sick, she laid the stick over her knees.

Whoever it was, they would have to come at her from the front now.

She waited for them.

Dawn was a smear of lavender and pale pink on the eastern horizon when Jericho stopped his Land Rover in front of Ellen's trailer. He thumped his fist against the horn impatiently. A moment later, she stuck her head out the door and came sleepily to the street.

"What's going on?"

"I need to get to the clinic. If you want a ride, get moving."

His voice was clipped, tense. Ellen scowled and looked up at the murky sky. "Now?"

He didn't want to waste time explaining, but he knew that his behavior was just odd enough to make it necessary. "I've got a bad feeling," he said finally.

Ellen's face changed. "About that Anglo doctor."

"That's right."

"Why?" she burst out suddenly. "Why are you doing this to yourself after what happened the last time you got involved with someone like her?"

He didn't look at her.

"Jericho, for God's sake! Anelle nearly destroyed you! Didn't you learn anything from that?"

"I learned to trust my gut feelings," he snapped. He had done it too late, but he had learned. If he had listened to his heart all those years ago, he would never have asked Anelle to live here on the Reservation. He wouldn't make the same mistake now. His heart was telling him something was wrong at the clinic. Maybe the isolation of the place had finally broken her the way it had Anelle. Or maybe it was something else entirely. Either way, he was going over there.

He put the Rover in gear.

"Okay, all right," Ellen said. "Give me five minutes. I need a fast shower."

"Use hers when you get there."

"I'd rot first."

"You know, if you weren't so damned stubborn you'd be a real sweetheart."

"Look in the mirror," she snapped and hurried back inside.

Jericho studied the horizon. After a long moment he looked at his watch, then he closed his eyes.

Was she right? Was the black feeling swelling in his stomach telling him that something was wrong at the medical trailers, or was it warning him to stay away from Lanie McDaniel, to end it before it began, before this devilish fascination destroyed him? The ominous feeling had started not long after she had left the sing. It had dogged him all through the night, making sleep elusive until he had finally gotten up and dressed, knowing he had to go out there.

Because something was wrong there, or because he wanted—needed—to see her again, because each moment away from her was becoming one in which he thought of her and wondered about her?

He didn't know and he couldn't trust himself. He didn't dare trust himself—Ellen was right about that. Once he had believed that Anelle only seemed fragile, that she could survive this land. And when she'd broken instead of bent in the hot desert winds he'd brought her to, the guilt had nearly killed him.

He scrubbed a hand over his jaw as the sky lightened slowly. He was beginning to think Lanie was strong enough, too—feisty and tenacious and relentless beneath her soft, city-girl exterior. But he had been wrong before.

Ellen came outside again, her hair still wet, holding a cup of coffee in each hand. He leaned across the seat and pushed open the door for her.

By the time the sky was blue again, Catherine's eyes felt as dry as the desert sand. Her back ached abominably, but her trembling had finally stopped, probably out of sheer exhaustion. When she heard a vehicle turn onto the side road, she waited dully for it to appear around the side of the trailer, too tired to even get to her feet, to be ready to run.

It was only the Rover anyway. *Jericho.*

A warm, pervasive feeling of relief filled her. Against all her better judgment, she felt safe now for the first time since she had returned from the sing. He was rock hard and capable, and no one could hurt her as long as he was here.

He got out of the Rover, saw her and threw his cup of coffee aside to jog in her direction. Catherine watched it roll in the dirt, oddly fascinated, then she looked back at him dazedly.

He was obviously concerned, and that made her feel warm inside too. She shook her head, clearing it. His alarm couldn't be for her. More than likely he thought another of his people had succumbed to *Tah honeesgai* and another death had left her reeling.

She tried to stand to meet him, but her legs wouldn't cooperate. He reached her and his strong hands gripped her arms, lifting her to her feet. She stumbled against him and thought she felt him stiffen.

The night before, she had craved his body close to hers. The night before, the heat of him had been wild and alive. Now it was solid, comforting, yet still something curled inside her in response. She was acutely aware of their thighs touching, of her breasts pressed against his chest. Something tingled inside her, tightening, ready, wanting.

"What is it?" he asked, his voice strained. *"What's happened?"*

She opened her mouth but couldn't find her voice immediately. He shook her a little and she motioned inside.

He went into the trailer and Catherine followed him. But he stopped suddenly at the foot of the bed and she bumped into him.

"It's dead," she muttered, her voice raspy.

He bit out a dark curse. "No kidding."

They heard footsteps behind them. They both spun about to see Ellen standing in the door. Her expression was jealous, pained, yearning as she watched them. Realization jolted through Catherine suddenly.

Ellen was in love with him.

Now that Catherine realized it, it was as plain as the nose on her face. She flinched, an odd pain shimmering through her. Had they been together since the sing had ended? Why should it matter to her if they had? Kissing her had been nothing more than a taunt, a test. He had said as much himself.

"What's going on?" Ellen demanded.

Jericho motioned to the bed. Ellen looked, then her face drained of all color. She backed up quickly.

"What the hell *is* going on here?" Catherine asked. It was *her* bird! What were *they* all shaken up about?

"Ellen, go get a box." Jericho snagged the stick out of Catherine's hand. "Give me that."

He got no closer to the owl than he had to. He nudged it with the stick, rolling it over. "It's been shot."

"I could have told you that."

"How did you know?"

She looked at him, perplexed. "I looked." She reached out for it again. "Here—"

"Don't touch it."

She shrank back, her own skin crawling at the tone of his voice. "I . . . I don't understand."

He looked down into her face. A single muscle moved at his jaw.

"The Navajo believe an owl is an omen of death. If you dream of one, if you hear one at night, someone close to you will die."

"But this one is already dead," she protested.

He didn't answer.

"*I'm* going to die?" she asked, jolting.

Ellen came back, carrying a box. She flung it at them. It landed on the floor, not far from Jericho's feet, and he used the toe of his boot to slide it close to the bed. Catherine knew in that moment that neither of them had left the bird for her to find. They were both too purely, instinctively terrified of it, and tying its beak would certainly have necessitated touching it at some point.

Jericho nudged it off the bed with the stick and it landed in the box with a dull thump. "Who've you ticked off lately, Cat Eyes?" he asked.

She looked at him incredulously. "Present company excluded?"

His mouth quirked again. "Yeah."

"I can't think of anyone."

"Haven't forced your services on anybody?"

"No!"

"Saved anyone who was supposed to die?"

"You know I haven't." Suddenly she understood what he was getting at. "You think I crossed paths with your wolfman. You think I made him angry."

Ellen paled even more. "He'll be coming after all of us then," the nurse breathed. "If something happened here at the clinic to upset him . . ."

She didn't like the nurse, but neither could she stand by silently while someone suffered needlessly. She opened her mouth to tell her that it wasn't their wolfman who had done this, it was Victor. The cloth, the bullet . . .

But she couldn't trust Ellen Lonetree, of all people, with a secret that could cost her her life. She closed her jaw again helplessly.

"What?" Jericho demanded. He was watching her again in that way he had, as though he could read her heart, her soul, her mind, if he only gave him enough time.

"Nothing," she whispered. "I just . . . I think you're barking up the wrong tree."

Something flared in his eyes. Suspicion? Her throat closed uncomfortably.

"Yeah?" he asked too mildly. "So what's your theory?"

"There are an awful lot of people who don't want me here," she managed. "Maybe someone's just trying to scare me off."

"It's not Navajo nature to scare you off. Unless they're wolfmen, they'll just ignore you."

Catherine shrugged helplessly. They were certainly doing that.

Jericho peered down into the box. "That thing around its beak mean anything to you?"

"I . . . no."

He looked at her sharply again, but then he only carried the box to the door. Ellen skittered out of his way and Catherine followed him.

"What are you going to do with it?" she asked.

"Burn it. Sing over it." He placed the box in the dirt outside and looked at Ellen. "I'll need something flammable and some matches. Anything like that in the clinic?"

"I'll look," the nurse said and hurried off again.

"Here? Now?" Catherine tried to think fast. Was it possible she could need the thing for evidence or something? She couldn't imagine why, and Jericho was not going to be delayed anyway.

"Can't leave it," he said. "He might come back for it. Wolfmen don't like to leave pieces of their work scattered about. He might come back for it."

"Then we'd find out who he is."

His eyes narrowed on her. "He won't come in human form."

Catherine's head spun. She was getting that disassociated feeling again. Reality was getting all tangled up with things that couldn't be, that belonged to another time and world.

"What will you sing?" she managed. "A whole ceremony?"

"No. There's a simple chant to make an enemy peaceful."

"Will it work?"

"Do you care?"

Yes, she thought. Yes, she did. Even considering that the enemy was Victor, she thought she could use all the help she could get, even if it was just Indian hocus-pocus.

She nodded, then a new thought came to her, making her feel ashamed.

"I'm sorry," she said quietly.

His brows rose. "For what?"

"For being so...so skeptical. I just realized that I'd probably get riled, too, if an atheist tried to tell me there was no God."

He was quiet for so long that she didn't think he would answer. He looked out at the craggy horizon and the looming mountain. Finally, he blew his breath out in a harsh sigh.

"Don't sweat it, Cat Eyes. This is a strange, ancient land. Back in the city you've got witches and ghosts. We've got wolfmen and *chindis*. Your people don't talk about them. Mine accept them as part of life. Sometimes it's hard to cross that line, even for those of us who were born straddling it."

Catherine managed a faint smile. "Well, I don't believe in witches and ghosts, either."

Ellen brought the things he needed. Catherine backed away to give him room to work. "I should take the Jeep back to Eddie Begay," she said finally.

Jericho looked up as he started the fire. "Yeah? And how are you going to find him?"

"Shadow said he worked in a garage in Shiprock."

"Which one?"

"How many are there?"

"Three."

She was getting irritated again. "Then I guess I'll just ask at each one until I find him."

The truth of the matter was that she needed to make a phone call. She didn't want to place it from the clinic, even assuming the mobile phone could handle long-distance calls. She'd never used one before and couldn't be sure, but she was certain that she didn't want this call to be traceable.

The fire was burning. The stench of the bird made her throat close and her eyes water, but it had no appreciable effect on Jericho. Maybe *he* was the wolfman, she thought wildly.

"How're you going to get back?" he asked.

Catherine hesitated. She hadn't thought of that.

"Hang on five minutes and I'll follow you."

Panic made her heart skip a beat. First of all, she didn't want to be trapped in that Rover with him for what—a hundred miles? And secondly, her instincts for self-preservation told her it would be best if no one saw her making the phone call. She had to decline the offer... but there really was no other way.

"How about if I go ahead and you can meet me there?" she said finally.

He nodded without arguing with her. "It's the Exxon."

"Thanks."

She was halfway to the Jeep when his voice stopped her again. She turned to look back at him. He stood, tossing the stick from hand to hand as the small bonfire leaped and spat.

"Just out of curiosity, what had you planned to do with this?"

"Beat the hell out of anyone who came within striking distance."

He made an odd sound in his throat and snapped the stick in half over his knee, feeding the pieces into the fire. Catherine flushed, then her jaw dropped.

He was laughing.

It was a deep, almost rusty sound that rubbed warmly across her skin and tickled something inside her. The reflex transformed him and left her reeling as no voodoo owl ever could.

She hesitated, but the broken burning stick *was* a pathetic weapon. She grinned and shrugged.

Jericho laughed harder.

Catherine kept her eye on the rearview mirror as she drove, expecting to find him coming up hard behind her. But apparently the chant he planned was long enough to suit her purposes. She made it into the town without him and dropped the Jeep at the Exxon station.

Eddie wasn't in, but she wrote him a note of thanks and left it in the office with his keys. Then she went next door to a motor inn that advertised a coffee shop on the sign outside.

She heard mingled voices, tangled languages, as soon as she stepped into the lobby. She followed the sounds. The coffee shop was packed. Tourists with children sat at the counter among Anglo businessmen and Navajos in jeans, cowboy hats and neat bolo ties.

Civilization. She passed through it reluctantly to a pay phone on the far wall, wishing she could sit down and join them for a while and talk about innocuous things such as the weather here.

Instead, she placed a call back to Boston. "Horace Schilling," she said when the line picked up, then she was put on hold again until the man's rich baritone came back to her. "It's Catherine Landano."

There was a brittle silence as this sunk in. "So where the hell are you?" Schilling asked.

Catherine bristled. "Watching out for my own hide," she snapped. "I didn't fare very well when you guys were doing it."

His lack of a response was all the agreement she would get. "How are you?" he asked finally.

"Alive. Are you tracing this call?"

"I can."

That told her all she needed to know. She would have to make it quick. "Where's Victor?"

"Right here in Boston."

"You're absolutely sure?"

"He'd have his bail revoked if he left."

Catherine gave a wild little laugh. Still, after everything, the authorities underestimated him.

"Check and make sure," she said. "I'll call you next week. When's the trial?"

"December seventeenth."

"For my attempted murder, or for the whole thing?"

"We're still trying to piece together corroborating evidence on his associations and that business about the senator. We can't take it to trial on your testimony alone. It wouldn't even pass the grand jury."

They had told her all this before, and Schilling knew it. He was just rambling, trying to keep her on the line.

"If Victor is there," she interrupted, "watch him closely, and I think you'll find something to prove out his associations. If he's there, then he's got one of his goons out here, trying to frighten me. There'd have to be some kind of contact between them, wouldn't you think?"

"Where's here?" Schilling asked without answering.

"I'll call you next week."

Catherine disconnected hard and fast and wondered if she had talked too long. She had a sinking feeling that she might have. Then it vanished under the assault of a hot, probing sensation at the back of her neck.

She turned quickly. Jericho stood in the door of the coffee shop, watching her.

Chapter 8

He didn't say anything for a long time. They went back to the Exxon to get his Rover, then they drove a full eighty miles at a speed that had her pulse slamming. By then the tension of his stony silence would have had her blurting anything at all.

But he didn't immediately mention the phone call. "You need a gun," he said instead.

She looked over at him, startled. "I thought they were illegal on the reservation."

"Antiquated law tracing back to the days when the government didn't want us to arm ourselves for fear we'd fight back." Then his jaw relaxed a bit. "It's possible to get a special permit from the tribal council now. *Their* major concern is that visitors will come onto the Res and hunt out all the wild game that remains. Not to mention the fact that when people get drunk they tend to shoot each other."

"Oh." Catherine watched the sage and the rabbitbrush whiz by outside the open window. Slowly, her stomach unknotted. "Can you shoot a wolfman?" she wondered aloud. "Can you kill one by ordinary mortal means?"

What was she asking? Her problem was definitely Victor. She couldn't imagine how he might have known about the Navajo significance of the owl, but the bullet wound and that little gag on its beak left very little doubt. Even if she wanted to believe she had irritated the wolfman—and it was almost a preferable alternative—that piece of cloth wouldn't let her.

Jericho seemed to consider her question. "No," he said finally. "Not really. They can only be destroyed by magic or by fire. But that's not who you want to shoot, is it?"

She flinched, then it came to the tip of her tongue to lie. The fear she had been living with for so long now made her defensive. She wanted to feign confusion, pretend she didn't understand his question. But she knew instinctively that Jericho Bedonie would not tolerate a lie. He would shut her out again and this time he wouldn't thaw.

Catherine found that she couldn't bear the thought. She knew, somehow, that it would leave a gaping hole in her life. Perhaps this odd relationship would never lead anywhere; perhaps they were simply too different. There was his relationship with Ellen to consider as well. But if she lost him now, she thought she could be losing the tantalizing possibility of something more glorious and passionate than she had ever imagined.

"No," she heard herself admit quietly.

"Who then?" he asked.

She rubbed a hand over her eyes and shook her head. "I can't tell you that."

He took his eyes off the road to study her for too many moments. Then, to her surprise, he nodded. "Okay."

He would respect that, she realized. He was a private man and he would allow the same privacy in others.

"Don't rule a wolfman out, anyway," he urged. "They know things."

"I beg your pardon?"

"Whoever he is, he knows whatever you're not telling me."

Her heart lurched. "That's not possible."

He cocked a brow at her. "Think about your own ghosts and ghoulies."

"I told you I don't believe in them."

"Doesn't matter. They're supposed to be omniscient, right?"

She nodded reluctantly.

"Same goes for our wolfmen."

Catherine hugged herself against a shiver. If she could somehow manage to contact Schilling next week, if he told her the FBI had turned up no connection between Victor and a hired man, then that would almost force her to contemplate a supernatural alternative. She had been trained in science; she had an analytical mind that needed rules. She didn't want to be forced to step beyond them.

"I think," Jericho continued, "that our wolfman sees you as a threat. You tried to save Lisa, tried to interfere with his magic. He's warning you off."

"Then why not leave something that tied into her? Why leave hints of..." *What happened with Victor.* "Of something else entirely?"

"He's going for your most vulnerable point."

Jericho finally turned onto the clinic road and parked the Rover. He shifted a little behind the wheel to face her more fully.

"I'll talk to the council about a special gun permit anyway," he said finally. "No sense in leaving you with a blind side."

Catherine hesitated, then she blurted, "If you're willing to accept that the owl might be the work of something more mortal, then why can't you believe the same thing about the Mystery Disease?"

"Because I never saw the Mystery Disease sneaking in a phone call in Shiprock."

She flushed and fumbled for the door handle. But when she was out, she couldn't help looking back at him.

"Why are you doing this? Why are you helping me? I thought you wanted me to turn tail and run."

His gaze fell to her mouth and everything coiled inside her all over again.

"That would be safest," he said quietly. "But I'm beginning to think you're not going to do it."

He returned on a quiet afternoon, after Shadow had given Ellen a lift home. Catherine was alone, cleaning one of the back rooms. She heard his boots on the floor out front and her heart squirmed dangerously. She grabbed a paper towel to dry her hands and went to meet him.

"Lock up the clinic," he said curtly.

His arrogance irritated her all over again. When he snapped his fingers, everyone jumped, and he had clearly come to expect it. Catherine tossed the paper towel in a trash can and crossed her arms over her chest instead.

"No."

His brows shot up. "Come again?"

"The last time I checked, this place was under the jurisdiction of the IHS. Since I'm the only representative of the Service here, I guess I should be the one to decide when we close."

"Fine. Do it."

She fought the urge to stomp her foot in temper. "Why?" she demanded.

"Because I want to make sure you know how to use this gun, and I'm not going to do it here. I'm not in the habit of arming someone if it's going to come back to haunt me."

Her eyes widened. "You got the permit?"

He reached beneath his jacket to pull out a small revolver tucked against his waist. He held it out to her and she reached for it, but then he pulled it back.

"Target practice first."

"I can shoot it."

"Mind if I don't take your word for it?"

He turned away from her and went outside. Catherine hesitated. It truly irked her to let him win, but she wanted— *needed*—that gun. Suddenly she realized how very tired she was of being a victim, of running and hiding and fearing. She had to be able to fight back with something other than a flimsy stick, and she couldn't blame him for not wanting to give a gun to someone until he was sure she knew how to use it.

She flipped the Open/Closed sign on the window and followed him out. He was already clear across the parking area and she had to run to catch up with him.

"Where are we going?"

"There's a little canyon about a quarter mile from here. The walls should stop the bullets from going anywhere they're not supposed to."

"You're being a little overly cautious, don't you think?"

"Just saving myself some work. Ten-to-one Ellen and Shadow would have me replacing the clinic windows, if you shot them out. Then there are the innocent passersby out on the road to consider."

Catherine gritted her teeth.

They reached the canyon and climbed, sliding, down its steep walls. When they reached the bottom, she looked around. It was less than a city block wide, and maybe three times that long. Red rocky soil crumbled down from the sides, and the floor was littered with gnarled, water-starved juniper trees.

They were completely isolated here, out of view from the road and the clinic. Something tickled down Catherine's spine. She wasn't sure if it was trepidation or the titillating prospect of being so very alone with him again.

Jericho handed her the gun and pulled a full speed-loader out of his jeans pocket. "Go for it, Cat Eyes."

Her chin came up. "All right. I will."

She opened the gun and placed the speed-loader in position. Then she felt his hand in her hair.

Her heart slammed as he combed his fingers through it and fanned the curls out in the sun. She looked up at him, her throat going dry. Was he going to kiss her again? Did she want him to?

Yes. God help her, but she did. It was crazy to start anything with him. She had too many secrets and she had a life to go back to. He had Ellen. But when she looked at him, none of that seemed to matter at all.

He hadn't spent much time outdoors with her, Jericho realized. Now he noticed that her roots were a deep, rich copper color. They gleamed like fire in the sun, like the wild, inner flames he'd felt in her when he'd had that lapse of sanity and kissed her. Irrepressible, untamable, the color even glinted through the black dye. His stomach tightened.

"What . . . what are you doing?" she asked.

"It's not really black."

She thought of lying again, and again she knew it wasn't possible. "No."

He wasn't going to kiss her. He was simply probing again. She looked back at the gun in her hands, trying to remember what she had been about to do with it.

She dropped the speed-loader, the bullets spilling out into the sand. Jericho made an impatient sound, but in truth he was grateful for the diversion. He bent to scoop them up, but she dropped to her knees at the same time. When he closed his hand over the bullets, he found himself holding hers instead.

She went absolutely still. He thought he could hear her heart pound. Or maybe, he thought, it was his.

Damn her. Damn her for getting to him this way.

Finally, slowly, she looked up from their hands. Her eyes were so big, so green, with flecks of honey gold.

"Don't ask me this time," she breathed. "Just do it. I'm afraid to say yes."

An invisible fist rammed its way into his solar plexus.

He told himself to stand, to load the gun for her. His hand found the back of her neck instead, pulling her toward him. He told himself he could have withstood anything but that— a breathy admission that was stolen right from his own heart. But he knew the truth was that he would probably have touched her anyway, because something about her drew him like a moth to flame.

Of course, the moths always burned.

He ground his mouth down on hers, too hard, too punishing. Catherine made an odd sound in her throat, but it was not a protest. His kiss was like everything else about him, hard and sure, hot and dangerous, and suddenly she

craved it with reckless hunger because no one had ever made
her feel like this before.

She leaned into him, the gun sliding from her nerveless
hand. She dug her fingers into the sand to brace herself as
his tongue moved past her lips, sliding, urgent, demanding.
She opened to him, meeting it with her own, leaning more,
more, until finally his strong hands had to come up to hold
her arms.

Velvet and steel, she thought, and she shuddered again.

He growled and pulled her into him hard, twisting at the
last moment to drop her on her back in the sand. Then finally his body covered hers, and it was everything she had
wanted, everything she needed. He broke away from her
mouth to run his lips down her jaw, then he closed his teeth
with shattering gentleness on the sensitive lobe of her ear.
She cried out and drove her hands into his hair.

As black as midnight water, as soft as his breath, the only
soft thing about him. The curls slid through her fingers and
this time she felt his arousal hard against her belly. She
moved her hand there, amazed and a little frightened by the
way he could want her so completely, so suddenly. An agony of hunger slammed through her, because this *wasn't* all
she wanted. No, she wanted all of him, everything he could
give her, and sanity be damned.

She gasped as his hand moved up her hip, over her ribs to
her breast, covering her possessively. She arched into him,
pressing herself into his palm. He made a sound that was
half a groan, half the curse of a man who was lost. Then he
pulled at her shirt roughly, tugging it free of her jeans.

"Okay, Cat Eyes, let's go for it. Maybe we're both crazy."

She moaned something inarticulate then she froze. *The
scar.*

Something cold and jagged splintered suddenly inside her.
If he undressed her here, in broad daylight, he would find
it. Catherine panicked, pushing his hands away. "Please.
No. I . . . can't."

He reared back from her, confused, then his eyes blazed
with anger. "Could have sworn you told me not to ask."

"Yes...no." Suddenly her throat closed, aching painfully with the urge to cry.

Someday, when all this was over, maybe she could tell him. But not now. It wasn't only her fear, this time, that had her scrambling away from him. Suddenly she realized that if he knew about Victor and Victor *did* have a man out here waiting to see if she would talk, then Jericho could be in danger as well—if he shared her knowledge.

"I'm sorry," she managed feebly, but the response came from somewhere deep and raw in her heart and it echoed with real pain. Finally she grasped at straws. "I thought it would just be a kiss. I didn't intend for it to go any further."

His eyes narrowed. "Sure you did. You're a big girl."

Catherine flinched.

Yes, on some level she had known. She had known that if their mouths met it would not be just a test this time. It would erupt into something neither of them would want to control—it had almost happened at the sing and might have if they had been alone. But she had panicked then too, and this time some small, reckless part of her had wanted the decision taken out of her hands.

The part of her that had forgotten that Victor had forever marked her.

She grabbed the gun where it had fallen in the sand and scrambled to her feet. She had been as crazy to come here as she had been to meet him in moonlight at the sing. She would do what he had brought her to do, and then she would go.

He had set up targets in the middle of the canyon before he had brought her here, ten bottles perched upon various rocks. She rammed the bullets into the gun grimly and took aim. Breathing deeply, closing one eye to look down the sight, she blasted one after the other, then she lowered the weapon again.

"Satisfied?" she managed. "I promise you I won't shoot myself in the foot." She turned around to look at him. Jericho was staring at the shattered bottles, slack jawed.

It was too much. Her emotions were too exposed, too close to the surface, and they bubbled there. She laughed until she had to hold her stomach against the pain it brought.

Jericho's gaze moved from the bottles to her. He had never heard her laugh before, he realized. In fact, this was the first time he had ever seen her look truly happy. *What the hell were her demons?* He wanted to hold onto his anger, needed to curse every mewling, shrinking bone in her body.

But broken birds didn't shoot like that.

Slowly he got to his feet. "Not bad," he allowed.

"Not good, either." She gasped for breath. "I used to be faster than that, but I haven't practiced in a long while."

"Where'd you learn?" His voice was hoarse and he had to clear his throat.

He saw her hesitate, her smile trembling away. His temper flared again. "More secrets, Cat Eyes?"

"No." She shook her head. "No."

This was safe ground, she realized. Growing up with Paddy Callahan for a father had absolutely no connection to her life with Victor. Speaking of one would not jeopardize him with the other.

"My father's a retired cop," she said softly. "And one of my brothers-in-law is active on the force. They were both determined that Paddy's girls should know how to protect themselves."

His brows arched in that dry, skeptical look that was uniquely his. "Paddy's girls?" he repeated.

"Paddy's my father. I have five sisters."

He opened the gun, emptying the spent cartridges as though he was only mildly interested. But it was the most she had ever told him about herself. Of course, he admitted, he hadn't given her a lot of opportunity. Again, he told himself he didn't want to know.

"Your people are damned prolific," he answered.

"We're Irish-Catholic. Paddy's from the old country. For that matter, so was my mother." She was talking too much, almost babbling, but he didn't seem angry anymore and she was eager to leave that wrenching aborted moment in the sand behind.

"The Irish don't believe in birth control?" he asked finally.

"Actually, it's the pope who doesn't. What about the Navajo?"

"Excess is frowned upon. Only wolfmen accumulate too much of anything, even children."

"But you have a sister."

"Two's about the norm. So what about you? Do you do everything the pope tells you?"

"No, but I always thought I'd have a big family. It just seems normal to have a bunch of noisy kids gathered around the dinner table."

He shook his head. "Can't imagine it."

It was another difference between them, not that it should matter. She began walking back to the slope.

"So where's your mother?" he asked from behind her. "You said she *was* from the old country."

"She's dead."

Catherine pulled herself up the canyon wall. She paused at the top to get her breath back, then she smiled again, almost whimsically. "Paddy was a hard-drinking, hardworking man in his younger years. Mom kept him under dubious control until I was about sixteen. Then she died from complications giving birth to Erin—she's the baby. Kelly and Elaine—they're the oldest—had already left home and gotten married by then, so I grew up fast. I —"

"Elaine?" he asked.

Catherine hesitated. "That's right. She's four years older than I am."

"Elaine and Lanie. Two sisters with the same name. Guess you Irish have some convoluted traditions."

"Lanie is short for Delana." She wasn't lying. That *had* been her grandmother's name. Still, she felt herself flushing and she quickly starting walking again.

"So you grew up fast," he prompted, following her.

Catherine shrugged. "I had to take care of the three youngest girls. Erin was a handful—crawling by then—so I quit school."

"Thought you needed all kinds of degrees to be a doctor."

"Paddy blew his top when he found out and made me go back. He gave up drinking and used the money to hire a live-in housekeeper so I could do it. That's when I started applying for scholarships. It broke his heart when Mom died, and whiskey was his last remaining pleasure. I figured if he was willing to give it up, then I was damned well going to make it worthwhile."

He almost believed her...almost. There was a light in her eyes when she talked about her father. Maybe her name really was Delana, but he couldn't quite buy that she had gotten her penchant for french-vanilla coffee from the childhood she had just described. Even in the city, he doubted if cops made enough money to provide such luxuries for six kids. Besides, she'd said he'd had to quit drinking to afford the housekeeper.

They had reached the parking lot again. He stopped at his Rover. "So is he still off?" he asked.

Her eyes came around to him, startled. "Who? What?"

"Your father. Is he still off the booze?"

"Oh. I don't know."

Catherine bit her lip. This was getting into a whole different area. She couldn't tell him that she hadn't been in contact with Paddy since she had thrown all those scholarships and all that whiskey money down the drain to marry Victor Landano. As sure as the sun was shining, he'd want to know where Victor was now.

She forced her spine straight. "So can I keep the gun?" she asked, changing the subject.

His eyes searched her face, but then he leaned through the open window of his truck and brought out a box of ammunition. "You're lying through your teeth, Cat Eyes," he said mildly.

Her heart thumped, but she shook her head hard. "No."

Maybe she wasn't, he thought. Maybe she was just throwing up more shadows, telling him something, telling him nothing at all. He supposed he could find out. Shadow's friend with the health service was Jack Keller. He could contact him and learn what there was to know about Lanie McDaniel.

Assuming he wanted to. Assuming he had any inclination at all toward letting himself get all tangled up again with a woman who needed more than he could give her.

He watched her go. She headed back toward the clinic trailer, all long legs and slender, swaying hips. He thought of those satisfying moments in the sand and something hot gathered itself inside him again, even as he knew it was best that they had stopped when they had.

Suddenly he knew, again, that she wasn't really like Anelle at all. Anelle had not loved that fiercely. He had thought there was more depth to her because he had needed there to be, so he had denied his instincts. Lanie McDaniel, on the other hand, was all secrets and shades of gray and wary cat eyes. And by their very nature, secrets demanded strength and cunning to remain well kept.

Yes, he wanted to know what they were. But he wanted her to trust him with them. He wanted her to give them up on her own.

In the end, he thought, maybe that was the most dangerous thing of all.

Chapter 9

Catherine couldn't concentrate.

She sighed, looking blearily at the case notes Richard Moss had left on the clinic steps before she had come in. She assumed it had been him, because he had returned Lisa Littlehorn's clinic file along with them. They contained more information on the Mystery Disease than she had been privy to yet and she wanted very much to read them, but her mind kept wandering.

She had arrived late this morning because she had grimly remained in bed long after dawn had come. But she hadn't been able to sleep then, any more than she had all night, because her thoughts kept tangling and swirling. Images of Jericho's mouth on hers were interwoven with flashes of the owl and memories of her conversation with Schilling. It had finally occurred to her in the wee hours of the morning that if Schilling should be able to trace a link between Victor and a hired man, then that link would probably lead him directly to the health-service clinic as well.

If anyone found her, she preferred it to be the FBI. She wasn't entirely sure why she had tried to hide her whereabouts from them as well. It had just been an instinct. The bumbling ineptitude of some of their men had appalled her. Like most people, she had always assumed their agents were smooth, shrewd men of great expertise. She had learned the hard way that that wasn't necessarily true. She had lost a great deal of faith in them after Victor had shot her, so she had simply fled Boston without telling Schilling where she was going.

She groaned. She was such an amateur at these hide-and-seek games, she thought. However inept Schilling's agents might be, she was sure they were a lot better at it than she was. She hadn't even been able to figure out a way to avoid telling that health-service official who she really was. And it certainly hadn't taken Jericho very long to figure out that something was amiss.

Jericho. Impossibly, when she closed her eyes, she could still feel his hands on her breasts, his teeth at her ear, his breath hot against her skin. Then she heard the distinctive thump-*thump* of his boots on the steps outside and her eyes flew open again. He appeared in the clinic doorway and watched her expressionlessly for a moment. Catherine carefully lowered her feet to the floor from where she had been resting them on the desk.

Her pulse hitched. When had she become aware that he took those stairs unlike anyone else, that his footsteps had a quick one-two tempo because he always skipped the middle plank? She swallowed uncomfortably, not sure she wanted to examine the question too closely.

"You look like hell," he said finally.

That snapped her out of her daze. "You would too if someone was dropping dead owls on your bed."

He shrugged one shoulder. "No doubt. Listen, I need you."

Her heart slammed. "I beg your pardon?"

For the first time—and she thought maybe for the only time—his face actually seemed to redden. His gaze danced away from her uncomfortably, then came back.

"Ellen's visiting her boyfriend in Albuquerque," he said. Then he added unnecessarily, "It's Saturday."

Catherine's head began to spin. What was he saying? Was he *lonely* without the nurse? She dismissed that possibility immediately. No matter what his relationship with her was, she could not in a million years imagine this man being uncomfortable or lost without companionship. As private as he was, as stony and forbidding as some of his moods could be, he would never be dissatisfied with his own company.

She swallowed cautiously. "I don't think...I mean, I don't want—" His eyes narrowed on her face and she broke off.

"Go on. Spit it out. You don't think what?"

Her chin came up hard and her eyes flashed. "Okay. Fine. I don't want to fill the gaps while your girlfriend's out of town."

"My *what?*"

"Girlfriend, lover, whatever you call it in this part of the world."

He looked at her blankly, then his face hardened. "If she was—and I'm not saying she is—would you care to tell me what you thought I was doing kissing you, then?"

Catherine colored to the roots of her hair. God, how could she have misjudged him that way? Looking at him now, at his expression, it was perfectly clear that this was not a man who would treat an intimate relationship—any true relationship—so lightly. There was something too fiercely loyal about him. She remembered how he had looked out for Angie Two Sons, and the way Shadow could say almost anything to him and get away with it. She remembered the way he had wept for Lisa Littlehorn.

Why *had* he kissed her, then? Her blood began to pump hard in her ears.

"I don't know," she managed.

He raked a hand through his hair. "Where the hell did you get such an idea?" he asked finally. "Ellen and I are born to the same clan. If anything ever happened between us, it would be incest."

"Well, how was I supposed to know that?" she answered indignantly. "Besides, it hasn't stopped her from wanting you."

He considered that a moment, then he shook his head. "You're crazy."

"No," Catherine retorted. "I'm a woman. And women see things that go right over men's heads."

"Given this some thought, have you?"

"It's just obvious," she answered tightly. "If it were an animal, it would jump up and bite you."

She had indeed given it a lot of thought, though, and now that she knew the truth she was appallingly relieved. She was also very aware of his thoughtful, perusing eyes. In an effort to hide her expression, to do something with her hands, she got up and went for the coffeepot.

Jericho took three long steps and pulled it out of her hand. "No time for that."

She scowled at him. "Generally I have all day and not much to do with it."

"Not today. There's a sick little boy out near Standing Rock. I need you to run over there with me and take a look at him."

Her jaw dropped. "Me?"

"There's nobody else here."

She ignored that. "You want *me* to go treat this kid?"

"Don't make more of it than it is. The kid's sick, I have no license to practice, Ellen's in Albuquerque. As it is, I'm probably going to have to twist arms to get his mom to let you look at him."

"I'll go."

"Never doubted it."

He waited while she threw together some items she thought she'd need. When they were in the Rover, hurtling down the road at his usual dangerous speed, she looked over at him.

"Did it kill you to ask me?"

He gave a very small grin. "Just about."

"You could have just gone to him yourself. No one would have known, and I can't imagine that you care much about the law."

"I have a healthy respect for the law." His face hardened. "Never considered it, actually. I'm thinking about the kid. I figure all those scholarships must have taught you something. Maybe you know something to do for him that wouldn't occur to me."

"Probably," she answered, glad to take credit where it was due. "What's wrong with him?"

"Cold. Maybe the flu."

Catherine stiffened. "What kind of flu?"

"His head's all stuffed up. Stomach cramps, throwing up. His mom caught up with me down on the Crownpoint road. She was headed to the clinic over there. I told her to go home and I'd find someone to come see him. The guy at Crownpoint is even worse than Kolkline, and I don't know the Navajo working out of there. Different clan."

He was being unusually talkative, but Catherine barely heard him. "Drive faster."

He quirked a single brow at her. "I'm damned near going a hundred."

"It sounds like it could be *Tah honeesgai.*"

He didn't answer, but she felt a surge from the engine. She glanced at the speedometer. The needle inched up over a hundred.

"No," he said finally. "It's his *head,* Cat Eyes. *I* would have thought of that if she'd said his chest, that he was having trouble breathing."

She shook her head frantically. "Patients do that all the time. They're not trained to be specific. They'll *say* head because they're sneezing, but they'll forget to mention that they're coughing, too."

"He's throwing up. That hasn't happened with *Tah honeesgai* before."

"But it could. Cramps could cause it, especially in a kid."

He swore darkly. The needle worked its way to a hundred and ten. The engine shuddered.

"How old is he?" Catherine asked finally.

"I don't know. Ten or so, I'd guess. They're clan, but they live so far out I don't know them very well."

She bit her lip. "He's the youngest so far."

"If it's *Tah honeesgai.*"

But it was. Somehow she *knew* it was. She had managed to retain the dates from the other case files. The bug was gathering steam. It was striking more and more frequently.

She turned her thoughts grimly to saving the child. She hadn't brought the portable oxygen tank, hadn't thought she'd need it. She would do mouth-to-mouth if she had to. At least she had the things she would need for an IV.

"Where's Standing Rock?" she asked.

"We're just about there."

"How far from Albuquerque?"

"Two hundred miles."

She fought the urge to weep in frustration. As fast as Lisa had deteriorated, they'd never make it.

Think. "Do they live in a hogan or a trailer? Will they have a phone?" She had noticed one of the trailer conclaves outside of Shiprock and there had been telephone lines there. She could call for a helicopter again, she thought, but Jericho shook his head.

"Damn," she said.

"There's a hospital in Gallup. Thirty miles across the desert," he said. "We'll take him there."

"Are they familiar with the Mystery Disease?"

"They're going to be."

Suddenly he swerved hard off the road. Their speed had them practically airborne when the Rover hit a rocky expanse of ground. Catherine knocked her head on the roof and grabbed the armrest.

The brakes screeched as they reached the hogan and Jericho careened to a stop. She was out almost before the Rover stopped sliding, but he was right beside her. A young woman in jeans and a calico shirt came running outside.

Her eyes flew over Catherine and sought Jericho. "He's worse!" she cried. "What's happening to him?"

Jericho took her arm as they moved back toward the hogan. Quietly, without alarming her too much, he tried to explain. Catherine hesitated, then raced past them.

Finally the woman acknowledged her. She wrenched free of Jericho to see where she was going.

"No!" she cried. "Who is she? Stop her!"

"She's a doctor, Bessie. You've got to let her help him."

"She's *Anglo*. I want you."

"I can't do anything this time. I can't always. You know that. That's why I brought her."

Catherine didn't wait to hear any more. She ducked inside.

The boy was on a narrow bed pressed neatly against one wall. A man—presumably his father—stood beside him. He was too stricken to fight her presence. He moved aside and made room for her at the boy's bedside.

Catherine knelt there and felt her heart stop. She had been right. It was happening again.

She fumbled in her bag for acetaminophen, because he was probably too young to take a chance on aspirin. Once again, she felt the fury of helplessness. She was only an extern. There was so little she could do.

She looked down at the little bottle in her hand. No. Damn it, *no!* She was not going to lose this child too because Kolkline didn't give a damn, because this land was too big, because all the odds were stacked against them. She dropped the acetaminophen and rummaged for something stronger.

"Lanie."

She didn't hear him. She was too engrossed in what she was doing to pick up on a name that wasn't hers.

"Lanie," Jericho said again. His eyes narrowed when she didn't respond, but he wasn't surprised. *"Lanie!"*

She jumped. "What?"

"Are you allowed to do that?"

She met his eyes. "No."

He studied her, then he shrugged. It was a choice between her career or the child's life. She was going to save the child and even if he were inclined to, he knew suddenly that he wouldn't be able to stop her.

"Get the truck ready," she said. "Bring it up close to the door."

"Right."

He was gone before he had uttered the last of the syllable. Catherine got the IV hooked up, dripping precious fluid into the boy's veins. Then she bent over him to give him air.

Jericho's strong hand caught her shirt, pulling her back. "Don't."

She shot a wild glance at him and tried to pull away. "He needs help breathing."

"Not yet he doesn't. And Gallup's not that far. Let's get going."

Her head swam, but then she understood. He *wasn't* entirely ruling it out that *Tah honeesgai* was physically communicable.

She backed away from the bed, looking down at the child. Jericho was right. His breathing was labored, but he was still holding his own. It wasn't necessary to risk her own life yet. She would sit beside him and monitor him carefully. She would not leave his side as she had done with Lisa. At the first hint that he wasn't able to draw breath on his own, *then* she would take over.

Jericho lifted the child, blankets and all, into his arms. Catherine held the IV aloft, then she let out a startled squeak.

"Just a deer mouse," Jericho said. The tiny animal had scurried out of the bedding, startled when the boy's warm body was moved. Catherine looked after it, then back at Jericho, shaking her head. Who else in her Tufts class was practicing under such conditions?

Bessie was obviously embarrassed. "There's nothing I can do about them," she muttered. "I clean and clean, but when the nights get cold they still come in."

Catherine put a hand on her arm as they went outside. "It's like that all over." Of course, she thought, their passage was a good deal easier out here with no doors to impede their progress. But in the end, it was a tiny creature and could hardly do much harm. Lice and roaches would be far worse, but the place really was clean and there was no sign of either.

Jericho settled the boy in the Rover. His mother got in the front seat and Catherine slid in the back, half squatting on the floor beside him.

"Jericho, you need to call University right away, as soon as we get there. Have them send someone over who's familiar with this thing."

Jericho made a wordless sound of agreement.

"Bessie, it's best if you go to the desk and fill out the paperwork. They'll want some, even in this case."

"Yes," the woman agreed in a small voice.

"I'll stay with him and tell the doctor what I've done so far."

"You don't have to do that," snapped Jericho.

Catherine didn't answer. He looked in the rearview mirror and saw her staring dully out the window, her hand protectively on the boy's chest. She would do it, he realized. Not only was it in her patient's best interest, but she was such a damned stickler for rules. But he knew she wouldn't do it easily. Her expression was wrenching, pained.

He bit back a curse. He thought of her father and his booze money and the scholarships. She was going to throw everything away, and he realized that the prospect nearly strangled him.

The Rover jerked and lunged from side to side as they reached a road and climbed onto it. Catherine braced her weight against the boy to keep him from jolting off the seat. Finally, they pulled up in front of the emergency door of a hospital.

Jericho lifted the boy out of the backseat and Catherine struggled to take him from him. "You've got to call University," she reminded him.

"He's heavy."

"Yeah, and I couldn't shoot a gun, either," she snapped.

He let her take the child, if only because something hard and breath-robbing had punched into his gut. In that moment, he finally knew that she wasn't a broken bird at all.

He wanted to dwell on that, needed badly to mistrust it, but there was no time. Bessie was already at the desk and Lanie—or whoever the hell she was—was pushing through

the swinging doors to the treatment rooms, staggering a little under her burden.

"Stretcher!" he shouted. Behind the desk, white-hatted
heads snapped up. He pointed where Lanie and the boy had
gone, then he went for the telephone.

Who was she? *What* was she, besides too selfless and
stubborn for her own good?

He had to find out fast. Whoever she was, he was starting to care far too much about her. And the deeper he got,
the more her secrets scared him.

Chapter 10

Catherine returned to the emergency lobby an hour later. She slumped in the seat beside his and rubbed a hand over the back of her neck, where a dull ache was starting.

"Ready to go?"

She looked at him, startled. There was something odd, something even tighter about his voice than usual.

"I want to see how this turns out," she murmured.

"You can call from the clinic."

"I could also wait here. Go ahead, if you've got somewhere to go. The CDC is here now. One of those guys can give me a ride back."

"I don't have to be anywhere," he snapped.

Catherine scowled at him. Even he seemed to realize that his tone was unnecessarily harsh. He went on with deliberate control.

"You look like you're ready to collapse."

"I am, but I won't. I just need some caffeine. Is there a cafeteria around here?" She pushed to her feet again, looking about at the signs and the red arrows on the walls.

"No doubt," he answered, "but I wouldn't count on french vanilla."

She gave him a grimace that wasn't quite a smile. "I can make do when I have to."

They made their way down a long hallway leading to another part of the building. She must be weaving, Catherine thought, realizing that she hadn't really slept in two nights. Her arm kept brushing Jericho's, and warmth slid sweetly through her. Then she realized that he wasn't moving away from the contact. Somewhere over the course of the past couple weeks, a sense of camaraderie had settled between them. She hadn't realized how precious that was, how very much she'd wanted it, until it had happened.

He got them each a cup of coffee, snapping at her again when she started to dig in her jeans pocket to pay for her own.

"Since when does the IHS give salaries? Shadow said you were working for free."

"Room and board," she corrected.

"Keep your money."

She looked at him curiously as they sat at a table. "Do you work?"

He scowled at her. "You know what I do."

"I mean besides the sings."

"The people pay me."

"Yes, I know, but you don't seem to do very many of them. Two since I've been here."

"It's more than singing in this day and age." He hesitated, clearly struggling to explain to someone who wasn't Navajo. "It's...being there for people. It's taking water to the elders who live alone and can't get around, and trying to get kids to come back from the cities when they leave the Res and break their parents' hearts. It's picking Lance up when he passes out at the windmill. Sometimes the people give sheep or blankets or pieces of turquoise. Sometimes they've got money to spare. It doesn't cost much to live out here."

"I've noticed." The truth was, she hadn't felt the pinch of her drastically altered income at all. She was still doing fine with the money she had managed to squirrel away during those last horrible weeks with Victor, when the FBI was supposed to have been protecting her.

"Did you tell the doctor what you did with the medicine?" Jericho asked, changing the subject.

Catherine nodded slowly. The pained look came back to her eyes.

"So what happens now?" he asked.

She tried to shrug as if it were of no great import. "With any luck, I'll just be written up. He'll send a letter to the American Medical Association, and probably one to the Service, too. They'll go in my file, then I'll write one explaining the extenuating circumstances and that'll go in, too." She bit her lip. "It might affect my getting a residency. Then again, it might not. I'll just have to wait and find out when I start applying."

His eyes narrowed again. "Where're you going to apply?"

Catherine sighed. In truth, she hadn't given it any thought yet. Simply getting this externship had in itself been a minor miracle.

"I don't know," she admitted.

He scowled. "*When* do you apply?"

"When this post is over."

"How much longer is that?"

He was shooting questions at her like an inquisitor. What was wrong with him this afternoon?

"Four weeks," she answered, then she thought about it, surprised again at the way time flew here. "No, a little over two now, I guess," she amended. *About the same time Victor goes to trial.* But that was another bridge she'd cross when she got to it.

Jericho stood, draining his coffee, tossing the cup into a nearby trash can. "Let's go back to the desk and see how Louie's doing."

Catherine rose as well, carrying her cup. "Is that his name?"

"I think so. He's got a brother, and I lose track of which is which."

They went back down the corridor again, arms brushing, hips bumping, until he finally held open the opposite door for her. He wore another blue chambray shirt, the sleeves rolled up on his forearms. Apparently he had left his ever-present jacket in the truck. Catherine watched his muscles ripple as he stretched to step out of her way. She fought that damned instinctive urge to shiver again.

He went to the front door, staring out through the glass at the gathering twilight. Catherine went to the desk, but her eyes kept drifting back to him.

"Miss?"

"Oh—yes." She jumped and turned back to the nurse who was trying to get her attention. "The Mystery Disease victim, the little boy, how's he doing?"

"Are you a relative?"

"I'm an extern up on the Res. I brought him in."

"Oh, of course. Well, I don't have any new information except what you admitted him with."

"Can I go check on him?"

"I don't see why not."

She looked back at Jericho. He was still standing at the doors. She shrugged. She would only be gone a minute.

She went to the examining rooms, but the one Louie had been in was empty now. Her heart constricted. She grabbed a resident as he made his way down the hallway.

"Do you know what happened to the little boy who was in there?"

"The CDC moved him to ICU quarantine. Fourth floor."

She found an elevator and went up, repeating the whole process with a floor nurse. Worriedly, she glanced at her watch. She had been gone a lot longer than a minute, but she couldn't imagine that Jericho would go anywhere without her. Then again, he had been acting more like a bear than usual this afternoon.

She was directed to Louie's room. It was connected to the corridor by a little chamber where she hurriedly pulled on scrubs and a mask, then she slipped quietly inside. Three doctors were working on him, but they showed no urgency. Bessie was there, and she seemed calm under the circumstances.

"How is he?" she asked. One of the doctors looked back at her. "Richard!"

He smiled warmly. "I'd hoped you'd turn up. I saw your name on the admittance forms." He left Louie's bedside and came to meet her. "He's stabilized," he told her. "Vital signs are good. He's not out of the woods yet by any means, but I think he'll make it. He's breathing pretty well with the help of the regulator."

"Yes." She had noticed.

"The speed with which you acted is commendable. I'd say you saved this one."

Catherine managed a smile. "My methods won't win accolades, and as far as the speed goes, I had help."

He scowled. "Help?"

"Jericho Bedonie. Have you met him?"

"The name doesn't ring a bell." He brushed past the subject, clearly not interested in pursuing it. "Questionable methods have been overlooked before."

"I hope so. I had no choice."

Richard hesitated. "I wouldn't even include mention of it, but this patient's file will be gone over with a fine-tooth comb. Any treatment must be listed meticulously, especially as it appears he might live. The CDC will want to know why."

"I understand." She looked at her watch again. She'd been gone thirty minutes now. She had to get back downstairs.

"Are you ready to leave? Do you need a lift? I'm just about finished here."

Catherine shook her head. "Jericho's waiting somewhere."

Richard grinned good-naturedly. "Do I detect competition?"

For a moment she only gaped at him. *Competition?* For that to be the case, Richard would have to be in the running and Jericho would have to be interested in her as more than...than what? How *was* he interested in her? She thought of the way he had kissed her and the fact that he wasn't tied up with Ellen after all, and her pulse skipped.

Richard watched her expression change. "Ah, I do."

"No." She shook her head, if for no other reason than there was no rivalry possible between the two men. They were simply too different for them both to appeal to the same woman, any woman. Richard was suave, smooth. Jericho was rough and brutally honest, unapologetically male.

She managed a small smile. "I'd better find him."

"I'll try to pull the interview on this one, too. Maybe I'll see you soon."

She was already backing into the chamber. "That'd be fine."

She hurried past the nurses' station again, absently noticing a man standing there in the ever-present boots and jeans. But his jeans were pressed, his boots were unscuffed and he was reading a chart. Something about him made her hesitate. She looked at him closer, frowning.

"Is this all you've got?" he asked the floor nurse.

The woman answered with forced patience. "That's the admitting form, Dr. Kolkline. The rest of the paperwork is down in his room with the doctors who are working on him."

Catherine felt her blood drain. She felt cold.

In the next moment, rage burned through her. It made her pulse thunder and her hands clench. She took a step closer to him.

"Dr. Kolkline," she repeated carefully.

The man looked up at her. "Yes?"

"Abe Kolkline? You're supposed to be working out of the Shiprock clinic on the Res?"

He nodded, then a wary look came over his face. "Who are you?"

"I'm your new extern."

His expression cleared into a jovial look she knew all too well. Paddy had once been able to drink with the best of them.

"Tracked me down, did you? I've been meaning to get out there—"

"Then why didn't you?" she spat.

Surprise flew over his well-worn features. "Now hold on a minute, young lady."

Hold on. Yes, she had to do that. Catherine closed her eyes, trying to get control of her dangerous temper. Her chances for a residency were already tenuous at best. For all she knew, Kolkline had some significant clout with the Service, and if that were the case, it would be like pulling teeth to get a recommendation out of them if she blasted him.

But what kind of reference was she going to get anyway? Not only had she defied laws and medical ethics to treat Louie, but she had been working for nearly a month without supervision because this man never bothered to show up.

Hold on? Like hell she would.

"Has it occurred to you that you're being grossly unfair to me?" she demanded. "I came here to learn. I can't do that without you. I came here to save people, but I've already lost a patient and I blame you for that, too! Do you even know a teenage girl *died* out there because she was stricken with this damned disease and there was no doctor to treat her? I couldn't give her anything but aspirin!"

She realized, appalled, that she was going to cry. The tears were hot, brimming, but she blinked them back furiously. She had given Louie something stronger than aspirin, and he had lived. But while she had been hung up on rules, Lisa had died. Maybe the difference meant nothing, but guilt strangled her.

Then it was washed away by fresh fury. If Kolkline had been there in either case, they were decisions she would never have had to make.

"Those people out on the Res might not know they need you," she snapped, "but you're the only qualified medic they have in that area. If you're not interested in serving them, then why don't you go somewhere else? If you're not interested in practicing, then why don't you just retire?"

But she knew. Of course, she knew. His hand shook badly as he held the chart. His eyes were bloodshot and a network of broken capillaries marked his cheeks and his nose. The smell of cheap whiskey came off him in waves.

Like her, he was hiding in a place where even the wind could get lost. Unlike her, he was hiding from life itself.

Catherine let out a deep, shaky breath, then she jolted at the sharp sound of singular applause coming from behind her. She whipped around to see Jericho standing in front of the elevator.

He was clapping at her outburst, but his face was stony. Was he approving or mocking her?

"My advice to you," Kolkline said hoarsely, "is to get out of medicine while you still hold some high ideals."

She spun back to him. "Thanks to you, I might not have a choice. But I'm here for two more weeks, and in the meantime I don't need you. I'd be more than satisfied with a phone number where I can reach you to approve prescriptionary medicines."

"So be it," he said tightly. He grabbed a piece of scratch paper and wrote on it in a spidery hand. Catherine snatched it from him.

"Thank you." She stalked past Jericho, shooting him a warning look. "Don't you dare say a word."

She got all the way back to the parking lot before she remembered that they had come in his Rover. She waited at the truck, feeling foolish.

He arrived a few minutes later, unlocking her door silently, looking at her only long enough to quirk a brow. She got in and waited as he slid behind the wheel and dropped a brown paper bag on the seat between them.

"What's that?" she asked.

"Thought you told me not to say anything."

"Since when do you listen?"

He laughed. The tension shimmied out of her. The rough sound of his voice seemed to reach inside her and soothe her soul. She managed a tremulous smile.

"Is your temper an Irish thing too?" he asked dryly.

"Now that you mention it."

"Kolkline had it coming. Won't do any good though."

"I know. But at least I got his phone number." She folded it and slid it into her jeans pocket, then she was appalled to realize that her throat was closing again over unshed tears.

"God," she groaned. "Everything's sliding right through my fingers like sand. He'll report me, too."

Jericho's gaze sharpened at her strangled tone. "Something tells me he doesn't contact the Service very often. He's got his own skeletons to protect."

Catherine nodded. It was all she could manage.

He was driving on the roads this time. She looked around dully and realized they were back on U.S. Route 666. But then he suddenly turned off, heading east onto the desert. She held on to keep from hitting her head again, scowling.

"Where are you going? The clinic's over the other way."

He didn't answer. The Rover hurtled up through a rocky gorge before coming out on a low butte. She looked up through the windshield. Catherine felt her breath snag. She had never seen so many stars in her life. They looked different here than they did even from the isolated medical trailers. They danced and twinkled, close enough to touch.

"Come on," he said, pushing open his door, grabbing the bag.

Catherine hesitated, then followed him. "If you're going to abandon me up here, I guess there are worse places to die," she muttered.

His laughter came again, low and amused. Then he took her hand.

Her heart jolted. Such a simple gesture…and such a huge, telling one coming from him. But what did it tell? More about her own feelings than his. He guarded his so ferociously, but something hot curled inside her even at the contact of their hands.

They went to the edge of the butte, their fingers linked. Then Catherine gasped again. Below them, the desert was alive.

She saw a bright, beady pair of eyes dart in and out of a shadow. There was no moon, but the stars gave more light than she ever would have believed possible. She had always thought the night was a clutching thing, a pervasive darkness, but she was wrong. A hawk glided past on his way to the desert floor, a magnificent shape just darker than the sky.

"She's not always unforgiving," Jericho mused. "Sometimes she's at peace, just breathing with the rhythms of life, and in those times she can soothe you."

Catherine started to ask who he was talking about, then she understood. He was speaking of the land as if it were a woman he knew intimately and loved. She supposed, in a way, that was true.

He dropped her hand to open the bag. "Figured you might need some soothing," he went on.

"But Louie is going to live."

"I know. I checked while you were among the missing. All the more reason for this." He pulled out a bottle of wine, a still-packaged corkscrew and a bag of Doritos. "The survival rate isn't high with this thing, but it looks like we claimed one small victory against it. Congratulations, Cat Eyes."

"A celebration," she murmured. Her voice sounded high, oddly pitched. She wondered if he noticed.

She was moved almost beyond speech. It was a gesture Richard Moss would have made carelessly. But from this man, she knew such kindnesses came deep from the heart...just like when he had taken her hand. Both would have been thought about and pondered, because he didn't do anything casually. More than that, he would have had to have bought this stuff in that quick half hour when she was upstairs.

Yes, it had been deliberate. Her heart moved again hard.

"Thank you," she managed.

He lifted a brow at her as he worked with the corkscrew. "You're too easy."

"I beg your pardon?"

"Ever occur to you that a man might have ulterior motives?"

This time her heart slammed. She admitted to herself that he wouldn't need the wine.

She swallowed carefully. "Do you?"

"Yeah. I thought it might loosen your tongue."

She stiffened and he was close enough to feel it.

"I don't get drunk."

"Never?"

"Once or twice in college."

"And what did you do then?"

She grinned suddenly. "I passed out. If I said anything, I did it in my sleep."

"Did you have secrets then, too?"

Her smile faded. "No."

He handed her the bottle for the first swig. She gulped, suddenly needing it, then her eyes widened. It was a very good, very crisp chardonnay. He dwelled in a dark world of mystical incantations, yet he was sophisticated and sensitive enough to chose the perfect wine for a night when the stars looked alive.

Good wine, Doritos, and not even a paper cup in sight. Something about him was starting to call to her in far more than a physical sense. She knew it should frighten her, but it just left her... defenseless.

She exchanged the wine for the Doritos. Jericho took the bottle, moved a bit closer to the edge and sat. After a moment, she joined him.

"You're not Lanie," he said finally.

Her heart drummed. "No."

"Who then?"

"If someone asked you, what would you tell them?" she countered. "Would you say I'm Lanie McDaniel, or that you think I'm someone else?"

"Who'd ask me?"

She licked her lips, then shook her head. "I'm not sure."

"What the hell have you done?"

She closed her eyes briefly. Suddenly she wanted to tell him everything so badly she ached with the need. She trusted him; she could no longer doubt the sanity of it, she simply did. She knew he would stand by her, protect her. If he genuinely liked her, then he would be that kind of man. He would do it, or he would die trying.

Something cold dashed through her. That was exactly why she couldn't tell him.

"I was in the wrong place at the wrong time," she whispered finally. "Before that I made some horrible, very naive choices."

She thought she saw him flinch. "It happens," he said shortly.

They stared out at the starlit desert for a long time in silence. Then he put the wine bottle aside very deliberately. Something about the gesture made her pulse start scrambling again.

"What are you doing?"

"I'm going to make a naive choice and pray that it's not horrible. You going to go crazy on me this time, Cat Eyes?"

She had to stop this, and knew she wasn't going to. Somewhere along the line, the decision really had stopped being hers to control.

"No." She let the word out on a shaky breath.

"Good," he said very quietly. "Because I'm going to make love to you. When you're hot and wet and naked in my arms, maybe the only secrets left will be ones that don't matter."

Chapter 11

The air was becoming cool since the sun had set. When Jericho leaned closer to take her mouth, the contrast made the heat of him seem enough to burn her.

Everything about him was slow this time, she thought, as if he would give her time to panic, to run, to change her mind even though she had said she wouldn't. She wanted this. She wanted to be naked and feel his warm breath on her skin, she wanted him to brand her with his own special fire. She wanted it as she had never wanted anything before in her life, and if she was wrong in her instincts about him too, then she would pay for it later.

She found his broad shoulders with her hands, trying to pull him closer, but he didn't deepen the kiss. His hands closed around her waist, holding her away, keeping her from moving. Yet she could feel the tension in his grip, the hunger. *For her.*

Then she understood.

"Last chance, Cat Eyes." His mouth slid to her neck and his voice was thick and raw.

"No," she breathed.

"No, as in stop, or no, you don't want the easy out I'm giving you? I'm not going to let you take me halfway again."

"I don't want you to stop."

He caught her hand, raising it to his mouth. He ran his tongue across her knuckles and she clenched her fist as something wild and unexplored tightened inside her. He turned her palm up and put pressure on her wrist until her fingers flew open again. Then he bit down gently on the spot his own fingers had touched.

Need screamed up in her—crazy, yes, but so much stronger than anything she had ever known before. She cried out and pulled away to bury her hands in his hair again.

He watched her face change, her eyes seem to darken with turbulence. She had made him feel again, had made him want, when he had learned long ago that it was safest not to want a woman too much. She had slid into his world like one of the water pixies that the Navajo believed lived below the streams. They were delicate and dancing, and he'd thought she was far too fragile to survive the demands that he knew he could make. Yet here she was, coming back at him, as hungry as he was. And so, for this time at least, he would be hers.

He had intended to love her with finesse and care. But she finally managed to push against him and the heat of her punched into him. He knew then that he could only be the man he was. While their tongues met roughly, he pulled at her T-shirt where it was tucked into her jeans. She shrugged out of her jacket even as he pulled the shirt over her head.

She wore no bra, but he had noticed that before, noticed without wanting to. She had in the beginning, but then the ageless simplicity of the land seemed to have caught her. Now he ripped his own shirt off as well, buttons spattering, and dragged her hard and suddenly against him.

Skin to skin. How long she had wanted this without even admitting it to herself! She pressed against him, savoring the smooth-hard texture of his chest, then his mouth stole the last of her air.

Catherine felt pain bite and fade as his lips crushed hers against her teeth, but she dug her fingers deeper into his skin, unwilling to let him stop. He lowered her into the sand, until the full, hot weight of him settled atop her. His mouth moved to her cheek, her ear, then behind it to a place that was exquisitely sensitive, though she had never known that before. He buried his face there as he tugged frenziedly at her jeans.

She lifted her hips to help him, her hands fumbling with his belt. Then they were naked, wrapped together, and his hand closed over her breast again. His breath was intimate and warm and damp against her neck, and it made everything coil inside her so tightly it was a new kind of agony.

His thumb found her nipple and stroked there. Then he touched his mouth where his thumb had moved, drawing her in between his teeth. She pressed his head there urgently.

"Yes," she breathed. *"Yes."*

Her wanting rocked him. In that moment, if never again, she wanted him more than she needed breath. There were no games, no pretensions, no lies. There were no mewling sighs and ladylike whimperings. She was what he had wanted for so long, the woman he had always hoped for but had stopped expecting to find.

His jaw clenched hard as he eased away from her. Not yet. Not now. She wouldn't whimper and complain, but she deserved more. If for no other reason, she deserved everything he could give her.

She wrapped her legs around him, refusing to let him go, and he knew he was lost.

Catherine dug her fingers into his skin where the hard, perfect angles of his waist tapered down. "Now," she moaned. "God, please, now."

He rose above her, and his strong, hard face filled her vision. He gave a guttural roar of defeat and plunged into her. In the last moment he had the stunning sense that he was sealing his destiny.

She had never dreamed that it could be like this. Raw and hungry, needs discovered and quenched in the same breath, new ones exploding and demanding to be met. He filled her and she felt herself closing around him. With his arms strong and straight, he drove into her until there was nothing but pounding urgency, until her nails dragged frantic trails in his flesh.

Harder, faster...she thought she screamed, but her breath was snagged, trapped somewhere in the tensing, tightening knot inside her. The stars swirled above her, sparkling and winking even when she finally closed her eyes. Then they erupted in color, as the knot inside her broke and shattered.

His arms came hard around her, and he followed her over the edge.

"Be careful." His voice was muffled against her neck. "Look over your right shoulder."

She did, and her breath flew out of her body again. Vertigo swam through her. *"God."*

"I'd guess he probably has something to do with the fact that we're still up here. The pope must have put in a good word for you, Cat Eyes. I'm going to move now. You stay still."

He eased off her. Catherine couldn't have moved if she had wanted to. Her eyes were glued to the butte edge where it fell away sharply, just inches from her right hip.

The cold air rushed at her when he was gone, but she didn't care. Then he took hold of her left hand. "Roll toward me."

She didn't roll—she leaped, coming to her feet in one motion with a death grip on his hand. Then she stared at him as he bent to grab their jeans. He was as calm as if he had just risen from his own bed.

"Didn't you know?" she gasped.

"I did."

"Then why didn't you move us away from there?"

"Can't say it was uppermost in my thoughts. Besides, it added an edge to things."

"You're out of your mind!"

He gave her that look again, too serious, too steady. "Must be." He handed her her jeans. "You sorry?"

If she was, then he was all wrong about her, and for a moment he felt something like real fear roll inside him where there had been nothing but hunger and heat before. Once he would have taken her for the type who would have worried and fretted about what road this might lead them down. But he thought that the Cat Eyes he had come to know would simply accept that they were on it and navigate it as best she could.

"No," she answered, and he breathed again. "But I might have been if I had died for it." She looked back at the butte edge again.

A corner of his mouth lifted. "Could have sworn there were a couple moments there when you wouldn't have cared."

No, she thought, she hadn't cared about anything at all but him. Too late, she ran her hand fleetingly across her scar as she zipped her jeans. It really was little more than a flesh wound, an angry red crease. Still, she had no doubt that if he looked at it closely in the light, he would know it for what it was.

Jericho's eyes narrowed as he watched her hand skim that place at her hip. Was that what she had been so skittish about the first time he had nearly undressed her in the canyon? A surgical scar? He'd noticed it—had felt it really—when he had pulled her jeans off, but then he hadn't given it another thought. But it must embarrass her, he thought, even if such self-consciousness didn't fit with what he was coming to know of her.

Then again, there was that unaccountable part of her that had developed a taste for french-vanilla coffee as well.

"I've got to go by the windmill yet," he said as he finished dressing. "I can't take you with me."

She pulled her jacket on. "I've met Lance."

"Yeah, but you embarrassed the hell out of him, Cat Eyes. No offense, but you're not high on his hit parade at the moment."

She flushed, then shrugged, helping him gather up the wine and the Doritos and trash. "Nothing I like better than long, lingering romance after sex."

He grabbed her arm as she bent for the paper bag, pulling her upright again. "I can't give you that," he said tightly. "I'm not that kind of man."

His eyes were so intense that something began heating in her all over again. "I know," she said quietly.

"I won't bring you flowers and I won't serenade you at your bedroom window. Hell, I don't even know what's going to happen between us next. But I'm game to find out, if you are, and I can promise you this..." He had both her arms now, tight in his hard hands. "If you ever decide to let me in on your secrets, I'll protect them. I'll be there if you need a friend."

Catherine swallowed carefully. "If I doubted that, I wouldn't be here."

He was quiet for a long time. "No, I don't think you would."

Finally he dropped her arms. "Come on," he said, going back to the Rover. "If Lance starts on a second bottle I'll never get him sober, and Ida'll feed him to the goats."

They bounced back down to the road, crossed it and headed over the desert again bearing west. It was a short ride as the crow flew. Moments later, he pulled up in front of the trailers. He went into the clinic to get what he needed for Lance's inevitable headache. Catherine waited for him outside.

He closed the door hard behind him and thumped down the steps again, pausing in front of her. His mouth quirked in a smile, then he brushed his lips very softly over hers. It almost undid her. He might not bring her flowers, but he had a special sweet-hard romanticism all his own.

"See you in the morning," he said quietly. "Sleep."

She sighed. "I'm beat. Even if my brain says no—" and she was pretty sure it would "—I don't think my body will cooperate."

"Go inside before I leave so I know you're safe."

"Bogeymen and *chindis* again?" she quipped, but in truth she didn't mind. She was so very tired of looking back over her own shoulder all the time. It was like a yawn after a long, hard day, to have him do it for her.

She left him and went to her own trailer. He waited until she had locked the door behind her, but Catherine only went to the side window, over the sink, to watch in the darkness as he drove off.

He headed north on the main road. She watched until his taillights faded to pinpoints in the distance, then she let out a shaky sigh. She didn't even know where he lived. Where would he go to close his own eyes and sleep? To a hogan, isolated in the desert? To one of the trailer conclaves, so he would be accessible to the people who needed him?

She had known a multitude of things about Victor—or thought she had. How could she possibly be falling for a man when she didn't even know where he lived?

The thought jolted her. She hit the light switch over the sink to dispel it with the darkness, then she recoiled with a thin shriek.

The sink was full of water. Floating lifelessly on top was an effigy doll of herself.

She shook her head. "No," she whispered. The door had been locked. She'd had to find her key to get in. She whipped around again, her nape prickling, but no one was behind her.

She hadn't noticed in the darkness, but the trailer was a shambles. Hot, furious tears welled in her eyes. She turned back to the sink, plunged her hand into the icy water and grabbed the doll. She was loathe to touch it and just as afraid not to look at it more closely.

Its neck was skewed at an awkward angle, clearly broken. Catherine moaned. Clippings of what looked to be her hair were glued to its head. She ran her free hand spasmodically through her own. *How?* She hadn't even slept in two nights! How could anyone have possibly gotten hold of her hair without her being aware of it?

Then she noticed that the doll was dressed in a crude imitation of the swimsuit she had worn on the day she had finally fled from Victor, blood seeping from the crease in her side. Her head spun badly and she had to grope her way back to the bed to sit down before she fainted.

She leaned over and put her head down between her legs. The message was clear. She had been inordinately lucky to escape the first time. The next time would be a different story.

When her head felt clearer, she straightened again, looking about. Then she scowled at the ransacked condition of the trailer.

Had the intruder been looking for something? She had nothing here that Victor might feel it was important to get back—nothing but the last of the thousand dollars she had saved in the weeks before she had run. She stood up and reached beneath the mattress, pulling out the envelope, counting it with shaking hands. Roughly five hundred dollars after airfare and expenses. It was all still there.

She frowned at the blanket on the bed. It had not been ripped back as it might have been if someone had torn it apart to search for something. It was sort of wadded in the middle. She looked about again. The table was knocked over—but it had been unsteady to start with. The refrigerator door was agape, and some food had been dragged out. She grimaced at the small bag containing the last of her coffee. It was torn open and destroyed.

Suddenly she stiffened. A faint scratching sound came from the bathroom.

She hurried away, back to the other side of the trailer. "Who's there?" She was amazed at how forceful her voice sounded. But then, she wasn't totally at the intruder's mercy, she realized. She had Jericho's gun.

She slid open one of the kitchen drawers. Her hand closed over the weapon and she found the speed-loader without taking her eyes off the bathroom door. She rammed the bullets home blindly and aimed it, but something was wrong here.

The door was ajar and that bathroom was *small*, barely big enough for her to turn around in without bumping into

her shadow. The light was off, but surely if someone were
in there she would see them.

Suddenly the shower curtain ballooned and the little
plastic rings at the top rattled.

"Come out of there," she snapped. "Slowly. So help me,
if your hands aren't up over your head, I'll blast you."

The intruder cooperated. The rings rattled again and it
half leaped over the bottom lip of the enclosure, getting
hung up halfway before it wrestled its way free again.

A possum?

Suddenly Catherine was shaking so badly her teeth
clacked together. She put the gun down carefully on the
counter.

A possum. No wonder the place looked less searched than
simply torn apart.

"Shoo," she managed. "Go on." Then it occurred to her
that it might be rabid. Wild nocturnal animals normally
showed more fright when they were trapped, especially in
such light. But this one only stared back at her with shiny
little eyes. It didn't look dazed and panicked at all, but
measuring.

She took up the gun again, moving carefully for the door.
She reached sideways, struggled with the lock without
looking at it, and flung it open.

"Get!" she tried again.

Its upper lip trembled. It bared its teeth, snarling, then it
launched itself toward her.

Catherine screamed and pulled the trigger. She hit it, she
knew she hit it. Droplets of blood spattered on the bed behind it. It squealed, a sound that froze her blood. Then it
flew past her out the door.

She whipped around to look after it, watching to see if it
would drop. The gun was only a .22, but the possum wasn't
a big animal. Yet it seemed to gather steam as it ran, going
faster and faster and faster, finally disappearing into the
desert. Slowly, carefully, Catherine closed the door again.

She couldn't think. She didn't want to think. In the af-
termath of adrenaline, she swayed with fatigue.

She took the remaining bullets out of the gun, returning them meticulously to the speed-loader, and stumbled back to the bed. No, not there. She looked at the blood, at the doll she had left there, at the rumpled blanket, and her stomach churned.

It didn't matter. She wouldn't sleep tonight either.

She sat down on the floor, her back to the kitchen cupboards. She drew her knees up and hugged them to her chest.

Sometime before dawn she surprised herself. Her head fell forward and she dozed out of sheer exhaustion.

Chapter 12

She woke with a cry when the door crashed open. Her head snapped up and she banged it squarely on the wood behind her.

"What's wrong?" Jericho growled. "Why aren't you at the clinic?"

Then he seemed to notice the condition of the trailer. His gaze shot around and he crossed to her, hauling her to her feet. His hand found her hair and he pulled it just enough that she had to look up into his face.

"When did this happen?" he asked more quietly, but his voice still vibrated with tension. "Are you all right?"

"I'm fine. I found it this way when I got in last night." She intended to ease away from him, if for no other reason than caution. It still troubled her that she was falling for him, fast and hard, when she knew so little about him, when she didn't even know where he went at night or who he went there with. But she found that she was reluctant to let go of him. She realized that whether she knew myriad details about him or not, the only times she hadn't been afraid in these past months were the moments she had spent in his arms.

She dug her fingers into the worn leather of his jacket instead. Then she flinched when he snapped at her again.

"Why didn't you yell for me to come back?"

"The way you drive?" Then she shook her head and sighed. "I didn't turn the lights on right away. You were long gone before I saw what had happened."

Finally, she let go of him and stepped away. "Where's Ellen?" she asked. She went to peer through the door he had left open, but she didn't see the nurse outside.

"How should I know?" He looked around at the trailer again almost bemusedly.

"Didn't you bring her this morning?"

"Thought about what you said and decided it might be better if she got her car fixed. I called Eddie Begay from home and sent him over to her place."

The news should have cheered her, but it only made her gnaw her lip. "Could she have done this?"

His gaze came back to her and it was blank. "Ellen? No way."

"But Shadow told me she doesn't like Anglo externs and doctors."

Jericho thought about it. "Well, she doesn't. They don't respect her native talents so she has a hard time respecting their views. But she wouldn't try to scare you off. For one thing, even if she got rid of you, the IHS would just send another to take your place. It's not you personally she doesn't like, but the whole situation."

"But what about... I mean, if the service sent someone else, that person wouldn't necessarily be one you'd... you'd..." She flushed and trailed off. She didn't know how to finish.

His mouth quirked. She realized he was enjoying her discomfiture.

"One I'd what?" he asked softly, crossing to her. He put his hand under her chin and tilted her head back again. "I thought about you all night." He studied her face for a moment, looking for something, then his lips grazed hers.

"Yes, that," she breathed.

Suddenly his mouth closed over hers, fully and hot. His tongue slid past her teeth, and her womb ached with wanting him. *Now?* How could he possibly make her react like this when someone was hunting her and rabid animals were running loose in her trailer?

His mouth left hers. "You do something to me, Cat Eyes," he said huskily. "Next time will be different, I promise you."

"Different?" She felt dazed.

"I won't let you drive me past control. I'll love you all over until the sun comes up."

Her heart slammed and her blood swirled and she was ready for him again. She dug her fingers into his waist. "Will there be a next time?" *Tell me there will. Tell me it's now.*

He gave a hoarse laugh. "No doubt."

Suddenly she felt him stiffen. She twisted to look over her shoulder, following his gaze. He was staring at the effigy doll on the bed.

"What's that?"

Catherine shrugged, feeling oddly fragile. "I didn't have a chance to tell you. Apparently I had two intruders—one who left that and one who did this." She waved a hand at the trailer. "The latter was a possum—rabid, I think."

He let go of her, crossed to the bed and grabbed the doll. "It's your hair." Red glinted through the black curls in the sun that came through the window.

"I . . . it can't be."

He bit out a dark, violent oath. "The hell it's not. Tell me about this possum."

"It was in the shower, rummaging around in there. When it heard my voice it came out and I shot it." She stiffened at the look on his face. "Did you have to promise I wouldn't shoot animals to get that permit? It snarled at me. It was going to bite me. I had no choice."

"Where?"

"Where what?"

"Where did you shoot it?"

"Dead on."

"And?"

"It ran like hell."

He looked at the blood spattering the bed, noticing it for the first time. "Where's the bullet?"

"The bullet?" she repeated dumbly. "Well, it's there someplace, I guess. It would have to have been a clear-through shot for it to run like that. At least with people, the fatal ones are usually those that get trapped inside, tangling up with vital organs."

He began tearing the bed apart. He shook the blanket and the sheets, but nothing fell out. He threw them at the middle of the floor and examined the mattress.

"Do you see it?" she asked. Her voice was oddly strangled. His furious intent was touching something inside her, eliciting a violent panic that was beginning to make her shake.

He didn't answer, just tossed the mattress aside, as well, yanking at the frame where it sat braced on the cinder blocks. Everything fell to the floor with a clatter and a thump that jarred the trailer.

There were no bullet holes in the wall behind it, none in the flooring. "You're sure you were facing this way?"

"There was blood on the blanket," she protested.

He swore again.

"*What?*" she demanded. "You're scaring me."

"It's in him. He took it."

"Took it? *Who?*"

"That was no possum, Cat Eyes. It was our wolfman. Ten-to-one you walked in on him and he changed."

"Changed?" She croaked the word, then shook her head. "No."

"You think a rabid possum wandered in while someone else was leaving you the doll?" he demanded.

"I…" She trailed off. The explanation *did* reach—a lot—but there was no other that made sense. And she couldn't—wouldn't—start believing in witches, Navajo or otherwise.

Except… the way it had run. "Oh, God," she breathed. Her head spun, struggling away from what she was not willing to accept. "When the wolfman scare started getting bad, the people all said they saw dogs and wolves running as fast as cars. This was a *possum,*" she said.

"A wolfman can change into whatever he wants to change into, whatever the situation demands," Jericho said grimly. He looked around the trailer again. "This is an inconvenient place for a wolf or a dog."

Catherine dragged a chair over from where the table had once been. She sat down hard.

"First Lisa, then Louie. And you saved Louie," Jericho went on, almost to himself. He bent and scooped the doll up again from where he had dropped it on the floor. He turned it over in his hands. Its head lolled.

"So this is what he's going to do to you next. If you get in his way again, he'll break your neck."

Catherine looked at him dully. "No."

He didn't seem to hear her. "No more, Cat Eyes. You've treated your last *Tah honeesgai* patient."

Catherine paled. "Don't. Don't do that."

Something in her tone brought his eyes back to her. "Don't do what?"

"Don't give me ... orders ... and ... ultimatums."

Jericho studied her sudden pallor, then he looked to her hands where they were clenched and trembling. His face hardened dangerously. "I'm trying to protect your hide."

"You're way off base," she blurted. "It's not what he's going to do to me, it's what should already have happened, and it's *not* your wolfman."

He waited for her to go on. She couldn't. She realized, horrified, that she had said too much already. She turned away from him to hide the confusion and panic in her face.

He closed the distance between them in a heartbeat, spinning her around to face him again. He was as angry as she had ever seen him. His black eyes blazed. His jaw worked. She struggled against him, suddenly frightened of him.

He wouldn't let her go. "What is it with you?" he snarled.

Her pulse went crazy. She went very still, because to fight him brought pain where he gripped her. "What do you mean?"

"You make love to me with all your soul, with everything inside you. So why won't you talk to me?"

There was a low, groaning sound from the door. They both jerked and looked that way. Ellen stood staring back at them, her hands braced on either side of the doorframe, her eyes wide and aghast. She made another strangled sound and turned and fled.

Catherine felt the strength leave her legs. "Well, if she's responsible, now you've done it." But she knew it wasn't Ellen. She had been grasping at straws, and Jericho was not going to be sidetracked anyway.

"Answer me," he said angrily. "How can you give so much, yet so little?"

"You haven't exactly offered a wealth of information about yourself," she retorted. She wanted to get as mad as he was. She *needed* her temper now . . . but the look on his face was only tearing her heart out.

"It didn't matter to you last night," he said tightly.

"No," she raged. "And apparently my past didn't bother you much then, either."

"What are you saying?" His voice was deadly calm. Her heart thundered. She pushed her chin up.

"Maybe it was just sex. You don't need a lot of talk for that."

"Damn you." He crushed the doll in his hand. She was startled to realize that he still held it. He hurled it at the sink and it plopped wetly into the water again.

"I don't need this," he muttered. He headed for the door, slamming it hard as he left.

The trailer vibrated. Catherine felt as if her life were draining slowly, helplessly out of her. She wondered if there were any more numbing words in the English language than those.

It was early afternoon when she stepped out of the shower, grabbing a towel from the hook on the back of the door. She had spent the morning trying to put her trailer to rights again, and if she was exhausted before, she was practically dead now. The shower hadn't helped.

Then she heard a bang from the other room and her heart skipped. *Jericho*. He had come back.

She found the energy to fling the door open, but it was only Shadow working to get the table to stand upright again. When Shadow heard Catherine, she looked up and the table toppled over once more.

Shadow shrugged. "It wasn't much good in the first place, I guess."

"I used cinder blocks to put the bed back up," Catherine managed. "There's more where they came from. I just haven't had a chance to go outside yet to get them."

Shadow nodded and looked at her more closely. "How are you?"

Catherine gave a high-pitched laugh. "All things considered?"

"That bad?"

Her laughter died as abruptly as it had claimed her. "Yes."

"So what's going on around here? Ellen's over in the clinic acting strangely, Jericho barged in on me this morning yelling like a maniac and you're taking a shower in the middle of the day instead of working—not that you don't deserve a day off. It's like someone put a hex on this place and everyone's gone crazy."

"It's *not* your wolfman," Catherine snapped, frustrated.

"I didn't necessarily say it was."

Catherine went still as she rummaged through a suitcase for clothes—the one thing Shadow *hadn't* been able to produce was a dresser. She looked back at her and realized that the woman had absolutely no idea what was going on. Apparently, no one had told her about the owl or the effigy doll.

Catherine filled her in shortly as she dressed. Sooner or later, she reasoned, Shadow would find out anyway. Her response was predictable. The color drained from her face.

"The possum *ran?* Full of lead?"

"I'd put my money on it being rabid." Catherine sighed. "In fact, I'm going to call the health department and report it."

"I don't think it'll do much good."

"Maybe not, since I don't have the body." She pulled her boots on, then she frowned. God help her, but she was beginning to suspect everybody.

"How'd you manage to get in here?" she asked, keeping her voice idle.

Shadow didn't take offense. She sat on the floor and crossed her arms on her knees. "Your door was unlocked. Do you mind? There's just sort of a come-on-in attitude around these parts, and Jericho said you needed help cleaning up here. I knocked, but you didn't answer."

Catherine shook her head. "I don't care." She hesitated. She didn't want to ask, and couldn't stop herself. "What was he yelling about?"

"My brother?" Shadow's eyes narrowed in a look much like his. "He wanted to know what I knew about you."

Catherine sat on the bed and covered her face with her hands. "What did you tell him?" she asked, her voice muffled.

"There's not much I *could* tell him."

"Your friend with the health service isn't Ed Bunn?" That was the man she'd been forced to confide in. She splayed her fingers to look at Shadow, waiting for her answer.

Shadow shook her head. "No. Jack Keller."

Jack—whoever he was—had apparently told Shadow that she was Lanie McDaniel, then. Her secret was still safe in that corner, if no other.

"Does he hold a grudge?" she asked finally.

"Who? Jack?"

"No, Jericho."

"Depends. Did you hurt him or someone under his wing?"

"Him, I guess." God, what she wouldn't give to have those words back. It was her temper, her wretched temper . . . and it was so much more, so much she couldn't control.

"Then he'll probably hold a grudge a couple days short of forever."

In the next moment, Catherine was crying. She was appalled at herself, and there was absolutely nothing she could do about it. The tears welled up so fast, so hot, that they spilled over before she could blink. Then she was sobbing, burying her face in her hands again.

She *never* cried. It was just that she was so tired, and so much had happened to her. She was wrung out, emotionally and physically.

And she knew that wasn't it at all. So did Shadow.

The woman stood and went into the bathroom, coming back with a wad of toilet paper. She nudged her shoulder. "Here. Blow. You know, nobody tells me *anything*."

Catherine took the toilet paper and managed a watery smile. "Thanks." She appreciated Shadow's no-nonsense attitude more than anything else.

"Well, this explains Ellen's funk." Shadow dropped down on the bed beside her.

"Ellen's in love with him," she muttered, blowing her nose.

"So are you."

Catherine stiffened to argue the point, but finally she only let her breath out on a shaky sigh. "I don't know yet. I've been wrong before."

"So has he. That's why he's so touchy."

Catherine's eyes cleared sharply. "Tell me."

Shadow hesitated, then she shook her head. "I can't." She stood and started pacing. "It's not the Navajo way, Lanie. You've got to understand that we make it a habit not to speak for anybody else. We don't presume to know how anybody feels or why—even if it's kin. For instance, if you asked Eddie Begay how his mother's feeling, when you know she's got a cold, he'll just tell you that she's home today. He'd expect that if you wanted to know badly enough you'd go find her and ask her."

"I see."

"I could tell you why I *think* Jericho's angry, and I'd probably be right. But I could be wrong, and that wouldn't be fair to him."

"So if I want to know, I should ask him myself." Catherine sighed.

"Well, in this case you can't because I can't tell you where he is. I don't know where he's gone."

Catherine flinched, wondering herself. But she felt marginally better than she had all morning. "So does this same respect apply to visitors living among you?" she asked.

Shadow nodded.

"If someone came here asking about me, nobody would tell them anything?"

"Well, they'd probably just say you work at the clinic. Why? Who's going to ask?"

Catherine got to her feet, as well. Her heart felt wretched again. God, she was tired of this, of the subterfuge and the worrying and the lies.

"As for your first question, I can't tell you. It's not a matter of trust," she added quickly, "especially in light of what you've just told me. It's just . . . I'm not sure yet that it wouldn't put you in danger. You're better off not knowing. Jericho too, though he won't believe it."

"Have you told him that?"

"No, but he hasn't actually given me a chance." She remembered where the conversation had gone the night before, when they'd broached the subject, and she felt a flush creep up her neck.

"Anyway, as for your second question . . ." She paused and blew out her breath. "I don't know that yet either, but I'm going to find out. Can you give me a ride into Shiprock?"

"Sure. I'd say it's probably best all the way around if you kept out of Ellen's way today. You know, as beautiful as she is, she has wretched luck with men. Jericho's clan so nothing could ever come of a relationship between them, but she's still got to be hurting. And when she hurts or gets upset, her tongue gets . . . sharp."

"I've noticed," Catherine said dryly.

She gathered up some change that had been lying on the kitchen counter. Going all the way into town to call Schilling was probably a waste of time, but she had to talk to him, had to find out if Victor did have a man out here watching her.

The time had come to tell Jericho, she thought, feeling something tremble inside her. How *much* she could tell him remained to be seen, but she knew that if she kept hiding this secret from him she would lose him, whether she had actually lied to him or not.

If it wasn't too late. Suddenly she felt like crying again.

She asked Shadow to drop her off at the motor inn. Her friend raised a brow but asked no questions.

"I have to run over to the feed store and pick up some grain. It should take me about half an hour. Will that give you enough time?"

"More than enough," Catherine answered. "I only need about five minutes."

"Well, that rules out an illicit lover's tryst."

Catherine laughed for the first time all day, but it was a shaky sound. She figured she already had more than she could handle of that sort of thing.

She watched as Shadow's truck darted off down the street. When it turned a corner, she went inside the coffee shop again.

"Horace Schilling," she said into the phone, then, when he picked up, "It's Catherine Landano. Well?"

Significantly, she thought, he didn't ask where she was this time or beat around the bush to allow time for a trace.

"Victor's here. In Boston."

"You've actually seen him?"

"Better than that. We've also got his voice on tape. He's had several meetings that we managed to gain some foreknowledge of, and we were therefore able to wire his discussions. None of them pertained directly to you."

"Directly? What does that mean?"

"It means that he met with his lawyers and some associates to discuss his possible defense, should you repeat what you overheard."

"I already have."

"He doesn't know that. He hasn't been charged yet with anything other than shooting you, and that's a fall he's willing to accept. He and his pals all go into this business with the understanding that they're liable to go away for a few years at a time. It's the big chunks of their lives they kill to avoid. Charges like racketeering, money laundering, anything that would threaten the whole organization. Attempted murder and assault with a deadly weapon will only get him five-to-ten. He'll probably be out in two with good behavior."

Catherine took a shaky breath. A million implications were flying around in her brain, and some of them were making her feel cold inside. "So he hasn't spoken to anyone he might have on my tail?"

"No."

She felt colder. "*No one?* He's not after me now?"

"No."

"Someone is," she breathed.

"It's probably your imagination."

"No." No, it definitely wasn't.

"Well, it's not Victor Landano. He's not planning on making his position worse unless the situation becomes critical. Meaning that as it stands right now, he's looking at two years, not even maximum security. If he puts someone on you and the authorities find out, he's looking at five. If he kills you in cold blood after the first attempt, he's looking at a minimum of twenty, and I'm talking *parole.* Life or gas are more likely. And you're gone. You've tucked your tail and run. What are the odds that you're going to come back and squeal? Why kill you until you try?"

"So I'm safe until he's charged with . . . with the other."

"That's his plan."

"You've got that on tape?"

"Yes. At the very least, if you go down, you know he's going to hang."

Somehow it wasn't comforting. "You've confirmed his associations then."

"To *my* satisfaction. We're still busy. The DA will want more for the grand jury, but it's a simple matter of putting the pieces together now."

Her blood drained. "So he *will* be charged with the business about the senator?"

Schilling finally hesitated. "Yes."

"When?"

"Probably within the next couple of weeks."

"Oh, dear God. Then they'll come after me."

"Catherine, not even his father is exceptionally pleased with the fact that Victor allowed you this knowledge. The family's doing some active damage control. If Victor goes up for the murder of the senator, Daddy will tell him goodbye. From all indications, he acted on his own on this, without the family's approval or cooperation, except for the flunkies he used. They're not going to make matters worse by gunning you down after the fact, when the damage is already done. *You* didn't screw up. Victor did when he allowed you to learn what he'd done. Victor's the one who'll be punished. I really don't think you have anything to worry about."

"You said that before," she answered, strangled.

"But now we're in a much better position to protect you if we have to."

Catherine thought about that a moment, then she understood. "You *do* know where I am."

"We know you're in New Mexico and that he's not."

She closed her eyes. "It doesn't matter anymore, does it?"

"You'll be all right."

"I'm not going to testify."

"On which?"

"On either. It's not worth risking my life to come back there to testify on the attempted murder charge if he's only going to do two years for shooting me." It made her angry—the cops had certainly never bothered to tell her that.

But in the end, she had far more serious concerns and it was too much of an effort to hold on to her temper.

"Well," Schilling said, "the attempted murder thing's a criminal charge under the jurisdiction of the local cops. It's not my problem, and as far as I know the cops don't know where you are. I won't plan on telling them. That's the least I can do to thank you for handing me Victor Landano, especially since your disappearance isn't costing the government anything. Normally it requires the U.S. Mint to hide informants in this sort of situation, but you took off on your own."

"That's big of you," she managed.

"As far as the other charges are concerned—the federal issue of racketeering and the senator's murder—your testimony would be hearsay anyway. Now that we've got proof, we don't need you any longer. Get lost, Catherine."

"I thought I had."

"Then stay lost. Stay there. Start over."

She hung the phone up very carefully, turning around, looking out over the coffee shop. No one was watching her this time. She went to the counter for a cup of coffee, desperate to warm the ice inside her. She didn't know if she wanted to laugh or cry. Relief tried to lift the weight off her shoulders, but fear wouldn't let it.

She wasn't in danger...yet. She had two more weeks, give or take.

No one was following her, warning her to keep quiet, watching her and waiting for her to talk. Victor hadn't sent anyone yet.

She thought of the possum and suddenly she felt faint. She didn't bother to go back to the pay phone to call the health department and report it.

Chapter 13

Three days later, Ellen was still distraught. Catherine couldn't bring herself to care. Except for the times when he had been doing his sings, it was the first time since she had come to the Res that Jericho hadn't appeared in the clinic.

The place had a hollow, cold feeling without him. *Where was he?* It frightened her how much she needed—wanted—him to come back. It wasn't just because she felt protected when he was near. His absence left a gaping void inside her, and the sure knowledge that she had hurt him only gnawed it wider.

When she heard a vehicle out front around lunchtime, she leaped up from the desk to look out the window. Her heart sank slowly down to her toes again. It wasn't Jericho.

"He won't come back, you know." Ellen said. "Not until your tour is up. He'd be crazy if he did. Your kind is nothing but trouble and he has the scars to prove it."

"I know," Catherine murmured, more from a faint need to fight back than anything else. She got the desired effect—Ellen blanched—and it made her feel instantly awful.

"He *told* you?" Ellen asked disbelievingly.

He hadn't told her anything more than she'd told him, Catherine thought. God, what a strange attraction they shared, all built on hunger and shadows . . . and, she allowed, instinctual truths. She *knew* the kind of man he was, saw his strength and loyalty every day. No words had been needed to tell her of those things, and they had been enough to make her love him.

She was saved from trying to explain to Ellen—even if she were inclined to, which she wasn't—when she recognized the woman getting out of the truck that had just arrived. "It's Bessie," she said, startled.

Ellen went to the other window to look out. "Louie will be getting out of the hospital soon. She'll want pollen to protect her hogan from further trouble." She moved back to the shelves to get it as Bessie came inside.

She had another young boy with her—presumably Louie's brother. They hesitated self-consciously in the door and the boy tried to hide behind Bessie's legs.

"Here," Ellen said. "I've got the pollen all ready for you."

Bessie flushed. "I'll need that too, but I came for the doctor."

Shock flew across Ellen's face, but it was nothing compared to what Catherine felt. "Me?" Catherine asked.

"She's not a doctor," Ellen snapped. "She's an *extern*. If you want that kind of help, I'll try to find Kolkline."

She was halfway to the phone when Bessie stopped her. "No. *She* saved Louie, not that other man." She pulled the little boy forward. "This is Leo," she told Catherine. "His school sent him home last week until I give him tetanus."

"Give him— Oh." Catherine grinned. "You want the shot."

"And they said I need some kind of form to take back to them to prove it."

"Okay. But I still have to call Kolkline," she cautioned, "just to get him to approve it."

"Just so long as that man doesn't stick him. He made a bad bump on Dana Strong Deer's arm. Her mother told me."

Catherine sighed. "That's because it's not supposed to go in the arm." What had Kolkline been thinking? But then, he had probably been drunk, not thinking at all.

She went to the phone and tried the number he had given her. No answer. She tried University, but he didn't respond to his page. Catherine was too glad of a patient, of anything to take her mind off Jericho, to care. She got one of the emergency-room residents to okay the shot—dubious protection at best, but she figured her externship was already screwed to the wall anyway.

She filled a syringe and motioned Bessie and Leo into one of the exam rooms. "Okay, drop your drawers, big guy."

The little boy thrust his chin out. "I want Jericho."

Catherine grimaced. *Oh, so do I.*

"He can't," Bessie told him. "He's up on the mountain."

Mountain? "Where?" Catherine demanded.

Bessie looked at her oddly, then something in her expression must have touched the woman in her. "Beautiful Mountain," she explained. "That big one on the horizon right outside. Uncle Ernie has a hunting cabin way up top. I saw Jericho two days ago and he said you could do the shot. He's not allowed to do it anyway. The school won't take the form with his signature."

"No...I mean, yes, that's right." Finally, reluctantly, Leo pulled down his jeans. Catherine hunkered down to give him the shot. When she straightened, a wave of dizziness swept her so badly she had to close her eyes.

It was getting to the point where if she didn't sleep soon, she really was going to collapse. *Oh, Jericho, come back.*

"What does he do up there?" she asked. She went to a drawer in one of the cabinets to get the form she would need, citing the Emergency resident's name first, then signing her own.

"He goes there when his life's been unbalanced."

"Unbalanced," Catherine repeated, giving her the form. Her stomach cramped painfully. Oh, God, what had she done to him with those few short, nasty words, with her evasions? It had just been her temper and her panic!

Did he care that much?

"Our people believe that when trouble comes it's because we've gotten out of balance with nature," Bessie went on. "Since nature can't be changed—it just is—we have to bring ourselves back to peace with it."

Trouble, Catherine thought. Maybe Jericho's didn't have anything to do with her after all. Maybe he was worrying about *Tah honeesgai.*

Somehow she didn't like that any better.

She went with Bessie and Leo back to the front room. Bessie looked embarrassed. "We have no money, but my husband will bring a sheep the next time he comes out this way."

Catherine was taken aback. What on God's green earth was she supposed to do with a *sheep?* What was she supposed to tell the Service? Presumably, they would want to be reimbursed for the cost of their vaccine at least.

"That'll be fine," she answered. She'd figure it out later. She still had five hundred dollars left. "How's Louie?"

Suddenly Bessie grinned. "Great. He wants to come home. Those nurses want him to, too. He sneaked out of that room and gave them all a scare."

"Boys are something, I guess." Catherine thought she and her sisters had been a handful.

"Oh, they are. I think the Holy People have a special place in the afterworld for their mothers. It's a place where we can close our eyes sometimes."

Catherine laughed, then, suddenly, she felt self-conscious. "Thanks," she said. She motioned at Leo. "No one's actually wanted my services before."

Bessie shrugged. "Our people have learned not to trust the government too much. We always get burned—we lose leases on our mining lands, get cheated out of thousands of dollars for those houses they tried to give us in our land dispute with the Hopi. Our kids get bumps on their arms. Trust takes time."

"Yes," Catherine agreed. Yes, it did. And sometimes it just . . . happened.

Bessie finally left with Leo in tow. The little boy got half-way to the truck, then turned back to wave shyly. Catherine felt her heart constrict and she waved back. Apparently she had passed muster with him as well.

She stayed at the window for a long time, watching them go. Only then did she realize that Ellen had left too. Finally, she thought, she could get something done without sparring with the nurse and explaining her every move to assuage her suspicions.

Still, she didn't leave the window. She kept staring up at Beautiful Mountain.

The rain started in the late afternoon. The first drops spattered angrily against the window, taking Catherine by surprise. She had almost forgotten the fury of the first downpour that had greeted her arrival here, and she had given up hope of ever seeing the brown Ford again. But now she wondered dismally if it was going to get pushed even further down the wash.

The clinic remained deserted. She sat at the desk, resting her chin on her hands, watching as the rain gathered momentum. It hurled itself against the windows and drummed at the roof.

The angels are crying. That was what her mother had always said. Suddenly, she could hear her voice again as clearly as if she was standing beside her.

Catherine wished fervently that there really was such a thing as *chindis*. She would give anything for some of her mother's practical advice right now. Mary Callahan had never allowed her life to be turned upside down by a man—or by anything else, for that matter, Catherine thought. She had always been a serene, quiet presence in the midst of Paddy's blustering and the chaos of six children in one small home. She always knew just the right thing to do in any situation.

Catherine covered her face with her hands. "Oh, Mama," she groaned, "what have I done?"

Everything had seemed right at the time... repeating faithfully to the FBI what she had heard, trying to the best of her ability to do what they had asked of her. It was her country, after all, and she had been raised to respect and honor this land that had taken her parents in. But then it had failed her, so she had run—straight into the arms of a hard, uncompromising man with a heart of gold. She had never intended to get involved with him, had known it was the worst possible thing she could do under the circumstances.

Some things are stronger than we are, Catie. Fate has her plans and there's no sense fighting her.

"I know, Mama. I know." Mary had always said that when it started to look as if you were going to sink, it was time to stop fighting and swim with the tide.

She was sinking. Fast. And Catherine was so very tired she *couldn't* fight anymore. She could only pray that sooner or later Jericho would reappear and give her a chance to explain.

Sleep, Catie. Everything seems better when the sun comes again.

Catherine finally put her head down on the desk and did exactly that.

The storm made the mountain road nearly impassable. It had never been graded, was really no more than tire ruts, but the sand still slid downward in oozing waves of mud. If he had any sense at all, Jericho knew he would pull over and hike the rest of the way to his house.

But he had been gone for the better part of two days, and he told himself he needed to go by the old windmill. So he kept easing the Rover gently down the trail, his foot on the brake to slow himself when gravity and the mud pulled with too much momentum. He kept going even as he knew he wasn't going to be able to get back up the mountain tonight, not until the sun came again and dried everything out.

No big deal. It had happened before. It was a price he had known he would pay often when he had built on the slope.

He made it to the windmill. Lance was nowhere in sight, but he had left a half full bottle propped neatly against the brace. Jericho got out and stood in the downpour, staring at it.

He had known Lance wouldn't be at the windmill in this weather.

He grabbed the bottle and tossed it into his truck. He'd come this far, he thought. He should probably run by the clinic trailers and make sure everything was all right there as well. They were right on the way to Shadow's hogan, and he would have to bunk down there for the night.

He got in, slamming the Rover's door hard behind him. What the hell was he doing?

Trying to find balance, he thought. Trying to find peace. He hadn't gotten it in Uncle Ernie's hunting cabin. The Holy People had barely spoken to him. They rarely did when they knew the answers he sought were right in his own heart and all he really had to do was look inward and find them. If he had ever doubted that, he would have gone straight to the old man himself instead of wasting time in the solitude of his cabin.

But the thing he couldn't get past was that Lanie had a point, and he'd just needed to think about that. He *hadn't* told her a damned thing about his own life. He didn't like to talk about himself; some things were private. And the past was past...but sometimes, like *chindis,* it woke up and haunted you.

His past had come alive again lately. It was impossible to love again and not reckon with old horrors.

Love again. How had he let it happen? Then he realized that he probably had never had any say in the matter. Fate just *was;* when it started spinning, a man was helpless. Fate was nature. Nature could not be changed.

Lanie "Cat Eyes" McDaniel matched him, he thought. Somehow, on some inner level, they fit nicely and the secrets hadn't stopped it from happening. It just *was,* and he was not going to get balanced within himself until he got balanced with her first.

No small task, he thought, his jaw hardening.

Not only was there the issue of whatever it was she wasn't telling him, but she was going to leave. Soon—in less than two weeks now. This externship thing would be over and she would go off somewhere to take a residency. Back to one of the big cities where she belonged, maybe even the city she had come from, sandals and all.

The pain that brought to his heart was strong enough to take away his breath for a moment. Then it came back in a harsh burst as he drove around the canyon where she had shot the tarnation out of those bottles. The land rose there, and when he reached the top of the rise he saw that the lights were still on in the clinic trailer. His brows knit.

He looked behind it. Her place was dark, though ten o'clock had come and gone. He knew she usually went to bed early—he had passed by here a thousand times in the past few weeks and all the lights were always out by this time. So something else had happened. Something was wrong.

He cursed himself viciously. He had been a fool to leave her unprotected, to go seek balance that he had known from the start he wasn't going to find at the cabin. He brought the Rover to a hard stop and hurried up the steps, easing the door open cautiously this time. Once again his breath left him as he realized that she might not even be alive. That doll . . .

The possibility almost crippled him when he saw her at the desk, slumped over lifelessly. For a moment, pure, unadulterated terror made it impossible for him to move.

"Lanie," he growled hoarsely. *"Cat Eyes."*

She didn't stir, but he finally managed to do so, crossing the room in three long, hard strides, grabbing her, wondering how it was that whenever he lost something too precious there was never an issue of an Anglo God or Navajo Holy People, only *someone* bigger and stronger than he was, some higher being. And God help him, he needed Him now.

Catherine screamed at his touch.

The sound stunned him, and he actually staggered backward a few steps. She leaped to her feet, then her legs went out from under her, seeming to simply fold as if someone had neatly and surgically removed the bones from them. He made a fast move to grab her again, but the desk was in the way and she sank to the floor with a tiny, helpless gasp.

"Jericho." She shook her head like a little dazed animal. "Jericho?"

Catherine tried to scramble to her feet again. She made it halfway before the room began to spin. She had to hold onto the desk to keep from going down again, but then his strong hands held her and it felt so good, so right.

She dug her fingers into his leather jacket, clutching him. "You're all wet," she said inanely. Of all the things she wanted to say to him, *needed* to tell him, where had she come up with that?

"And you're sick," he answered too harshly.

She scowled before her temper came back. She held onto it this time—marginally. "I'm exhausted. I haven't been able to sleep at all. Someone's trying to drive me crazy, and then *you* disappeared, and now you just wander back in and grab me—I thought you were the damned wolfman, and all you can say is I'm sick?"

He absorbed her outburst with one raised brow. "You don't believe in wolfmen," he said finally.

She let go of him and sank weakly into the chair again. "I don't know what I believe anymore. I don't—if it's not—oh, who knows?"

His other brow went up. "Whatever you say."

She looked at him, her eyes narrowing as her heart skipped a beat. Yes, he was back, and suddenly it occurred to her to wonder what that might mean.

"Did you get balanced?" she asked cautiously.

He looked vaguely surprised. "Who told you where I was?"

"Bessie."

"Did you ask her?"

She hesitated. "More or less."

He nodded once, as though this pleased him, but then he took a step backward, away from her. He ran his hand through his hair. "We've got to talk."

"I know."

Again, he looked surprised. "Not now," he said finally. "Why not?"

He took yet another step away from her. Now that it was possible, now that she didn't appear to be fighting it, he felt even more out of sync than he had when he had driven up to the cabin. Why?

Because I'm scared. The realization jolted him, left him reeling. For the first time in a very long time, something mattered to him more than life itself, and it terrified him that he could lose it. He could tell her about Anelle, clean up the slate, at least on his side . . . and she would probably still go away.

"Because you're in no condition to talk," he said finally, and that was true, too. "Go back to your trailer. Get some sleep. Real sleep, not hunched over a desk."

Catherine snorted. "With one eye open, to see who's going to sneak in and leave me a present this time?"

He swore darkly. "I'll hang around outside."

"All night?" Her jaw dropped. "That's ridiculous."

It was. He closed the space between them suddenly. "All right," he said. "I'll stay with you. You'll sleep, I'll watch the door. I was going to go to Shadow's anyway. Can't get home until the storm clears."

She let him pull her as far as the door before she dug her heels in. "The storm's cleared," she murmured.

Belatedly he realized that the rain had indeed stopped. "The roads are still washed out."

"So drive over the desert."

"Can't."

"Why not?"

Finally he realized that she was deliberately baiting him. Yeah, they matched.

"Do you want me to leave, Cat Eyes?" he asked quietly.

A very small shiver went through her. "No." *I want to know where you go when you leave here.*

The shiver undid him, weakening him, dissolving all the common sense that had taken him away in the first place. It made his fear seem small.

He pulled her into his arms, closing his eyes, resting his chin on top of her head.

"Good," he murmured. "Because the hell of it is, it took me a long time to get here and now I really don't want to go back."

Chapter 14

Their feet stuck to her porch. Jericho looked down, scowling, and Catherine straightened her spine.

"Flour," she explained a little defensively. Just enough of it to turn reasonably tacky in the rain that had dashed this close to the building.

He watched her as she dug the key out of her jeans pocket. "Ancient Irish custom?"

"No. If anyone breaks in again, I want to see what their footprints look like."

"All right." He wasn't going to point out that what she'd probably find were paw prints or claw marks. Not now. In the morning they could tackle it all again.

They went inside and he watched her stretch with a yawn, with unconscious grace. Like a cat. Her sweater pulled taut across her breasts and he thought, no bra again. Suddenly, morning seemed a very long time away.

He brought his eyes deliberately back to her face. He was going to make her sleep. He had to, for her sake and for his own. Later, when they had straightened some things out, there would be ample time to sink into her again...he hoped.

"Go on," he snapped. "Use the bathroom. Do whatever it is you have to do to get ready for bed. I'll stay here by the door."

She watched him closely. Something both hot and cold sliced through her at the look on his hard face . . . wanting all tangled up with stony caution. He was that kind of man. He certainly wouldn't rush on to ground that even a reckless man would fear.

Nor could she entirely blame him.

"Okay," she said carefully. She backed up for the bathroom, her head whirling. She brushed her teeth and undressed down to her panties, washing up, then she pulled on a robe she had left on the back of the bathroom door. But when she came out again he was still standing where she had left him, watching her with a wooden expression, a single muscle moving in his jaw.

She clenched her hands into fists. "I lied," she whispered. "Just let me tell you that much now at least."

Impossibly, his face hardened even more. "About what?"

"It wasn't just sex . . . it didn't feel like that."

Her words hit into him like an iron fist. "And you know what 'just sex' feels like?" he asked tightly. He didn't think he wanted to know. He had always been relatively confident in his masculinity; he had never been a jealous man, not even with Anelle. But now jealousy clawed through him in a stunning ambush.

It showed on his face. Catherine paled, then her chin came up. "I know what it feels like to just go through the motions." She had gotten shot for it. "I know what it feels like to grit your teeth and pray to God it's over with soon. But with you, I wanted it to go on forever."

He was reasonably sure he could have withstood anything but that—a hushed admission, but somehow strong, somehow defiant. He closed his eyes again. "Lanie . . ."

"Catherine," she said softly.

"Cat—" He was going to choke. Had he *known* when he had called her that? Had the Holy People been whispering malicious little hints in his ear? Fate was nature and nature was inevitable, he thought.

"My father calls me Cat. My mother called me Catie."
She crossed to him slowly, shrugging. "Lately, since college, I've gotten used to Catherine."

She fiddled nervously with the belt to her robe and prayed that the truth—even this much of it—would in no way endanger him. But Fate had plans of her own, and she couldn't fight her any longer.

"So." She dropped the belt. "Do you still want to wait until tomorrow to talk?"

Suddenly talking was the last thing on his mind.

It was necessary, vital, to do it before he got in any deeper. But he was already sinking fast, and the closer she got to him the more his balance was restored. The scent of her—some clean floral soap—filled his head. The warmth of her reached out and stroked something inside him. And in that moment everything felt right again—he couldn't even remember why he had gone to the mountain in the first place.

With you, I wanted it to go on forever. And he had promised to love her all night, after all.

"Yeah," he said hoarsely, "talking can wait."

She sighed and closed her eyes. Relief made her sway into him. He caught her and she lifted her arms to his neck, holding on tightly, seeking his mouth, needing the reassurance that he was back now and that somehow everything was going to turn out all right.

His hands held her hips, then left them to tug hungrily at her belt, pulling it loose. Her robe fell open and he groaned like a man dying a slow, sweet death. His hands swept upward to cover her breasts and she felt her nipples grow hard and tight beneath his rough palms.

She tore her mouth from his. "Please, Jericho, please."

His arms came around her, and she felt herself being lifted and carried. The room was spinning oddly again, but she couldn't care. It righted itself anyway when he laid her on the bed and kneeled over her, because then there were only his eyes, black, fathomless, so intense. His gaze moved to her hip...to the scar hidden beneath a silky puddle of her robe. It laid open in a long, narrow swath between her breasts.

There was no darkness this time, no sweet protective cloak of night. The trailer lights blazed.

"Okay if I take this off?" he asked quietly, his fingers tugging at the lapel.

Catherine nodded slowly and held her breath.

He slid both hands across her breasts, baring them. Then he followed the path with his tongue, running little circles around a nipple. Finally he pulled back to look at her, but his eyes didn't linger on the short red welt. They came right back to hers as he shrugged out of his jacket, then his shirt.

He turned away to sit on the side of the bed and get rid of his boots and his jeans. He stood and faced her again, looking down at her, and then she knew what she had been missing in all that darkness. She filled her eyes with him until her throat ached. His body was hard, the planes of his chest tapering to his lean waist, then to the black nest of hair there and the full evidence of his arousal. His thighs were strong and she saw that he had a scar there of his own, an old one. A small leather bag hung on a piece of braided twine around his neck. She realized that he must always wear it hidden beneath his shirt.

She had known, somehow she had known that he would look just like this.

She reached out a hand to him and moved over to make room for him on the bed, but he kneeled over her instead. If he made love to her forever there would never be time to talk, he realized, and she would never have a chance to go away.

The thought brought a brief surge of desperate anger. He ground his mouth down on hers and tore her robe the rest of the way off. His hands went to her body as though to brand every curve, every long, lean line, to make them his own. She was strong and limber, and he could feel her muscles grow taut and trembling beneath his touch. Oh, how she trembled, and how it undid him. He found the elastic of her panties and tore them roughly down over her hips, then he settled his weight on top of her, rolling, carrying her with him until she was above him.

His hands cupped her bottom, then he kneaded the back of her thighs and coaxed her legs apart. All of her. All of her would be his...now, for this night, and curse tomorrow. He ran his fingers up between her legs and found dampness and heat. He couldn't believe the fire in her could catch so easily—for him, not for any other man.

Catherine felt his breath melt over her. His mouth began to touch her skin as if she were something priceless, irreplaceable. The awe of such a thing rocked her. There was so much beauty in his world, so much that was sacred. That this man could consider her so special in spite of all that she had hidden from him shattered everything she had ever taken for granted about herself.

His tongue slid across her collarbone, leaving a trail of hot fire. Then his mouth moved to her neck, sucking harder and harder, as though to deliberately mark her. It was exquisite, sweet pain, but she wanted to touch him. She moved her arms to feel him, but he caught her hands in a lightning-quick grasp.

"Oh, no, Cat Eyes," he said roughly. "Lay still. This time I want all your secrets. This time you're going to give them up."

Her heart leaped in excitement, willing and wild. He found her mouth again and they rolled, legs twined, until her back came up hard against the trailer wall. Then he was on top of her again and his teeth closed gently over her nipple. He sucked and she groaned, arching into him. His lips moved, sweeping down over her belly and thighs, biting, licking, his hand stroking up along the inside of her legs again.

If she couldn't touch him, she would die.

She finally managed to wrench free of his grip and her hands found his shoulders, strong and broad, vaguely rough with fine hair. His calloused fingers found her warm, hot center in an assault that was both gentle and invading, sweet and relentless.

She heard a raw cry of need explode from her own throat. She would have pulled back from him—it was too much, it made her want him too desperately, it brought him so dan-

gerously, intimately close to her heart. But fate was taunting them, laughing wickedly, and when he pushed her legs
open further she knew better than to fight him.

His mouth moved lower, trespassing on all her secrets. It
brushed over her belly, her muscles contracting in delicious
agony, then closed over her most sensitive flesh. Catherine
groaned, then she gasped, then she lost control of her voice
completely.

His tongue probed and laved, circled and slid, until her
nails dug into his shoulders and she arched backward. He
was satisfied—she was his.

He came up over her again, giving the devil's own grin
when she would have protested, laughing quietly when she
tried feebly to push him back down. But he was aching,
bursting, and they had forever, even if it was all crammed
into the space of one night. He would sate her, then himself, then both of them all over again until she wept.

He had promised.

He drove himself hard into her warm, waiting folds. It
was an act of pure lust, of primal need and uncomplicated
love. She stiffened in shock, then flowed over him, bucking
beneath him to meet his each thrust.

His. Now, for a time.

He felt her body pulsing, accepting, going over the edge,
and he let himself go with her. Emptied, spent, he collapsed on top of her with a groan.

It was a long time before she found her voice again.
"Sorry?" she asked, the way he had asked her the first time.

He had rolled onto his back and her head was settled on
his shoulder, her right leg twined with his. She thought she
felt him stiffen, but she couldn't be sure.

"Should I be?" he asked finally.

Catherine thought about it. "No." It came out on a long
breath. "Maybe scared."

"I am." He said it so simply, unashamed.

"You don't know the half of it yet."

"Tell me later."

Impossibly, he rolled on top of her again, and impossibly, she was ready for him. He slanted his head to kiss her again, fully and deep, then he captured her breasts in his hands, squeezing. He ran his thumbs over her nipples until they hardened once more, then he rolled her over, his teeth closing gently at her nape.

She cried out and rose to her knees, and he plunged into her yet again.

Dawn was tinting the sky when his mouth finally left hers for the last time. Jericho watched the window for a moment with a satisfied half smile, then he lowered his face to the side of her neck, tasting the place where her pulse moved erratically.

"Catherine," he said quietly. It suited her much more than Lanie, he discovered. It was dignified, classic, strong....

"Mmm?"

"Just out of curiosity, are you going to let your hair grow out now?" He braced his weight on his elbows to wrap one wild corkscrew around his finger and study it in the new light. Banked fire, he thought, embers not quite dying.

He wondered if he would be there to see it.

Catherine didn't answer. He looked down at her face again. She was asleep, snoring gently.

He eased away from her and sat up. "That's it, Cat Eyes. Let it go. I'll watch the last of the night for you."

She didn't wake until nearly noon. She did it with a start and a jolt, because something felt wrong. Then she realized what it was. The television was on, static spitting out from the single channel it almost received.

Jericho was sitting in one of the kitchen chairs, his boots braced on the rickety table. When she heard her stir, he looked her way.

"Feel better?"

She lifted one shoulder. Certainly she felt better than she had when she had first put her head down on the clinic desk the night before. And there were sweet aches and tender spots in places she hadn't known she had. That made her smile fleetingly, but the truth of the matter was that she could lie back down and probably sleep the rest of the day away.

"I'm not sure," she murmured. She sat up, leaning over the side of the bed to find her robe. "No bogeymen? No presents?" she asked. "Did you manage to sleep at all?"

He didn't answer. She looked back at him, pulling the robe on. He was staring hard at her.

"What? What's wrong?"

He got up slowly, frowning, coming toward her. He had said last night that he had no regrets. She had told him she would talk, and, God help them both, she would keep her word. So why was he staring at her like that?

She noticed that he had left a coffee cup on the table. "It's not even french vanilla," she mused. "That stuff is gone."

"Exactly how *do* you feel?" he asked finally.

He sensed something wrong with her, the way he could always feel a storm coming, the way he knew when one of his patients was going to die. Beneath his jeans and his leather jacket, he was a man whose dreams whispered to him much as they had to his ancestors. He had finally accepted that years earlier, and now he could not deny that there was a dark miasma of something . . . something evil . . . hanging about her.

He scowled. How long had it been there? He couldn't be sure. The night before had been numbing in its intensity. It could have been there then and he had simply not felt it.

Catherine watched him strangely. "I have a pounding headache, but it's nothing a few aspirin won't fix," she answered finally. "I'll swallow a couple as soon as I get to the clinic."

He made a sound deep in his throat. She couldn't tell if it was approval or irritation.

"I've got to take a shower," she went on. He was starting to frighten her. Maybe when she was finished, he would be his old self again.

She stood and the trailer tilted. She gasped and sat down again hard.

"What?" he growled.

"I'm just dizzy." He was watching her as if he were waiting for her to change color, and she was getting tired of it. "Not surprising, considering the stress I've been under lately. I'll give myself a B12 shot, too."

"Won't do any good," he said quietly.

Something shuddered through her at his tone. Paddy would have said that someone had walked over her grave.

"Why?" she asked a little breathlessly.

He decided to tell her, and the hell with her reaction. "There's something wrong about you this morning," he said. "Something dark."

She gaped at him, finally understanding. "You think your wolfman put a spell on me?"

He made a deprecating sound. "Now he's *my* wolfman again."

"I don't care who he belongs to," she snapped. "I haven't seen hide nor hair of him since that possum ran out of here, assuming the damned thing wasn't just rabid in the first place."

Suddenly she closed her eyes, getting a firm hold on her temper. She didn't want to argue with him. She couldn't bear for it to happen again. She stood carefully, and she was fine this time. She gave him a weak smile.

"So far so good. Look, if I feel worse, I'll tell you, okay?"

He nodded. "Dream last night?"

"During which blink?"

His mouth quirked. "This morning, then."

"I was too tired to dream."

Maybe she just didn't remember, he thought. "Go ahead. Take your shower."

"Care to join me?"

This time he smiled fully. "Care to get to the clinic?"

She sighed. "I think I've already made up for all the time I didn't take off. I guess I have to."

"Yeah, I guess you do. Besides, I already took one."

She raised her brows. "And left me unprotected?"

"Left the door and the shower curtain open."

She should have known.

He watched as she finally went into the bathroom. He had, to his reckoning, at least fourteen things he had to do today. Very rarely did he disappear for several days at a time. That being the case, he decided another day wouldn't matter. He wanted to keep an eye on her, stay close by. He would accomplish what he could by way of the clinic telephone.

He went to the door and pulled it open, scowling down at the porch. The flour hadn't actually been a bad idea, he allowed, but the only marks in it were their boot prints.

Chapter 15

Jericho couldn't feel Catherine's trouble any more. His eyes went back to her again and again, but there were just too many distractions in the clinic—the phone ringing as his calls were returned, people dropping in who needed his help for one thing or another. And then there was Ellen.

Each time he caught her looking at him with those stricken eyes, something stabbed through him. He was angry with himself. Had he somehow encouraged this? But more than anything he was sorry. He hated the thought that he had hurt her. She was like a sister to him; he knew her foibles and knew that she had done her share of suffering. He hated the idea that he had somehow been the man to hurt her again.

Finally he looked back at Catherine, where she was typing a letter to the service, trying to explain about Bessie's sheep which was currently tied to his Rover. Her brow was furrowed and her hair was more disheveled than usual because she kept running her hand through it. But then she would shake her head and laugh. Boggled by the task, but willing to tackle it.

God, he loved her. So what now?

"I'll pay them for the vaccine," he told her.

"No need." Without looking at him, she held up a twenty-dollar bill that had been laying on the desk. "I've got it. I just don't know what to do with that animal."

"I'll take it down to some folks living just south of here. It's a breedable ewe. They'd kill for it. In the meantime, Shadow's bringing some feed for it."

"What about Angie Two Sons?"

He raised a brow at her. So she had been a lot more aware of him and his conversations in those early days than she had let on.

Maybe there was hope.

"Angie's taken care of now," he answered finally.

Catherine kept typing and Jericho finally picked up the phone again. Ellen muttered something unidentifiable about Albuquerque and left.

Jericho continued to watch Catherine sporadically as he spoke to one of the boarding schools about a boy who had run away. The boy's parents were beyond distraught and had asked Jericho to try to find him. He got engrossed in the call, then he heard her chair scrape back and he shot another glance her way.

His heart staggered and almost stopped. He hung up fast.

"You feel worse."

It wasn't a question. Her skin looked as fine as parchment. It was beginning to take on the bright, almost ethereal flush of fever.

She sighed. "Now that you mention it, yes."

"Why didn't you tell me?" he demanded. He realized he was less angry than scared...plainly, emasculatingly scared. What was even more frightening was that she apparently felt too ill to fight back.

"It just hit me when I stood," she explained, seeming almost befuddled. "I was concentrating on the letter."

Jericho pushed back his own chair so hard it toppled over with a clatter. Catherine jumped, then swayed again. "Come on," he snarled. "We're going up the mountain to see Uncle Ernie." He thought he might be too close to her to do her any good himself.

"I don't think that's a very good idea," she answered in a small voice, sitting again.

"Why not?"

"Because I think . . . maybe I ought to stay close to medical help." She waved a hand around the clinic. "Everything I might need is here."

"Not everything," he snapped. He went to kneel in front of her, searching for something in her eyes. His attention was too focused on his own suspicions to consider what she had just said.

"You haven't had *any* dreams lately?" he prodded.

"Jericho," she said with forced patience, "I've barely slept. I'm worn down. Vulnerable to bugs."

Who close to her had died? He searched his memory for anything she might have said, then he remembered. "Your mother."

"What about her?" Catherine asked blearily.

"Have you seen her lately?"

She looked at him incredulously. "She's *dead.*"

"I know."

Suddenly, her heart constricted. She shook her head. This was incredible. Insane. She knew what was wrong with her and it struck terror of its own into her soul, but it had nothing to do with voodoo and *chindis* and—

But suddenly she remembered what he had told her about *chindis. The dead get up and go about their affairs at night. Sometimes they go to their kin, trying to warn them of sickness, of their own imminent deaths.*

"She didn't warn me about anything!" Catherine wailed.

He tried to pull her up again. "Come on. We're going."

"Jericho, for God's sake, it's *Tah honeesgai!*"

That froze him. His hands seemed to go cold where he held her arms. Something happened to his eyes that she could scarcely fathom, could not even begin to believe.

"You're sure?" he asked hoarsely.

"Listen to me." Her breath was starting to come in short, scraping wheezes.

"Then we'll go to Gallup, Albuquerque."

"No," she whispered. "Call for the helicopter. I'm going to lie down."

She made her way unsteadily to one of the exam rooms. After a moment he came in behind her. For the first time since she had known him he looked lost, helpless, and something screamed in her to protect him because she knew instinctively he could handle anything but that. He needed something to do, she realized, something that would let him feel as though he was fighting back.

"Out on the shelves, there's a strong antipyretic," she said. "Pink oval pills with a black *M* on them. Third shelf up from the bottom, second bottle from the right."

He went and got them, bringing them to her with a cup of water. "Now what?" he demanded harshly.

"We'd better... get the oxygen rigged up while I can still tell you how to do it."

She watched his hands as she instructed him. They were so strong, capable. He should have been a doctor, she thought wildly, and then in the next moment she remembered the way those hands had felt on her body the night before. *Please, God, let me feel them again.* She couldn't die. They hadn't even talked yet, she thought irrationally.

"Okay," she gasped. "Leave it there...so it's close when I need it."

"What about the IV you used on Louie?"

"We'll need ... that too."

It was getting so hard to breathe, and her stomach was cramping enough to take away even the air she had. She didn't know if it was fear gripping her there, or *Tah honeesgai.* How far gone was she?

"You'll have to...put it in. I can't manage with one hand."

She braced herself for the pain, telling him how to find a vein, waiting for it. She knew he had never done this before. But the needle slid in like the kiss of an angel, and that made her want to cry.

"Thank you. Set it... set that upper clamp... to the first little black line."

There was one more thing. Terror filled her soul, but she had to face facts, couldn't pretend. Jericho himself had said the survival rate of this thing wasn't high. She had done for herself all the things she had done for Louie. She had used an even stronger antipyretic, had the oxygen ready, but...

"Get...something to write with," she urged.

He looked at her oddly, but he did as she asked. He started to hand her the scratch paper and the pen, but she waved him away.

"Write down this number." She gave it to him, reciting carefully. Her brain felt foggy. The antipyretic wasn't working.

"What's this?" he growled.

"Paddy's phone."

His face went slack, all the beautiful, hard lines of it. Catherine had to look away.

"If...I don't make it, somebody has to give permission...for an autopsy. The CDC needs—"

She choked off as he grabbed her, coughs spasming through her. He shook her anyway, lifting her half off the table. "*No*. Don't talk about it. Don't even let it into your mind." Then he realized what he was doing to her and lowered her again with a ragged groan.

"Got to...be prepared..." she insisted. He leaned close over her.

Those shaman's eyes. If they were the last thing she ever saw, then maybe this lifetime had been enough.

His gaze burned into her as if he would convey his own life into her, his own soul. "Listen to me," he ordered. "The Navajo believe—*I* believe—that all life is the spirit. You medics keep trying to heal the body, but there's a whole hell of a lot more. *Listen to me.*" His fingers dug painfully into her arms when she closed her eyes.

"If the spirit is strong enough," he began, "it can resist death, the same way it can give up and die when there's nothing wrong with a man's body. That's why the sings work. Are you hearing me?"

She managed to nod.

"*Promise me.* Promise me you won't let yours give up."
Suddenly his hand shot out, sending the oxygen mask and
the tank crashing. "*You won't need it.* Tell yourself, damn
it, make yourself believe you won't need it!"

"Try," she agreed. She had to close her eyes. She couldn't
hold them open anymore.

"For once in your stubborn Irish life believe in another
way than the one that was taught to you as a child," he finished hoarsely. "Damn you. I thought you would run, but
this is a cowardly way to do it."

She was angry, so angry at that, but she couldn't find her
voice to argue with him.

"Don't leave me, Cat Eyes. I'm not through with you
yet."

It was the last thing she consciously heard, and the
sweetest.

They tried to stop him from getting on the helicopter with
her. Jericho grabbed the arm of a CDC doctor as that man
started to turn away.

"You've got two choices," he said with deadly calm.
"You can let me in there, or you can die now and I'll take
your neat little suit and your badge and no one will know
I'm not you."

"Get in," the doctor said tightly, after some thoughtful
hesitation.

The helicopter lurched and lifted. Jericho settled himself
beside Catherine's stretcher.

She didn't know he was there, at least not on any cogni-
zant level. But maybe she had heard him at the end before
she had fallen unconscious. It was all that would save her.
He knew that in a cold, rocky spot that had settled in place
of his stomach.

The wolfman had finally gotten to her. Even while she
had been sprinkling that stupid flour, he had been reaching
for her.

It was so simple, and so far out of the realm of anything
she could accept. To Jericho, it was as clear as the sun that
was even now setting, and the truth strangled him. The land

he loved, one of the People he lived for, would steal something precious from him yet again . . . but this time he truly did not know how he would forgive it.

"Why didn't you run, Cat Eyes? Damn it, why didn't you just go home?"

But maybe, maybe that stubborn strength would save her.

He found her hand, twined his fingers into hers, and chanted low beneath his breath so only her spirit could hear him. He would go through every chant he had ever learned and before this night was over he knew he would repeat them.

Finally she groaned, and he took it as a good sign. Then his heart stopped, paralyzed.

"Hey," he snapped at one of the paramedics. "Get over here."

A young man scrambled to Catherine's opposite side, working on her with a flurry of hands. "Fever's spiking," he said. "Did anyone give her anything for it?"

Jericho told him about the little pink pills. "She's a doctor. Almost a doctor," he said, then his mouth thinned. Because he couldn't take that away from her, because he would let her go so she could finish the dream. He had known it would come to that all along.

Catherine began thrashing. The medic tried to lash her hands down with little strips of fabric attached to the sides of the stretcher. Jericho caught his arm. "Don't do that."

"She's delirious," the man protested.

"She's not an animal."

The medic backed off, not wanting to tangle with him anymore than the CDC doctor had. He had overheard their conversation outside. "Okay, okay. Hold her down yourself then. But if you let go, she'll hurt herself."

"No, she won't." A heartbeat later, he wasn't so sure. What was she saying? And who the hell was Victor?

Terror strangled him more tightly than it had since this whole nightmare had started. It was the kind of fear that was helpless, horrified, impotent. Because he couldn't battle this demon for her. This was an old one, one that lived only in her memory, one that should, by all rights, already be dead. Now, in the throes of her fever, she was living it all over again.

Victor. Jericho struggled to control her as she fought him violently. He was awed at her strength, at her panic, and knew she wasn't fighting him at all. She thought he was the other man, undoubtedly the one she had gone through the motions with.

Suddenly he understood, made some sense of her garbled words. He used all his strength to hold both her hands with only one of his own. Then he shoved up her T-shirt and found the button and zipper on her jeans.

That scar. He had barely paid attention to it the night before, but some memory of it had lingered . . . something not quite right about it. . . .

A bullet wound. He had seen them before and this one was unmistakable, now that he knew what he was looking for. Disjointed thoughts banged wildly through his head. She had let him take her robe off anyway, had trusted him with it. His throat closed. *God, if it was too late . . .*

He would kill Victor if he ever found him. He would do it with his bare hands, and he would smile.

The helicopter began dropping. The doctor came back, pushing him out of the way. They were in Albuquerque, and she was still alive.

Still alive . . . believing . . .

Jericho followed them as they carried her inside. Then, at the swinging doors leading to the treatment rooms, a nurse barred his way.

She was quite possibly the largest woman Jericho had ever seen. "I'm with her," he said hoarsely, motioning past her to Catherine's stretcher.

"No, you're not. Dr. Weatherly told me about you." Her voice was like the rumble of a she-cat protecting her young.

Jericho scowled. "Who's Weatherly?"

"The CDC doctor who brought her in. You're staying right out here. And if you lay a hand on me, security will come running."

Jericho raked a hand through his hair. What had the CDC doctor told her?

Oh, hell, he had threatened to kill him.

He held up both hands in surrender. He considered that even if she didn't call for security, she could definitely hurt him. And anyway, Catherine was safe now. God, let her be safe.

There was nothing more he could do for her, and if anything, he would be in the way now. The doctors would be swarming around her, treating her body, forgetting her spirit and soul. She would hang on anyway. She had to. She had heard him.

He backed up, clamping down on a surge of temper as the nurse's gaze moved critically over his long black hair, then went to a spot on his chest. He moved one hand to grope there and found his gall bag, the medicine pouch he always wore around his neck beneath his clothing. It had slipped out from under his shirt when he had been struggling with Catherine. The nurse stared at it distastefully.

"We must maintain a sterile environment beyond these doors."

Oh, lady, you and I will tangle later. "Sterile or not, you might want to go in there and see if those doctors need you."

Her jaw fell and her fleshy face went red. Jericho left her that way and went back to the lobby.

It was near dawn when Weatherly found him. He approached him with obvious reluctance, and Jericho pushed to his feet to meet him.

"You aren't family, are you?"

Jericho's blood went to ice. "Why? Is she—" *Not again.* He couldn't finish.

"I think she'll be okay," the doctor said. "But if you're not kin, I can't admit you until she asks for you. She's asleep right now, so you'll have to wait."

Something shook through him violently, relief and a fierce pride. She had fought back to him. She had heard him.

The doctor was still talking. He dragged his attention back to him.

"Her fever broke about an hour ago. This thing is fast. It strikes while you blink and vanishes just as quickly. Ms. McDaniel is sleeping restfully. She spent the night in an oxygen tent, but now she's breathing pretty well on her own." The man shook his head, twin spots of high color coming to his cheeks. "I wish to God I knew why. Why her? Why Louie Coldwater, and none of the others?"

They'd believed. "She recognized the symptoms fast in both cases."

"But that was the only similarity. We don't even know how they're catching it."

"Because you're not listening."

Jericho left him and went to the pay phone on the far wall, digging for the scrap of paper in his pocket. He had forgotten he had it until Weatherly had mentioned kin. Now he frowned down at it, rubbing a hand over his dry, gritty eyes.

There was no reason to place the call now.

And there was every reason in the world.

He picked up the phone, looking at his watch only after he had punched in his calling-card number. Twenty past six. Was there a time change involved here? He didn't even know what city she had come from. Was it L.A., where it was an hour earlier?

The line rang and there was a click on the other end as it was picked up. Too late now.

"Mr. McDaniel," he demanded.

The responding voice had a definite if fading brogue. It was also hard-nosed and suspicious. "I should hope like hell not. Died twenty years ago, God rest his soul."

Jericho pulled the phone away from his ear and looked at it a moment. Okay, so McDaniel hadn't been real then, either. "Who are you, then?" he asked.

"Hold on, boy. I have a pretty pertinent question of m'own. Who are *you?*"

Boy? How long had it been since anyone had had the courage, the audacity, to call him that? Jericho waited for his temper to surge—and heard himself laughing.

Catherine was alive. Finally, the full magnitude of that sank into him. His air left him slowly. Emotion rushed in to fill the void, sweet and tangled, warm and unimaginably wonderful.

He found his voice. "I'm calling because of your daughter." He remembered then that the man had a slew of them. "Catherine."

There was a long moment of silence. "Cat," Paddy said softly. "Would you be a saint or the devil?"

"Plenty of folks'll tell you it's the latter."

The man didn't miss a beat. Jericho found himself liking him.

"So it goes, it does. Where is she, then?" Paddy answered.

"The hospital, but she's okay now."

There was a pregnant pause as this sank in. "Saint Mary's?"

Saint who? "No. University."

"Never heard of it. Here in Boston?"

Boston. So that was where she had come from. But why didn't Paddy know she was in New Mexico?

Jericho felt himself losing the thread of clear communication again. "Albuquerque," he responded warily.

"What'd she be doin' there?" Paddy was just as cautious.

It came to Jericho slowly. Her father didn't even realize Catherine was performing an externship on the Res. Why? He filled him in.

"And then how'd she come to be in a hospital?" Paddy demanded.

Jericho chose his words carefully, putting it together in his mind as he spoke. "We've got a bug out here. The Indian Health Service was grasping for externs, residents, anyone willing to come out here and risk contagion to practice. She was running from something. Guess she thought the risk was worth it. She caught it, but she's resting comfortably now." He thought of telling him about the wolfman and her spirit, and decided against it. Something told him this man already knew all about her spirit anyway.

Paddy absorbed this. "If she's so comfortable, how come it's not her I be talking to?"

Both of Jericho's brows lifted. The man didn't miss a trick. "She's asleep."

"Not holding grudges?"

Grudges? "How long since you've spoken to her?"

Paddy let lose with some colorful swearing that had Jericho's brows going up, and he wasn't easy to shock. "Four years, I guess it'd be now—since she married the s.o.b.," he rasped.

Married. The single word punched into him hard, robbing his air all over again. Through everything he had imagined, through everything he had feared, such a possibility had never occurred to him. *Married?*

"Is his name Victor?" he asked tightly, trying to control the rage that wanted to choke him.

"Victor Landano."

"He's trying to kill her." A few more pieces were coming together, finally, jaggedly, fitting the only way they could. "I think he's already tried. So she came here, hiding. Told everyone she was Lanie McDaniel."

"Good name, that," Paddy mused. It was clear his own thoughts were spinning.

"I need to know about Victor," Jericho said. "I need to know why he's coming after her."

Paddy cleared his throat. "Haven't the foggiest. Why don't you ask her?"

Because for all those times I thought she was a broken bird, I was the one who was really a coward. Because when I had the chance two nights ago, I shied away from it…shied away from losing her.

He wondered what she might have told him about Victor Landano if he had let her talk then.

"I'm not sure there's time," he said finally.

"Umph," said Paddy. "So what *do* you know about her?"

Jericho thought about it. "She's got a temper and it can cut a man clear to the bone—sort of a wild thing that just gets away from her sometimes. She laughs when you don't expect it, and she's stubborn and stronger than she has a right to be. She handles a gun like a vigilante, and she takes things in stride even when they make her stumble. She plays by the rules—too religiously. It's almost like her first instinct is to tell authority to kiss her sweet little Irish butt.''

"That's m'girl. Never liked Victor myself," Paddy added, suddenly congenial and talkative. "She met him her last year in medical school, and somehow he talked her out of finishing. Damned hardest worker you'd ever want to see, that girl. Can't figure how he made her do it."

Jericho did. Suddenly he remembered the pallor of her skin that day they had fought, the way her hands had clenched. Victor had given her orders and ultimatums.

Paddy sighed. "He's a rich guy, slick good looks. I didn't like his hands—too soft. Looked like he hadn't worked a day in his life. You can't trust a man with soft hands. Personally, I always thought he was the Maf-ee-a." He spat the word like a long, drawn-out curse, accentuating every syllable.

Jericho felt his blood chill again. He thought of the depth of her fear, of the meticulous care she had given her secrets. It made sense.

"I think she was just starstruck by him," Paddy continued. "He went after her hard and swept her off her feet, he did. Seems like she was ashamed, 'cause she wouldn't face me after that. Guess she might of thought I'd blow my stack again, too. 'Cause I sorta did, there in the beginning, but that's what fathers are for. You gotta blow up now and again to make a girl think twice of what she be doin'. I guess Cat thought and did it anyway, then she didn't come around the house again. You say she's sleepin' now? And she's doing her doctorin' again? She gonna call me herself now, you think?''

Jericho wondered. He could hear the depth of the man's longing clear across two thousand miles—a longing he knew instinctively he'd never tell his daughter about. Stubborn Irish tempers could go a long way—on both sides. He imagined Paddy's "sorta" blowup had been something to see, and Catherine wouldn't have taken such a thing quietly.

Then he caught sight of the gargantuan nurse waddling back toward the emergency desk. He thought briefly of the discomfort of having another man fight his battles for him and decided he didn't mind if it got him where he needed to be.

"I'll pass on the word, but I need you to do me a favor," he said suddenly.

"It'll have to reach a way," Paddy answered. "This here's long-distance."

"It'll reach. There's someone here I need you to talk to. They won't let anybody into Catherine's room unless they're kin. Guess you just got yourself an ambassador."

Paddy laughed loudly, a good burst of sound. "Put 'em on the phone." Then he sobered. "Victor ain't gonna get to her again, is he?"

"Not if I have anything to say about it."

Jericho waved the nurse over. She approached distrustfully and disdainfully. Jericho handed her the phone and headed for the swinging doors.

She shouted after him, but he ignored her. He pushed through the doors and waited for a moment, but security didn't come after him. Having taken a good read on Paddy, he didn't really expect them to.

He poked his head into each room until he found Catherine's. It was a busy hospital with few available beds. They hadn't moved her upstairs yet. He sat in a chair by the window and stretched his long legs out in front of him to wait.

She finally stirred around breakfast time. He bided his time until she focused on him fully.

"Welcome back to the land of the living, Mrs. Landano."

Chapter 16

Catherine's first reaction was shock. It galloped through her briefly, then she was furious.

She grabbed a glass of water from her bedside table and hurled it at him without thinking. He ducked quickly sideways and it missed him, but the glass shattered against the radiator and the water splashed across the wall.

"Feeling better?" he asked dryly.

"First of all, I told you to call him if I was *dying*."

"You were."

She ignored that. "Secondly, if you're going to jump all over me for something, if you're going to close me out and get that hard, hateful look on your face, then it seems to me there's plenty I've legitimately done to make you angry, that you don't have to reach for things that aren't true."

"I'm not hateful."

"And I'm not married, you stupid, mule-headed—"

His face got hard, and she choked on her voice.

"Go on," he urged darkly.

"Never mind." She clenched her jaw and shut up.

He rose from the chair, turning his back on her to look out the window at another sun-swept day. But he knew that if he touched the glass, it would be cool now. Winter was coming, a time when everything died.

"I'm ready to listen now," he said finally, too quietly.

Catherine blew out her breath. Everything was unraveling. Nothing made any difference anymore, and she would have told him even if it had. Somewhere along the line it had become painful, an ache, to keep it all from him.

She just didn't know where to start.

"I *was* married," she breathed.

"Gathered as much." He nodded at the sky.

"It was a mistake... I knew that almost from the beginning, but my family never believed in divorce."

"The pope again." Still, he didn't turn.

"That's right. So I stuck with it. And then one day in August I sent my car over to the garage for a tune-up. Victor was in his study. He saw my car leave, but apparently he didn't realize I wasn't driving it. He was on the phone and I went to ask him what he wanted for lunch. And I... heard something."

His eyes came back to her sharply, almost as though he knew this was the place where she was inclined to keep holding back. Catherine swallowed carefully. No more. No more secrets. Victor wouldn't stop to ask how much Jericho knew. If he were so inclined, he would kill him—regardless of what she did or didn't tell him.

"Senator Davies had opposed Victor on some business deal. So Victor had him killed. That was what he was talking about, where to... oh, God... what to do with the body. Someone had screwed up and it wasn't where it was supposed to be and Victor wanted it moved."

There was no appreciable change on Jericho's face. Catherine rushed on.

"He didn't see me and I went back to the kitchen, but I was shocked, didn't know where I was going, what I was doing. I had a pot of soup on the stove and I dropped it and he came into the kitchen. I made some kind of an excuse, didn't let on that I'd heard anything. But he knew... he knew.

"The next day I went to the cops and they notified the FBI. I called them myself from a public telephone in town and thought I could just tip them off or something, like in the movies. But it didn't work that way. The next thing I knew I was there in their field office and they wanted me to go back to that house, to keep living with him, to try to get him to talk about it. They wanted me to pretend that everything was fine between us, that what he'd done didn't bother me. They said they could protect me, that nothing would happen. I gave them permission to wire the house so they could listen in on everything and tape it. They said they needed 'direct evidence' and that everything I'd told them so far was just hearsay. They needed to hear it for themselves."

She paused, shuddering a little, remembering. "They said that if at any point I was in danger, they'd hear it and come running. They... kept saying they needed proof. They said they'd take care of an annulment for me, quietly and simply and fast—trying to stay married wasn't even an issue for me at that point. The pope doesn't approve of murder either. And since Victor essentially married me under false pretenses, not telling me of his true background or what he really did for a living, an annulment was all I needed. They said it wasn't necessary for me to go through all the messy red tape of a divorce."

She'd given the single explanation he'd needed so much to hear. Divorce, annulment—it didn't matter which. She was no longer Victor's woman. Jericho's eyes narrowed as he waited for the rest, already knowing, hurting for her in a place he hadn't known he had. *Just going through the motions.*

Catherine sighed, thinking. "All I had to do was live there a few more weeks. Then they said they would help me disappear. But it didn't work that way. I mean... I got the annulment, but Victor knew something was wrong. I'm not good at hiding my feelings."

"No," he agreed, and her eyes flashed to him. She gave him a sick smile.

"Sex had always been . . . sporadic between us. I realized so early on that I didn't really love him, and I tried to avoid it. But after I knew what he had done, what he was—I just couldn't stand it anymore, couldn't bear for him to touch me at all. So he knew something had changed and he knew what it was, and he tried to kill me."

"He shot you."

"I had some warning. I was in the pool, doing laps. If he had just come up to me and pulled the trigger, I...wouldn't be here talking to you. But Victor isn't like that. He has a very strong ego. He had to make sure I knew why I was dying. He just stood there, holding the gun, explaining it to me like he was discussing the weather. I ran into the house and that was stupid, but I made it upstairs and locked myself in a bedroom and by the time he shot the lock out I had gotten a window open. The pool was right there on that side of the house so I dove in."

Jericho's brows arched and he felt fresh horror, new disbelief, another sense of awe shimmy through him. "From the second floor?"

"I'm a good swimmer."

"You could have broken your neck." Suddenly, he remembered the doll.

Catherine nodded. "Of course I could have. But if I was going to die, I was damned well going to do it on my terms. I was going to go out fighting."

Laughter escaped him, a harsh, short bark that got cut off as she went on.

"So much for the FBI's protection," she said bitterly. "I couldn't go to Paddy, not even to warn him. I couldn't go to any of my family, because I figured Victor would look there first. I was alone. The only chance anyone had was if they were completely in the dark. Maybe Victor wouldn't hurt them if he was genuinely sure I hadn't told them anything."

"But he shot you. When'd he shoot you?"

"He came back downstairs and caught up with me just as I pulled myself out of the pool. I got as far as his car. The keys were in it, thank God. He always left them there, as though no one would dare steal it from him." She thought about that. "He was probably right. I think I was the only one in the world who hadn't ever suspected who he was ... who his family was." She shook her head. "Anyway, he shot just as I was scrambling into the car. I was sliding sideways at the time and the bullet just sort of grazed my hip, and I hit the gas and drove. I knew from med school that it wasn't fatal, just a flesh wound. So I kept pressure on it until I got into Connecticut, and I saw a doctor there. I used a charge card to buy some clothes—I figured Victor would follow the paper trail, but by then I'd be gone. And I had about a thousand dollars I'd managed to squirrel away after I talked to the FBI the first time. I figured I was going to need every penny I could get my hands on when the time came that I could finally leave that house."

He was looking at her oddly. "When'd you grab the money?"

She scowled as if he were missing something very elemental. "Before I jumped in the pool."

"Victor was chasing you with a gun and you stopped to get the money you had saved to run with?"

"I would have been in a fix without it."

He didn't know if he was shocked or if he wanted to laugh again. What had he told Paddy? *She takes things in stride even when they make her stumble.*

He looked at her again. His heart hurt. "So what happened in Connecticut?"

"I checked into a sleazy motel—you should have *seen* the people going in and out of there."

He nodded. He could imagine.

"And somewhere along the line I bought a Boston newspaper to see if there was anything in it about the FBI charging Victor. There wasn't, but there was a blurb in the national section about the Mystery Disease. It was like ... serendipity." She hesitated, watching him carefully now. "You know the rest."

Not entirely. "Who were you calling from Shiprock?"

"The FBI. I abandoned Victor's car because I didn't trust anyone anymore and I thought it was best if I just tried to disappear into thin air. But then there was the owl and that doll, so I figured someone had followed me anyway. I had to find out what was going on, where things stood, if Victor could possibly have put someone on my tail."

"And?" Jericho asked shortly.

Fear moved inside her again, like a snake winding its way coldly through her vital organs. "They say he's still in Boston. And I guess they got the proof they needed," she said quietly. "They should charge him with racketeering and on Senator Davies's death any time now. They don't think Victor will come after me until then." No, that wasn't entirely true. "Actually, they said that once it's a fait accompli, they don't think the family will send anyone after me at all. But they've been wrong before."

His face hardened in a way she had never seen before. "So it's not over."

"No," she breathed. "The owl, the doll—someone's out there. Someone knows. A part of me still believes Victor's got someone here, watching me."

"Either way, you're safe now."

There was something new about his voice, too. It made her feel more protected than she had ever felt in her life...and at the same time it chilled something deep within her. He would kill him, she realized. If Victor dared to come to this man's land to try to do harm to her, she knew without a doubt that Jericho would kill him.

Something jolted inside her, something like the horror and revulsion she had felt when she had first overheard Victor's phone conversation. She had been trained to save lives—the thought of taking one, even Victor's, was abominable to her. But looking at Jericho's face, his eyes burning at something far away now, she knew that this was an entirely different situation with an entirely different man. Victor's killing instinct had been cold and passionless. Jericho's was the fierce, hot will of a man intent upon protecting his own.

His own?

She hoped she was, with an ache that hurt. But then a host of new complications rose in her head and she had to push them away because she simply wasn't ready to deal with them.

"Maybe it really is just your... the wolfman," she tried instead.

"Could be." A muscle worked at his neck, tense and pulsing. "We'll find out."

"How?" she asked, not entirely sure she wanted to know.

He hesitated a little too long. "Because if it's the wolfman, it'll stop now."

"Why?"

He looked back at her, his brow creasing as he tried to explain. "Ever know a schoolyard bully?"

"Of course."

"Same thing. As soon as you stand up to them, they back off. You beat him, Cat Eyes."

She shook her head, feeling lost. "What did I do?"

"You're alive."

"But it was *Tah honeesgai*—" She broke off. Yes, it had been *Tah honeesgai,* and maybe... maybe its root wasn't organic at all.

She shuddered and closed her eyes, remembering how her mother's voice had come to her, not knowing what to make of any of it anymore.

"You need to rest," Jericho said.

"This time I won't argue with you." She felt as drained as if she had single-handedly fought the Crimean War. But her eyes flew open again when she heard him approach the bed. He looked down at her intently.

"Paddy wants you to call him."

Her jaw hardened and her eyes turned guarded. There was pain there, too. "Did he *say* that?" she asked suspiciously.

"What do you think?"

Her mouth looked like it wanted to smile, but God, she was stubborn. "I think he told you to make me call."

Jericho thought about it. "No. He asked me if you would."

Yes. "I don't know." She closed her eyes again, leaning her head back against the pillow. "He hated Victor."

"You're not married to him anymore. Bygones, and all that."

She lifted one shoulder in a shrug. "Doesn't matter. Paddy was right about him, and he's never been modest about that sort of thing. I'll have to eat a lot of crow."

"We'll handle it, Cat Eyes."

Her heart chugged, almost stopped. *We?*

But his eyes were distant again, thoughtful, and she knew his mind was off on another tangent. He probably wasn't even aware of what he'd said. He brushed his mouth over her forehead and was back at the door before her heart started beating again.

"Where are you going?" she managed.

"First I'm going to get someone I trust from the Res to come down here and stand guard over you. How long do you think they'll keep you here? How many days are we talking about?"

"I..." She felt dazed. She shook her head. "Louie was in for four days."

"So until about Friday?"

"I suppose. Where will *you* be?" Why couldn't he stay here himself?

"Keeping tabs on me, Cat Eyes?"

She flushed, then he grinned. It was a look still rare enough to steal her breath away.

"I've got some things to take care of," he said roughly. "I'll be back."

The door swished on a rush of air and he was gone.

We?

Jericho's parade of dubious bodyguards began less than two hours later. Catherine reminded herself that they were doing it for him, at his request, but there was still something touching about it. It was as though the People were closing ranks around her. She felt so secure, so sheltered and...bolstered.

Bessie's husband arrived first. He settled himself in the chair by the window, his back ramrod straight, a hand braced on each of his knees. He wouldn't look at her, but he seemed willing to talk.

"How's the ewe?" he asked.

Catherine wondered. The last she had seen of her, she had still been tied to Jericho's Rover. "She's fine."

"Old Lady Yellowhorse has a good ram."

He was staring above her to the place where the ceiling and the wall came together. "That's good to know," Catherine allowed, following his gaze.

"Makes good lambs with that ewe. 'Course, the old lady knows it and wants a lot of money."

"I'll keep it in mind."

Finally, it dawned on her that he wouldn't look at her because she was in bed. She was dressed to her chin in one of the horrendous hospital gowns they had given her and the covers were wadded all the way up to her breasts because she had been asleep when he came. But none of that mattered to this courteous Navajo gentleman at all.

She rolled over, putting her back to him carefully, dozing off again. Just before she did, she thought she heard him sigh in relief.

When she woke the next morning, Louie and Leo's father was gone. A young man of about twenty or so was sitting on the floor of her room poking at a pile of metal that laid on a horse blanket.

Catherine sat bolt upright, staring. "Who are you?"

He looked up at her. "Hey, you're awake."

She nodded, managing a smile. It wasn't difficult. He had an infectious friendliness about him.

"I'm Eddie," he explained.

"Begay?" On closer inspection, she realized that the metal bits he was sorting through were pieces of a car engine.

He nodded. "Hey, you know your Ford? It got washed away in that bad rain when you got here?"

Catherine nodded cautiously.

"Well, sorry to say, but it's a goner."

She shrugged. She had expected as much.

"You can borrow my Jeep, though, whenever you need to get around some."

She was touched all over again. "Thank you."

"Mind if I work on this stuff while I sit here? I take on odd jobs, you know, and I don't get much time off to work on them. I'll keep it real quiet."

"Sure," Catherine said. "That's fine." She hesitated. "Have you seen Jericho?"

He looked at her blankly. "You mean since he came by the garage yesterday to ask me to come down here?"

Catherine nodded, and Eddie Begay shrugged.

"Nope, but he sent this."

He rummaged underneath the coat he had thrown over the chair and came up with a rumpled paper bag. He carried it to her and deposited it in her lap. Catherine peered inside.

Coffee. Not french vanilla. Mexican chocolate. And a note with a single word. *Compromise.*

Something hot touched her eyes. Who needed flowers?

By Thursday, Eddie had been replaced by Grandmother Yellowhorse's son, Tommy, who was apparently ghost free now. Then Tommy left and one of Angie Two Sons' boys came. When Catherine woke on Friday morning, he was gone as well and a very old, very gnarled man was moving slowly around her bed in a circle.

Her eyes followed him warily.

His voice was reedy and thin as he chanted, and when he rounded the foot of the bed and came back toward her again she saw that his face was a road map, seamed with a thousand lines that told a million tales. He was frail and boney and he wore a baggy calico tunic that hung to his knees. His hair was gunmetal gray and grizzled, tufting up in places from two long braids that were anything but neat.

She was catching on now. This had to be Uncle Ernie. One by one, she was meeting all of Jericho's most beloved friends, his People.

"Hello," she said tentatively.

"Yutaheh," Uncle Ernie answered, waving a gourd over her head. When he wasn't singing, his voice was gravelly.

"Do you speak English?" It occurred to her that it was entirely possible that he didn't. He appeared almost old enough to have lived before reservation days.

Uncle Ernie smiled. "As good as you do. I prefer not to."

"I don't speak Navajo."

"You will."

Catherine's heart jolted. He spoke the way he might tell her that the sun would come up again. There was something about his eyes that made her think he could see clear into tomorrow.

She decided to change the subject. "Did Jericho send you too?"

"No."

"He didn't?"

"It wasn't necessary." He put his gourd away, tucking it into the waistband of his too-large trousers. She wondered how the gourd stayed there, how the pants remained up. "I heard you were here and I came," he continued.

He took some corn pollen out of the little pouch around his neck—at least she assumed that was what it was. She had heard a great deal about the stuff since she had come here. It was sort of a cure-all.

Uncle Ernie sprinkled his over her blankets. "He won't come back to you now," he said finally, satisfied.

"Jericho?" Her heart spasmed.

"No, the wolfman."

"Oh." She breathed again. "Jericho said he wouldn't bother me again anyway."

"And he is probably right. But now we can be sure." He tucked the little pouch into his shirt again. "Jericho will be here shortly, I think. He's on his way."

He went to the door, then paused, looking back at her in a searching way that reminded her of Jericho. Then he cocked his head as though listening to voices she couldn't hear.

"You must remember, Catherine Mary, to listen always to your spirit. You have found it, now you must use it."

The door swished again and he was gone. *Catherine Mary?* How had he known her full name?

Paddy had told Jericho, of course, and Jericho had told him. But somehow she didn't believe that.

She was alone for only a few short minutes, not even time to dwell on the old man's last words. Then one of the CDC doctors arrived to tell her that he was releasing her. By then, she had almost forgotten what solitude was like.

She dressed in the rare quiet once that man was gone, then she spun around again when a yet another knock sounded on the door. *Jericho?* Finally? But she couldn't imagine that he would knock.

"Come in?" she invited curiously.

Richard Moss stuck his head through the door. "Are you decent?"

"Generally."

He laughed and came the rest of the way inside. "I heard they were letting you go today. Do you need a ride back to the Res?"

Catherine hesitated. She did, but surely Jericho would reappear in time to give her one. She had no real reason to assume that he would... except for the bodyguards and the coffee and that last little "we" he had hit her with before he had left. He was a man who took care of his own.

Besides, the old man had said he was coming—she found she believed him intrinsically, through no reason she could put logic to.

"No." She shook her head, deciding to take the gamble.

"That's too bad. I'd hoped to say goodbye in a more leisurely fashion."

"Goodbye?" She blinked at him.

"I've been summoned back east by the powers that be."

"Oh." She tried to regret it, but she'd barely gotten to know him, after all. "Well," she said finally, "you said you didn't like it here anyway."

"But you've added immeasurable pleasure to my stay." A strange look touched his face. It was so serious, so out of character, she stared. "You're a very lucky woman, Lanie McDaniel."

"Yes," she agreed quietly. "I wonder why. I wonder how I caught it, and how I fought it off. But I assume someone from the CDC will be around to grill me sooner or later. Maybe, with my training, we'll be able to figure it out this time."

"I wonder. You know, I would have hated to have seen you die."

What an odd thing to say, she thought. But before she could reply, he, too, was gone.

She sat down on the bed, plucking thoughtfully at the blanket, waiting for Jericho. Uncle Ernie had been right. She scarcely had time to breathe before he pushed open the door. She had been right, too. He didn't knock.

"Kind of hoped you'd still be in that funny little gown. They really hang open in the back?"

Catherine pushed quickly to her feet, impossibly glad to see him, irritated by the way he had obviously assumed she would wait for him. And she had.

"You snooze, you lose," she snapped.

He cocked a brow at her. "Temper again?" He shrugged. "I've been busy."

"I imagined as much." Suddenly she realized that he wore a strange expression too, an odd mixture of regret and satisfaction and concern. "What's the matter? What is it?"

"Victor's dead."

Chapter 17

The color seemed to fade from everything in the room. Catherine didn't so much sit again as she sank, slowly and carefully, back onto the bed.

"Dead?" she echoed.

Jericho came to her, hunkering down in front of her. His shaman's eyes probed, intruded, tried to get behind her own. "That's right."

"Did you . . ." She couldn't finish.

His eyes sharpened even more, then they cleared as he understood. He wanted to be enraged, but the truth of the matter was that he had thought about it.

"Did *I* kill him? Is that what you're trying to ask me?"

Catherine nodded, her face white.

"No. I didn't have the pleasure."

Life returned to her limbs again slowly, tingling. "How then?" she asked.

"Do you want my theory or the official FBI version?"

"You talked to the FBI?"

"They have a field office here in Albuquerque, too. That's where I've been, for the most part. Straightening this out, or trying to. I figured that if Victor was still a threat, we were going to disappear for a while, but I wanted up-to-date facts.''

We again. She trembled.

"By the way, your Schilling is a jackass."

"They all are," she responded absently. "They're clones and they do everything by the book." Then she remembered Schilling's promise not to tell the cops where she was. "Schilling's not as bad as some of the others," she amended.

"Frightening thought." Jericho hesitated. "Victor went over the Storrow bridge. His tire blew out and he lost control of his car."

Catherine looked at him carefully. "That's what the FBI says?"

"That's right."

"Did *they* kill him?" Was such a thing possible? But Jericho shook his head.

"I doubt it. A fellow identified as Johnny Maverick was fished out of the bay this morning back in Boston. There's another body in the morgue with a bullet in the temple, name of Sly Camarrati. Know them?"

Catherine felt cold. "I knew a Johnny, but I never heard his last name. He...always wore a suit." Odd that she should remember that now.

"Well, it looks like the hits came from within the organization. Too many bodies. Are you going to cry or something?"

"Or something," she reflected. In truth, she didn't know how she felt. She didn't know how she *would* feel when the shock wore off.

Jericho watched her closely. Presumably, she had loved the man once. She had married him. And he was dead. She would have to be going through some kind of hell right now. But of all the things he knew he could stand, watching her cry for the bastard was not one he thought he could handle.

Catherine slid carefully off the bed, lowering herself to his lap.

"Ah." She sighed finally, vacantly. "Dead."

He held her and found that it was easy after all, even if she was mourning a man who made rage and jealousy slash through him like vicious, angry animals with unspeakable claws.

"It's over," he continued, as much to assure himself as her. "It's done."

"No, I don't think so."

He stiffened. "Why?"

"Did the FBI ever charge him?"

"Three days ago. That's what started the bodies dropping."

She began shaking uncontrollably. "And now everyone who was involved is dead. Except…for me. I'm next, then."

Her words were so simple, so accepting, they drove ice into his soul. It took him a moment to fight free of it, to drag logic to the forefront past his fear.

"Why bother to hit you?" he growled. "Even if you talked now, who would you implicate? They can't put a dead man on trial. And you're not a threat to the organization in any other respect, Cat Eyes. Unless I badly miss my guess, Victor probably assured them up and down and six ways to Sunday that he didn't let you know anything else. He wanted to placate them. He didn't want to die."

She trembled worse, trying to accept that. It was true. Who was she going to squeal on? It was over.

That was when she cried.

She did it so quietly he didn't notice at first. "They mopped up their mess, Cat Eyes, and you were only a speck on the wall." *Thank God.*

Catherine nodded, sniffing.

Finally, he looked down at her. "Ah, hell," he muttered. "You *are* crying."

"No, I'm all right." She swallowed carefully and burrowed deeper into his arms. "Now."

"Am I supposed to pull a handkerchief out or something here? I don't have one."

"I don't need one."

He thought about that a moment. "No. You don't."

His hard, strong hands wiped the tears from her cheeks and his mouth followed them, kissing the last traces of them away.

When he dropped her off at the clinic trailers, it took Catherine about thirty seconds to realize that he was going to leave again. His brows arched at the look on her face.

"Cat Eyes, there are about a hundred people on this Res right now who need a piece of me, and I've ignored them for a week."

"I know." And she had no desire to keep him from them. It was just...

She shook her head. She had talked and told him everything, and now the whole mess with Victor was over. Now she felt hollow and incomplete inside. She had been filled with that mess and now there was nothing to replace it, because she still didn't know where he went when he left here. Jericho moved through her life like the wind, undeniably powerful yet leaving nothing of himself behind when he went.

She wanted to ask him what he had meant by *we*. She wanted to ask him about the bodyguards and why he had protected her so fiercely, ignoring his people for days to dig to the bottom of things with the FBI. She wanted to know and didn't dare ask, because the wind couldn't be chained. If she had not learned anything else in this land, she had learned that.

She finally shrugged and turned for the clinic steps. What difference did it make? Finally, painfully, she faced that one nagging truth she had not been able to cope with while she was in the hospital. She was a week away from the end of this externship. No matter what he wanted, what she wanted, she would have to leave and he would stay. She could not imagine him dwelling in any country other than this.

It sent such a pang through her she almost stumbled, but she reached the steps before he called her back.

"Forgot your coffee."

She wheeled around and returned to the Rover as if he had her on a string and was simply reeling her in. She hated that and it made her voice sharp.

"Thanks again. For everything." She snatched up the bag through the open passenger side window.

"See you tonight."

She arched a brow in a look stolen directly from him. His smile was slow. It melted everything inside her.

"I'll be back, Cat Eyes."

She watched him drive off, then she finally went back to the clinic. She would put on a pot of this stuff, she decided. Then she would call Tufts and see when they were giving final exams. She'd intended to study hard while she was here, brushing up, trying to remember everything she had learned four long years ago. It would be incredibly difficult to pass those tests; she had known that from the start and knew, too, that she could do it if she tried hard enough. Maybe not the first time, but there was no law that said she couldn't take the exams again and again until she got them right. She had brought all her old textbooks to pore over, had driven all the way back to Boston before flying to Albuquerque so that she could get them out of storage. Then she remembered that they were still in a box in the old brown Ford, which was lost somewhere in a wash.

"Damn it," she exploded as she trotted up the steps. Then she stopped dead. The front room of the clinic was full of people.

She looked dumbly over her shoulder again, back outside. Ellen's Toyota was squeezed between an old truck and an older convertible. Farther out on the desert, a horse, complete with saddle, grazed beside Bessie's hobbled sheep. As odd as such traffic was around here, she still hadn't noticed before, because she had been so preoccupied with Jericho.

Which said a lot for the way he had filled her heart and soul.

She whipped around to look inside again. Several pairs of black eyes gazed back at her quizzically. Most of them were children, but there was a man with his arm in a crude sling and Lance was there too.

Lance?

"Uh, Jericho just left," she mumbled.

A few heads nodded mildly. One woman shrugged. Then Ellen came out of one of the back rooms, holding a syringe up to the overheard fluorescent light to check the dosage.

"Lance is first," she said flatly. "Kolkline is on the phone. He okayed the vacs, but you need to talk to him about the antibiotic."

"What antibiotic?"

"Lance got bit by a skunk up at the windmill."

"Oh." That explained the strange smell she had finally become aware of. She looked at Lance. He shrugged sheepishly. No one was sitting very close to him.

"Thought he was going to dig up my spare bottle," he explained.

Of course, she thought, feeling a very dangerous, very wild laugh work its way up her throat. If she let it out now it would be so close to hysteria that she would send everybody running again. She grabbed the phone instead and talked briefly to Kolkline about the side effects of the antibiotic.

She motioned Lance into one of the rooms while she talked. Then she hung up and looked squarely at Ellen. The nurse's eyes tried to slide away.

"Those kids by the door are next," she muttered. "Same thing as Leo Coldwater. The school sent them home because their shots weren't up to date. I guess they're running through their files over there."

"I see."

"I'll put them in a room and have them ready for you." She handed her the antibiotic shot, but Catherine caught her arm when she would have turned away.

Not everything had changed. Ellen gave her a scathing look and shook her hand off. "Don't touch me."

"No problem. But will you at least tell me what's going on here?"

The nurse didn't answer.

"Is Jericho responsible for this?"

Finally, Ellen snorted. "You've got to be kidding. He doesn't give much thought to the mechanics of things—like the fact that you've got to have something to do if you're going to stay put here."

"Stay..." Catherine was beginning to feel as dazed as she had before she came down with *Tah honeesgai*. "*You're* responsible for this?"

Ellen's eyes went hot and defiant, daring her to make something of it. Catherine did.

"Why?" she blurted, looking at the room again wildly.

"I don't want you here. I don't need you." Then she hesitated. "But there are some things they won't let me do, and you're a little bit better than Kolkline. If you stay, maybe they'll give him the boot back to Chicago or wherever it is he came from. And then there's Jericho. I won't see him destroyed again. I don't know why he wants you, but if he does then you better plan on hanging around. I'll be damned if *I'm* going to give you an easy way out."

Catherine backed away from her. The pang she had felt in the parking lot had been bad. This one drove through her like a blade of ice.

Stay? Shadow had talked of it once, but it had never been a possibility. She had started realizing that in the hospital. She needed a residency in a real facility. She needed to earn a living. She had less than five hundred dollars left to her name!

And she couldn't give up her career for a man again.

She felt sick, but she had given a lot of thought to Victor while she had been stuck in that bed, to Victor and their marriage and everything that had gone wrong. And she would die never knowing how she might have felt about him—how less torturous those years with him might have been—if he had not stolen her very spirit from her, if he hadn't coerced her into giving up everything she had worked for, turning her into a life-sized Victorized doll.

What was it Uncle Ernie had said? *Always listen to your spirit. You have found it, now you must use it.*

This time she did laugh, a choked, bitter sound. She would have left Victor anyway, because of what he was, what he was capable of. And she knew she would love Jericho until the sun burned clear of the sky. But she could not go back to being somebody's doll. Their whole relationship had been built upon their mutual responsibilities in this clinic. Without those, she was a shell, empty, nothing... not the woman he had finally befriended at all.

She couldn't do that. She needed to *be* something, to earn something for herself, even if it cost a piece of her heart that she would never get back again.

And she knew that would happen. God help her, but either way she would never be quite whole again. So what was she going to do?

"I'll...I'll see Lance now," she said, because if she didn't do something fast she would cry.

"He'll need something to pack that bite with, too," Ellen said tightly. "I'll take care of that end of it. Bottlebrush works best."

"Whatever," Catherine murmured.

Jericho didn't return until the night was at its deepest. Catherine had finally fallen asleep, curled up in bed while the single station on the television buzzed and spat at her with white noise.

At first she only stirred groggily at the thud of a vehicle door closing outside. Then her heart scrambled, as she recognized the sound for what it was. She sat bolt upright, fear an inherent part of her now.

Then she remembered. Victor was dead.

Still, the wolfman was presumably still alive, and pollen or no pollen she didn't think it was wise to take chances at this hour of the night. She got up and went cautiously to the kitchen for Jericho's gun, then she returned to the front window, keeping back from the glass, peering out.

The moon moved out from behind a rare cloud, spilling thin light down upon him. He stood beside his Rover, looking up pensively at the mountain.

She threw the door open and went out to meet him. "You could get yourself shot sneaking up on people at this hour."

"You knew I was coming." He looked at the gun in her hand. "Give me that thing."

She handed it over and he unloaded it, pushing the bullets into his pocket and sticking it under his belt. "We've got to talk."

Her heart leaped, even as she dreaded anything he might say now—dreaded it as much as she had once longed to hear any inconsequential little thing he cared to tell her. She looked down at her watch.

"Now?" she hedged. "It's one o'clock in the morning."

Jericho scrubbed a hand over his jaw. "Couldn't get back any sooner. I had a lot to do. Come on, let's sit over here."

He led her to a low knoll beyond the parking area, sitting to face the mountain. Catherine remained standing, hugging herself.

"It's cold," she murmured. "Why don't we go inside?"

"Because I think better out here. You can have my jacket."

She finally sat beside him and snuggled beneath it. Her heart was banging hard again, but he didn't say anything more. He just sat, staring up at the craggy peaks. There was snow at the very top.

"I live up there," he said finally. "I guess I never told you that."

A slow, warm peace began to seep through her, in spite of herself. "No," she said quietly. "You didn't."

Where to start? he wondered grimly. There was so much to say. In barely a week, she would be leaving. He didn't want her to go and knew she must; he needed her to come back and didn't dare ask her to. He knew that in some poet's mind somewhere there were the right words to say to make it happen. But they weren't in his mind—he had always been a man of watchful silences and quick action when the situation demanded it. Words had never been something he had cared much for.

Then he thought of a way.

"I saw a wolfman once when I was a boy."

Catherine straightened to look at him more closely. She didn't know exactly what she had expected him to say, but it wasn't that. Her skin prickled into gooseflesh even beneath his warm jacket.

"It happened at my outfit's summer sheep camp when I was about twelve. Me and my buddies were in charge of herding the sheep and the horses. I woke up one night because the flock was bawling, and I went outside. My knees were knocking together and I damned near wet myself because I knew a man in the camp had just had a run-in with some stranger from another clan. That's how it always starts. Strangers can be dangerous, especially if they're wealthy and they have a lot of sheep. We're taught from the cradle to take only what we need and to leave some behind for a man who might need it more. It's the Navajo way, and anybody who disregards it is suspect.

"Anyway, the stranger this guy tangled with was rich. And the next thing any of us know, the sheep are carrying on. My buddies all came outside too and we all saw it—sort of a figure of a man creeping away from the camp through the camouflage of the flock. And then he just...grew. He mushroomed in size and his shoulders got sort of hunched over, and he flew out of there faster than any car or animal could run."

He paused thoughtfully and Catherine waited, rapt.

"You've got to understand that I'd spent twelve years listening to stories about that stuff without really believing any of it—me and Shadow both. Kind of like the ghost stories you must have heard as a kid. Spooky and fun, but not real. We were educated at the public school in Gallup, not at any of the Res boarding schools. My family always felt that we had to be able to move pretty easily between the two worlds if we were going to survive, if we weren't going to end up drinking from a bottle of Thunderbird at an old abandoned windmill because all the old ways were gone and we couldn't accept new ones."

He paused to rub his jaw again thoughtfully, but his eyes were still far away. "My point is that I was schooled enough in modern ways to try to consider more practical explanations for what I'd seen. Damn, I tried, but there weren't any. Because when we woke up the next morning, the man who fought with that stranger was dead, right there in his brush shelter, cold as stone.''

Catherine gasped in spite of herself. "Was he old?"

His eyes came around to her. "No older than I am now.

"Things happen in this red-rock country, Cat Eyes. This land between the four Navajo mountains is sacred and old. Things happen here that can't—don't—happen anywhere else. If a person's going to survive here, it has to be with a mind that's as open and innocent as the sky.''

He wasn't talking about wolfmen now. Another shiver whispered over her skin, both hot and cold.

"Whatever's happening between us hasn't been open.''

"No," she managed.

"But I guess it's about as basic as the air we breathe. Every beast and living thing shares it, instinctual and stronger than sense. Attraction, sex, just growing bigger and wilder sometimes until it becomes . . .''

She held her breath but he trailed off, and she wasn't sure if she was relieved or sorry. *Until it becomes what?*

"Maybe it could endure," he went on, "if we never took it out of here, if we never took it past this sacred ground into a world of concrete and bureaucracy and expectations. But you can't do that, can you?''

She felt as if she were being strangled. She couldn't answer.

"That's about what I thought." His voice held an almost metallic edge of pain, so jagged it cut her as well. "So where will you go?" he asked finally.

"Back to Boston," she whispered. "I have to take some tests. After that . . . I just don't know.''

"Maybe you'll come back." And in the end, he still couldn't think of a better way to say it than that.

To what? she wondered wildly. "Do you want me to?"

He slanted her a wry look. "You know I do, Cat Eyes.''

Yes, she did after all. She felt it the way she had felt almost everything about him, the kind of man he was underneath all that early antagonism, the solid, strong goodness of his heart. She knew it the way she had come to love him without knowing anything about him, instinctively and with her soul.

"You said..." She paused to swallow carefully. "You said that mountain is sacred."

He looked up at it again pensively. "Yeah. It marks one of the boundaries of *Dinetah*, our land. We're the only tribe in America that ever went to war with the white men and ended up with the same ground we started with. There's a lot less of it than there was two hundred years ago, but we've still got the heart of it."

"Then love me here, Jericho. Make love with me while it watches."

His eyes came back to her, heating so fast, so strongly, it took her breath away. "I thought you were cold."

"I won't be." She sighed roughly and looked up at the mountain. "Maybe something special will happen," she whispered, "some magic, some miracle that can't happen anywhere else."

She pressed herself against him so quickly and quietly he never even sensed her moving. There was just enough moonlight for him to see her eyes before he lowered his mouth slowly to hers. He saw something there that made him ache. In that moment, she didn't just believe. She *wanted* to believe, desperately, fervently, with a passion that hurt.

She wanted a miracle. She wanted a way to stay. There wasn't one, but it was enough, more than he'd expected, more than he'd ever hoped to find. He covered her mouth with a groan, letting himself get lost in her again, refusing to accept that it could be the last time, because to think it would almost certainly make it so.

He slid his hands underneath his own jacket, then he laughed raggedly. No wonder she was cold. She wore a big, baggy T-shirt, but he realized for the first time that her legs were bare. When he had gotten here, she had been in bed, but he had wanted to sit outside, so she had.

She gave so easily; he thought he could understand how she had quit medical school for Victor. She gave of herself even as she elicited things from Jericho that he hadn't thought himself able to give.

He lowered her to the ground and settled on top of her, trying to warm her, but she slid and twisted away from him.

"No," she whispered.

Now what? But then he understood, and his mouth went dry. She tugged at his jeans and his shirt, and the gun spilled in the dirt.

"That damned thing...spends more time in the sand than we do."

She didn't answer. She settled her legs between his, her belly flat against him, an excruciating, sweet weight. He groaned as she slid downward, her nipples tight and hard through her T-shirt, teasing skin that was suddenly too sensitive, too hot. Then her hands closed over his shaft and her mouth followed. He growled something that could have been her name, plunging his hands into her hair.

She tortured him. His jaw ached with the pain of restraint. When he thought he would lose control anyway, she was suddenly above him again, tugging off her panties, moving up over him, but her mouth...still there was her mouth, moving across his chest now, his neck. He understood what she was doing and hated it even as he loved it. She was giving him something to remember, leaving something behind.

It was more than Anelle had done, but she had always been so much more woman than Anelle, even from the start.

Her legs were strong and smooth against his sides and her fingernails raked slowly and deliberately across his skin. He knew she was marking him as he had once tried to mark her. He was close to exploding, hot and rigid to the point of pain, when she finally came down on him and enfolded him.

He supposed turnabout was fair play, and he'd certainly tried to torture her the previous time, but he'd had enough of it now.

He rolled over suddenly, taking her with him, hearing her gasp, pressing into her again, fast and hard, when she was beneath him. He held her legs up and drove into her again and again until she wept his name and he knew it would echo in her heart a long time after she was gone.

Magnificent and silent, the mountain rose above them. Its shadows shifted in the moonlight as if it were breathing, alive, watching them.

Chapter 18

For a long time afterward there was only the deep black sky and the shadows of the land. Then an even colder wind howled down from the mountain and Catherine shivered.

Jericho closed his arms around her. He had been lying with them splayed out, like a man who had just been run down by something a lot bigger, a lot stronger, than he was. An ironic, almost pained smile pulled at one corner of his mouth with the thought.

"We'll go inside," he murmured.

"In a minute." Somehow she had the sense that once they got up from here, once they left this spot, something beautiful and amazing would be over.

But a minute was too long. Fresh wind blew, and it carried the scent of icy moisture this time. Catherine pulled away from him reluctantly and sat up, hugging herself.

"Another storm?" she wondered.

"It's the season for it." He sensed it too, she realized, that feeling that once they went inside, they would never be able to get back to a place, a time like this ever again. She could tell from his voice, and it almost made her moan aloud.

Suddenly she was desperate to forestall it. "I'll put some coffee on."

"No."

Her heart staggered. Was he going to leave then, right now? But she saw a small grin on his face as he looked for his jeans and the gun again.

"I'll make it," he finished. "The stuff you brew tastes like a warm puddle."

"It does not!"

"So you can't cook. No big deal."

"I can cook." She was feeling more indignant by the moment.

"Well, you can't roll fry bread."

That sobered her. Not the basic truth of it, but all the little innuendos inherent in it. This was a land of fry bread, after all.

They started back for her trailer. "There's a trick to the chocolate stuff anyway," he said finally as they went inside. "You've got to use a little bit of milk in place of some of the water, otherwise it's too bitter."

She sat at the table and watched him move around the kitchen area. He was so male, so large, yet as graceful as a cat. How was she supposed to go through each day without him in it?

She pulled breath in painfully. "You could come with me," she blurted suddenly, then she colored to the roots of her hair. It would be a huge sacrifice for a man to make, even for a woman he loved. And Jericho loved his people, his land, with nearly all his passion.

Yet he actually seemed to think about it. At least, he didn't answer for a long time. Then he shook his head, and though she had known he would, it still made her throat hurt.

"No way, Cat Eyes," he said finally. "I already tried that."

"Living in Boston?" She was startled, and the question was admittedly stupid.

"Albuquerque." He brought the coffee back to the table and drew up the other chair. He didn't look at her. "After school in Gallup, I went to the university there."

There was more to it than that. She sensed it like a black cloud, the way he must have sensed that something was wrong with her before she got sick.

"College is rarely pleasant if you take it seriously," she said tentatively.

"College was fine. But I tried to stay there."

"Why?"

"The women."

Catherine jolted. Something cold was trying to replace her blood. "What about them?" she asked carefully.

"They were just like you, Cat Eyes. Fine boned and delicate, with porcelain skin and crystal-clear eyes."

"Is that why you hated me at first?"

"No. That was why I *wanted* you at first, and why I hated myself for it."

She flinched, then she forced one shoulder up nonchalantly. "So I was just ... your type."

He leaned back, stretching his long legs out beneath the table. Words weren't so hard after all, he realized, once he got into the swing of them.

"That's what Shadow said the first day you turned up in the wash. Actually, you were a type I tried to avoid."

"It showed," she answered shortly, before she could stop herself.

"No doubt." He used his finger to inch his coffee cup around in little circles. "You get burned, you learn a healthy respect for fire."

"*I* never burned you."

"Ah, but you will, Cat Eyes, and I'm going to let you."

Suddenly he picked his cup up and swallowed deeply, as if it were laced with fortification instead of just chocolate. "Oh, hell, it wasn't just the women," he said finally. "Your world is one of available riches and opportunity. That bit me too. But look around this Res, Cat Eyes—really look at the women. They own the hogans, the sheep, they rule their families with hands of steel." He gave a short, abrupt laugh, but it wasn't entirely unpleasant. "Shadow pushes *me* around, and I don't even want to tell you about my mother. I took one look at all those Anglo girls, soft, dependent, *fragile* in comparison. I learned quick enough that few of them saw themselves that way, but I decided to marry one anyway."

Marry? Of all the things she thought he might be keeping from her, that had never even crossed her mind. She had always wondered where he went at night, not who he went home to. Her eyes darted helplessly to his left hand, to his ring finger, then she bit down hard on her lip when he held it up to remind her.

No ring.

"She's dead," he said flatly.

Catherine's head swam. She didn't know what to say.

"I turned my back on my roots, on my past, on my history, and I stayed in Albuquerque with her. She was a rich city girl and Mommy and Daddy laid the world at her feet. Her name was Anelle. For a while it was easy. For a while she was . . . joy. Then she got pregnant and she aborted the kid."

Catherine blanched. His face twisted with emotion, even now, even all this time later, and she could only watch, sick and spellbound.

She struggled for her voice. "But . . . there's little danger to that procedure nowadays."

"Danger?" he spat, and she recoiled a little at his fury. "For who? For the grandparents who were fretting over the social consequences of a child with Navajo blood? For the mother, who cared more for her parents' feelings than those of her husband? For the *father,* who didn't even know about it until six goddamn weeks later?"

Secrets. "Jericho—"

But now he had found words, and he wouldn't—couldn't—be stopped. Because finally, with each one that burst from him, he felt somehow purged of it all.

"When she finally told me, she said she wasn't ready for the responsibility of a family, that she was still a kid herself. But she couldn't tell me that with *conviction,* and I

knew her parents had talked her into it because they—*they*—
were suddenly so satisfied. It was as if something had been
eating at them for months, and all of a sudden they took a
deep breath and relaxed. The problem was disposed of." He
made a bitter sound. "And I responded like a caveman, like
the savage they thought I was. Anelle was different after
that, haunted . . . my God, she'd aborted her own child because of familial pressure. So I grabbed her by the hair and
dragged her out of Albuquerque, back here to the Res. I
brought her here because the land heals, and sometimes it
soothes. And sometimes it forgives."

Catherine was beginning to understand. "But she
couldn't forgive herself."

"No." He looked at her finally, his deep black eyes filled
with cloudy pain. "I will always have to wonder," he said
slowly, "if she would have managed it if she had stayed in
Albuquerque, if I hadn't dragged her back here. Maybe I
should have just let her go."

"You . . . loved her," she whispered. It brought a strange
kind of hurt, a jealousy of longing to be that woman, a
woman who perhaps hadn't known what she had.

Jericho seemed to deeply consider her words. "I was ob-
sessed with her," he corrected. "She was mine, the most
beautiful thing I had ever found. She was like a gem you put
away somewhere to keep it safe, and every night you take it
out to look at it and stroke it."

And oh, how those hands could stroke. Catherine wanted
to cry.

He raked his fingers through his long hair in that way he
had when he was struggling with something. "She didn't
belong here, and I guess I knew it right from the beginning,
a nagging little idea in my gut that I wouldn't look at too
closely. My instincts told me the land would destroy her. She
wasn't hardy enough for it, especially after what had happened with the baby. She was—in the purest sense—a city
girl." His mouth quirked in something that could have been
a bitter smile. "But instead of sending her back where she
belonged, I tried to change my land to suit her.

"I had some money saved from working in the city and I built her a house up on the slope, so she wouldn't have to live in a trailer or hogan. I took her to sings and tried to teach her what this country was about, some of its secrets. Bought her a decent car so she wouldn't feel so isolated here and I wouldn't have to worry about her breaking down God knows where. And in the end, she took it and drove it off the mountain."

Catherine gasped, but he only finished his coffee, setting the cup down with a decisive cracking sound.

"So now you get it, Cat Eyes. Yeah, I can see in your eyes that you do." He pushed his chair back. "The hell of it is, it took me a long time to come back from that, and it was the land that finally brought me around. That and Uncle Ernie. Teaching me the sings, teaching me where I belonged. I belong here, Cat Eyes, and you...don't. I'm not going to drag you away from what you want, what you *are*, and try to make you stay here. And I can't leave the people who saved me by needing me. And that," he said quietly, "is that."

He was at the door. She had to stop him. She had to make him understand.

I never burned you.

Ah, but you will, Cat Eyes, and I'm going to let you.

She couldn't tell him he was wrong. Because he wasn't. She understood perfectly what he was telling her, because she had already thought of it herself. To the best of his ability, he had shown her his world these past few weeks, had let her in and given her the kindest part of himself. It was there for her if she wanted it, if she thought she could live with it, stay with it without it driving her mad. But they both knew she would have to give up everything else to keep it, and that was a choice only she could make. He would not ask it of her; he wouldn't make it for her.

And she could not stand to be that hollow, that useless, ever again.

"But I love you," she whispered.

The door clicked quietly behind him. He was already gone.

* * *

After a few short hours in the clinic the next morning, Catherine knew that Jericho wasn't going to show up. He wouldn't thump-*thump* his way up the steps this time and throw his jacket over the chair. He wouldn't go to the mountain for a few days and come back, raging in as if the storm had blown him. He wouldn't carry her to the bed and love her until dawn.

He wouldn't do any of those things, because he was waiting for her to make up her mind. He wouldn't put himself through five final days of hell, waiting to see if what he had given her would be enough.

Catherine tensed her jaw and stared down stubbornly at the file in her hands, trying to read it. There was a woman in one of the exam rooms with an infected boil on her big toe and apparently it kept coming back. She had been one of Kolkline's rare patients, but then she had given up on him. Catherine needed to find out what kind of imbecilic, negligent thing he had done to her to make her decide she'd rather live with the pain.

But Kolkline's spidery handwriting kept smearing on the page, even when she sniffed quietly and got a tissue to try to circumspectly blow her nose. Ellen was watching her. Catherine finally straightened her shoulders and tucked the file under her arm, marching off to the exam room.

The woman sat on the table waiting for her, one foot clad in a tennis shoe, the other one bare. "Well," Catherine murmured, "no matter what Dr. Kolkline did, it only makes sense to clean it up first, don't you think? Maybe then we can see what the problem is."

She hunkered down in front of one of the cabinets to get some swabs and astringent. As soon as she opened the door, a startled deermouse darted out. Catherine cringed instinctively, then she let out nervous laughter.

"Don't let 'em bother you none," the woman said. "They're all over. More and more, the colder it gets."

"I know." Still, Catherine thought, she would have to clean these cabinets out well, the first chance she got.

She got what she needed and helped the woman move around so that her bad foot was resting on the table. She bent over it, then she looked up at her again sharply.

"What did you say?"

"When it gets cold, they come in to try to get warm. In the summer, they just stay long enough to hunt up some food, but in the winter they snuggle in. They're even worse up Two Gray Hills way this year. I got a niece living up there. She had to spend seventeen dollars last week on traps, and that man at the hardware place in Shiprock only takes cash. You don't, do you? Ellen said I could give you some of my turquoise."

"I beg your pardon?" Catherine breathed.

"Turquoise. I got plenty. My man makes jewelry. That okay with you?"

"I . . . that's fine."

Catherine cleaned her toe without seeing it and gave her some antibiotic ointment. *Two Gray Hills way. More and more, the colder it gets.*

Lisa had been up to Two Gray Hills country, although Jericho had decided it probably didn't mean anything. And Louie had had a deermouse in his bedding. The cases were escalating steadily with the colder weather. But how had *she* gotten it? The only mouse she had encountered was the one in Louie's blankets. It had never touched her, and if it had contaminated Louie's bedding, then Jericho and certainly Bessie should have gotten *Tah honeesgai,* too.

Unless it wasn't the mice that were transmitting it. Unless the contamination was in something they were leaving behind, in the clinic cupboards, in Louie's bedding, something the victims had direct contact with.

Their droppings. How many times had she shoved her hands blindly into these cabinets, she and Ellen too, but rarely Jericho?

Ellen.

She pushed the tube of antibiotic into the woman's hand. "You need to rub some of that in there two times a day, even if it hurts, Mrs. Nakai. And come back here next week. I want to look at it again. You can give me the turquoise later."

Except she wouldn't be here next week. And the toe was as infected as it was because the woman had refused to see Kolkline any longer.

But she couldn't think of that now. She hurried back into the front room. A few new faces stared back at her and Lance had returned to have his bite rechecked, but Ellen was nowhere in sight.

"Where's the nurse?" she demanded.

One woman smiled helpfully. "She didn't feel good. She went home."

"Oh, my God." She looked wildly at Lance. "Are you sober? Can you drive?"

He looked highly indignant. "I can *always* drive."

She doubted that, but she had no choice but to believe him. She couldn't imagine there was much traffic on the mountain anyway.

"You've got to find Jericho. Do you know where he lives?"

"Sure. I can see his house from my windmill."

"Then get him. Find him." *Please God, let him have stayed at home.* "Tell him to go to Ellen's and take her to University. Tell him I figured it out and it's the mice."

"The mice?"

She was losing them. They were all exchanging looks. She couldn't care. *"Hurry!"* She looked around at the others. "Come back tomorrow," she said abruptly. "The clinic's closed."

They began shuffling out, muttering and casting glances back at her. She locked the door behind them and leaned against it, her pulse clamoring.

The clinic had to be cleaned—top to bottom—before she let anyone back in here. Who knew where the mice had left deposits? But first she had to find some droppings. She went back to the exam-room cabinets. It shouldn't be hard.

She pulled on some surgical gloves, not sure if she had immunity now or not. But she was going to find out; she was going to know everything about this disease before the day was over. There were some droppings in the back of the cabinet the mouse had scurried out of and she knocked them into a plastic bag with a small scalpel and carried the bag to the front room, grabbing the phone.

She had to notify the CDC in Albuquerque. She intended to call them first, but then she hesitated.

It had taken them as long as an hour to get a helicopter here when someone was dying. Now it was already past lunchtime. She knew as sure as she knew her name that they would tell her they'd send someone out to collect the droppings tomorrow. To them, it would just be another wild lead that needed investigating. She was only an extern; she doubted if they would take her idea too seriously. They would look into it, of course, but with no great urgency.

But she *knew.* She was as sure as she had ever been about anything that the mice were spreading this thing through their feces. And while the CDC hemmed and hawed, millions of mice would be running all over the Res, leaving behind deadly little packages.

Catherine's head spun. When she thought of all those housewives cleaning under their beds, she considered it a major miracle that more people hadn't fallen victim to *Tah honeesgai* so far.

Her chin came up. The hell with authority and red tape, she decided. She was already in hot water with the Service and the AMA up to her cute Irish backside. She'd give them the droppings, but she decided she wasn't going to put her feet up on the desk waiting for them to respond.

She called Eddie Begay first. He seemed startled, then glad to hear from her. "Hey, you're home now," he said.

Wherever that was. "You said I could borrow your Jeep," she blurted. "It's an emergency."

"Yeah, okay, sure. I get off at five o'clock."

"That won't work. I need it now. I'll pay you for your lost wages." *Four hundred dollars and counting.*

"Well, sure. Okay, I'll be there as soon as I can. The clinic, right?"

"Right—no!" Her thoughts galloped ahead. "Can you go to the old Ford first—the one I left in the wash? There's a big box in the trunk with some books in it."

"Yeah, I saw that. They're pretty messed up, though."

"That's okay. Can you bring them here? Then I have something I need you to take to Albuquerque." Eddie could do the running, she thought, while she did the work.

She hung up and went to the window to look up at the mountain, then she sighed.

Ellen and Jericho would get to the hospital first—she hoped. She could probably ask Eddie to have Jericho call her. This was important. He'd want to know everything that was going on.

And that was just an excuse. She couldn't do it to him. She couldn't do it to herself. It was better to let him slip out of her life the way the wind stopped blowing . . . on a sigh, before she even realized it was happening.

The way he had closed the door the previous night.

But I love you. She closed her eyes, fighting the urge to cry again, then she squared her shoulders and went to look for the equipment she'd need.

That damned mountain wouldn't know a miracle from a mud pie anyway.

Chapter 19

Catherine's textbooks were decidedly worse for the wear. The pages had swollen to twice their original size from the water, and the covers were warped. Some rodents had found the paper quite tasty—either that or the missing pieces were keeping their young snuggly and warm somewhere. If it had been deermice that had hauled them off to their nests, she supposed it would be an ironic twist indeed. Almost as if they were far more intelligent than they really were, protecting themselves, fighting back.

But that was a spooky thought that led to things such as wolfmen, and there was no time for that now. She found her epidemiology books and spread them out on the counter in the third little clinic room which served as a lab. Then she leafed through a big tome that gave a little bit of space to almost every subject and found the part dealing with viral infections.

She propped up the book, open to the page she needed, but then her mind wandered again. She glanced down at her watch, her throat tightening. Half past six. She knew Jericho had arrived at University by now; Lance had come back to report that he had found him and had passed along her message. Maybe he would call her of his own volition to find out what was going on.

She groaned softly. He wouldn't and she knew it. No matter what the organic cause proved to be, he'd still insist a wolfman's spell was to blame.

She settled herself on a wheeled stool in front of the counter, spreading the rest of the droppings carefully on a pallet. When she finally straightened again, it was to stretch and to rub the small of her back painfully. She looked at her watch again.

Midnight. She smiled, a tight little grimace at first, but then it spread wearily. *She had been right.*

She had found out what she needed to know. The thing was viral, carried in the cells of a host, in this case an animal. Of course, it had taken her the better part of an hour to catch the mouse. The droppings hadn't been enough to work with so she had lured the tiny animal into a trap she had found in the storage closet, using some of Jericho's chocolate coffee for bait.

Don't think about him. She stood up to go to the other room and get the phone. It was time to call the CDC.

She had something now, something that would move them. She had managed to isolate the virion in the blood, but she didn't have the equipment or the necessary textbook pages to break down its proteins or acids. They could do that in Albuquerque, she reasoned, as well as render the virion incapable of causing disease. From there, they could create a vaccine or interferon. She punched in the number, hoping that at least one of their doctors would still be at the hospital. After all, Ellen—their latest case—was there.

She got Weatherly after a long delay. He had indeed been with Ellen.

Catherine identified herself. "How is she?" she asked, hesitating in the last moment, almost afraid to know. She and Ellen would never be friends, but she still cared fervently about her condition.

"Reaction time seems to make a difference with this thing," Weatherly answered. "This makes three victims now you've managed to hold back from death's door, including yourself. Good work.''

Good work. How long since she had heard those sweet, sweet words? They filled her almost to the point of bursting. She had *done* something, something important, something worthwhile.

Weatherly was still talking. She had to drag her attention back.

"She's not recovering as fast as you did, but I think she'll make it.''

Catherine found her voice. "Did you get the mouse droppings? A Navajo kid should have dropped them off.''

"Mouse droppings?'' He sounded genuinely perplexed. "No, but I've been with the patient all night. Perhaps they're down the hall in the office.''

"It doesn't matter. You'll need the blood, too. Can you send someone out here? I don't have a vehicle.''

"And I don't have the vaguest idea what you're talking about,'' he said apologetically.

"I've found it.''

"What?''

"The virion. The disease.''

There was stunned silence. Catherine rushed on to explain. "Anyway, people rarely come in contact with mouse blood, so I figure it's got to be in the droppings too, but I couldn't break them down with the equipment I've got here. If it were just the blood, then the disease wouldn't be able to strike with such frequency. But mice leave droppings everywhere. I haven't proven it yet. I'm going to have to inject a sheep we've got outside, but—''

Weatherly interrupted her. "I simply don't believe this. Why didn't we find it in the tissue of the victims?''

"Well, I would imagine because you didn't *have* any tissue. And maybe it didn't show up in our blood samples because it mutates with communication, segues into something more harmless looking, something that wouldn't have caught your eye.''

"Of course we have tissue,'' he said defensively.

Catherine scowled. "What kind? What did you take from me?"

"Not you. The victims we lost. We did thorough autopsies."

"But I thought Richard said the Navajo wouldn't allow autopsies."

"I don't know who Richard is, but it's not a matter of permission in a situation like this. The families don't have a choice. It's a plague, a threat to the general population. Autopsies are mandatory, required by federal law."

Catherine sat down carefully. "Mandatory," she repeated. Maybe Richard had been misinformed about the autopsies, she thought. But a CDC doctor would know that ruling inside and out. *Richard should have known.*

"That's right," Weatherly went on. "Listen, I don't have any staff here at this hour. There'll be a slight delay. You're at the reservation clinic, aren't you?"

"The one south of Shiprock," she supplied mechanically.

"And you're just an *extern?* I simply don't believe this," he repeated.

"I finished school, I just—I didn't take my final exams yet." Her head was spinning, her thoughts grasping. "I've been living out here. That's how I knew about the mice. Wait!" she said when he would have hung up. "You don't know who Richard is?"

"Should I?" the doctor asked.

"He said he was . . . one of you. Richard Moss."

"I think someone's been playing games with you, young lady. There *was* a Richard Moss with the CDC, but I can assure you he's not been in Albuquerque—at least not recently. He died six months ago of heart failure. He was an older man who wouldn't retire."

Her heart was pounding so hard she felt faint again for the first time in days. "But he was working on Louie. Louie Coldwater. In Gallup. I *saw* him at the boy's bedside."

"Well, I don't know who you saw. I wasn't in Gallup for that case. But it certainly wasn't Richard Moss."

"He brought me your files!"

"I should hope not."

"They're right here! They're—" She fumbled with Ellen's keys, yanking open the bottom drawer.

They were gone. They certainly had mopped up their mess.

She slid the door shut with numb fingers. "Never mind."

Weatherly seemed glad to drop the subject. "Go infect your sheep, since you're on such a roll. We'll need that, too, although you seem to be doing just fine on your own. I'll send someone to pick everything up early in the morning."

"I'll be here," she said vacantly.

He disconnected and she clutched the handset with white knuckles. Then she punched out another number. An emergency number. A very bland, very clonish voice answered.

"My name is Catherine Landano, and I've been working with Horace Schilling on a case involving my ex-husband," she said carefully. She had never chosen to call this number before—Schilling had told her it was for matters of life and death, manned twenty-four hours a day by a desk-duty agent. Now the voice on the other end of the line hesitated.

"That case has been closed, Mrs. Landano."

She ignored that. "Schilling knew where I was. How?"

"You'd have to discuss that with him."

"I can't wait to discuss it with him. I need an answer now," she grated. "I gave you guys everything you wanted—or I tried to. So cooperate with me. I just need one simple answer. Did you have someone out here tailing me, keeping an eye on me?"

Again, he hesitated. "No," he said finally. "We didn't feel the situation warranted that kind of expense. It's my knowledge that Mr. Schilling merely traced your calls."

"No one has been out here masquerading as a Richard Moss, a CDC doctor?"

A hint of a smug smile came to the man's voice. "We don't masquerade, Mrs. Landano. We are simply there."

That was about what she had figured. "Thank you," she whispered.

She disconnected carefully, hugging herself, starting to tremble.

Summoned back east by the powers that be. She had assumed—he had wanted her to assume—that he was talking about the CDC. *You're a very lucky woman, Lanie McDaniel. I would have hated to have seen you die.*

Victor *had* had someone out here, watching her, waiting for the word to take her out. And Richard Moss—or whoever he was—could have done it without her ever suspecting anything. Even Jericho and his bodyguards couldn't have protected her from him, because she'd trusted him. She thought of the way he had appeared on the plane beside her nearly six weeks ago, so effortlessly infiltrating her world. She thought of the way he had so seamlessly stepped into the role of a CDC doctor, appearing in a patient's room, removing their files. He had been *good,* damned good. He could have snuffed out her life in the blink of an eye, but the family had gotten to Victor first, and then they had called in his flunkies.

Now it was over.

Catherine considered how close she had come to dying and made her way shakily into the rest room, where she promptly threw up.

Dawn came and went before anyone appeared at the clinic, and then it was Shadow.

The woman stopped dead in the door of the exam room, her eyes widening on the ewe that laid on the table, an oxygen mask jury-rigged over its nose, an IV tube stringing out from one of its forelegs. Catherine looked up at her grimly.

"I had to infect her. I don't have to let her die. I guess I'm glad the CDC is late, because no doubt they would. Can you hand me that syringe over there? I'm having *no* luck getting pills down her throat."

Shadow did so silently.

"How's Ellen?" Catherine asked, injecting the ewe with an antipyretic.

"Uh, good. That wouldn't be the sheep that Jericho wants me to take down to those people living south of here, would it?"

Jericho. But then, she had known he wouldn't come for the animal himself.

"Sorry," she answered tightly. "I had no choice."

"Too bad." Shadow sighed. "They were counting on it."

"I'll buy them another one. Even if she lives, she might not be breedable." How much did sheep cost? *Three hundred dollars and falling fast.*

Shadow shrugged. "Actually, that's not why I came."

Catherine got the ewe stabilized. She stepped away from the table, bone weary. "You know, as far as sleep is concerned, this Res is worse than med school," she muttered. Then she flinched, remembering the nights she had stayed awake voluntarily with Jericho.

She couldn't think about him. Each memory, each thought, was like a knife in her heart. Each time it happened her throat closed so hard she wondered if she would ever breathe again. She dragged in air painfully, motioning to the front room. Shadow watched her closely.

"Let's go out front," she urged, looking at her watch again. "I need some coffee. Where the hell is the CDC? I expected them by nine at the latest."

"I don't know where they are, but I know they've spoken to the Service trying to find out all about you," Shadow answered, following her. "Jack caught up with me this morning at the coffee shop."

"Jack?" Catherine looked at her blankly as she brewed a pot of regular coffee. She had put the chocolate stuff away yesterday because she knew it would choke her now. *Compromise.* Oh, God, if only there was one.

"Jack Keller," Shadow was saying. "You know, my friend with the Service."

Catherine's hands went still and guilt flushed her face. "Is he angry? I gave Louie that medication weeks ago. I sent them a letter explaining."

"Yeah, and it brought a world of wrath down on Kolk-line's head. They don't keep very close tabs on the personnel in their clinics—they more or less work on an honor system. They had no idea that Kolkline was taking their money and literally doing nothing. And of course nobody on the Res was going to tell them. They never cared *what* Kolkline was doing as long as he wasn't doing it to them.''

Catherine nodded thoughtfully. "And they sure wouldn't care if the Service was getting fleeced.''

Shadow gave a fleeting grin. "Nope, they wouldn't. So anyway, the Service is going to send Kolkline packing. They want you to stay and take his place.''

Catherine sputtered hot coffee. She wiped a shaky hand across her mouth, but could do nothing about the tears, hot and painful, that sprang to her eyes. "I can't.''

"Why? If you want an official offer, Jack's going to call you later on today.''

"I . . . it's not that.'' And surely Jack knew it. Catherine made her way to the desk and sat down carefully. "Shadow, I'm an *extern*. Externs don't get paid, and I can't remain one forever.''

"But you finished school, right? Jericho told me what was going on.''

Catherine managed a wry look. "I thought you people didn't speak for others.''

"We don't. He didn't tell me how you *felt* about it, just why you had to leave.''

Catherine sighed. "I've finished school. Now I have, anyway. I needed to do this one last externship. And I have to go back and take final exams. And pass them. I was going to study while I was out here, but somehow I got sidetracked.'' She laughed a little crazily. God, had she ever.

"University gives the exams in May.'' Shadow shrugged. "Just thought I'd check for you. Just in case.''

"I didn't go to University. I went to Tufts.''

"Doesn't matter. Your grades are transferable.''

"Assuming any school would want me to transfer in. Assuming any hospital would want me for a resident. Shadow, I quit *four years ago*. That's a long time. And each year, more and more grads come out, looking for positions. . . .'' She groaned and covered her face with her hands.

"You've got a position," Shadow interrupted. "Right here. Ellen relented a little, didn't she? And you're pretty high on her hero list at the moment. You sent Jericho to her before *she* had even figured out what was wrong with her. You've got people coming to see you now and Jack says the Service will give you a residency and pay you for it. Not as much as Kolkline was getting, but he had a résumé, such as it was. And it costs virtually nothing to live out here."

"Not unless you keep buying sheep and hiring mechanics away from their garage," Catherine muttered.

"Jack says you can even keep the trailer if you want to."

"Wow, now *there's* an offer."

Shadow looked surprised, then she chuckled.

Catherine shook her head. "It's not just that," she said.

Shadow hesitated and said a silent prayer that her Holy People would forgive her this one small transgression—and that her brother would as well.

"You'll take a piece of Jericho if you go. I'd say he's finally warmed up to you in a big way."

Catherine blanched. "And I'll leave a piece of myself behind."

"So then why do it?" Shadow demanded, almost angry.

Catherine felt her temper tug too. "Because I have to. Because the Service and fate gave me this externship and an opportunity to start over. But *I* did something with that opportunity. I took it and I wrestled with it, and somehow, by some miracle, I was able to achieve something no one else had been able to do. I found the root of that damned disease, and now maybe a reputable hospital, maybe even a *top-notch* hospital, will consider me. I can't turn my back on that for a man again. I'd never be able to respect myself if I did it twice. And I'm just . . . not ready to love someone . . . until I can love and respect myself first."

And that was it, all of it. She shot up from the chair again and went to stare out the window at the mountain, hugging herself, knowing it was true and that no matter how much she might want to change it, she couldn't.

"I'm not learning anything here," she said faintly. "I want to *learn*, Shadow. I don't just want to be a doctor. I want to be a good one."

Shadow was quiet for a long time. "The hell of it is," she said finally, "you already are." She went to the door, then she hesitated again. "It seems to me that being a doctor shouldn't just mean book learning. Sure, that's important, but how can you teach someone to care? How can you teach someone to bend their minds a little and accept things such as fear and superstition and treat them as well? If it were possible, anybody with a high IQ could do the job. But they can't. Kolkline couldn't do it, and the guy over at Crownpoint can't, and none of the others before them could either. You did. Ellen said that you didn't bat an eye when she stuffed bottlebrush in Lance's bite wound. You told him to come back in a day or so and you would repack it."

Catherine flushed. She had.

"He wasn't too keen on the antibiotic shot," she murmured. "But he thought the bottlebrush might work."

"It will," Shadow said. "It's been working for centuries."

"The antibiotic will work, too. I needed to get him to accept that, so I relented on the other. I compromised." *Compromise.* Why wouldn't that damned word stop haunting her? Jericho had pretty much said that a compromise wasn't good enough. She needed to want to stay here with all her heart and soul.

"Well," Shadow said quietly, "I rest my case."

Catherine listened to her leave, to the sound of her boots on the steps, without being able—or willing—to look at her. She started to turn away as the woman crossed the parking area to her truck, but then another vehicle pulled in.

A shiny rental car. Catherine thought of the one Richard Moss had driven and she shuddered. This one was equipped with a horse trailer, emblazoned with the logo of a rental company. She sighed. She knew without being told that the CDC had spent all this time trying to find the trailer, instead of just asking Ellen or Jericho if anyone on the Res might have one available for loan.

She shook her head, knowing she would have done the same thing six weeks earlier, and went to meet Weatherly as he came inside.

"The ewe is in the back room," she told him, handing over what was left of the droppings and six vials of blood, all marked as to how far she had broken them down. "The disease took her faster than usual because I injected her right in a vein," she went on. "I don't know how we're going to get her to that trailer. She can't walk. So what I was thinking was why don't you just leave her here? That's her blood in vials four, five and six. I'll call a vet up from Albuquerque or Gallup, and maybe together we can save her." She truly hated to see the animal die when her only crime had been that she happened to be tied up outside at a very inopportune time.

Weatherly gaped at her. "Save her?"

"The ewe."

"Oh, well, we might need other things besides her blood."

Catherine shook her head. "I'm pretty sure you won't. Here. This is everything I figured out last night." She gave him a file she had left on the desk, listing all her research meticulously so they wouldn't have to waste time repeating any of it. But of course they would.

"Anyway," she went on, "if you *do* need anything else from her, just call me and I'll get it down to you somehow. She's not going anywhere for a while."

Weatherly took the file bemusedly and nodded. "That should be fine. Uh, how much longer are you supposed to be here?"

"Four days. But I'll leave you a number where you can reach me if you have any further questions."

"Actually, I have a number you're supposed to call." He groped around in his suit pocket until he came up with a business card. He gave it to her and she looked down at it bemusedly. It was from the CDC.

"Craig Wilson is our chief administrator," Weatherly explained. "That's his number there in Atlanta. He would like very much for you to give him a call. To be quite honest, Ms. McDaniel—"

"Callahan," she corrected absently. "Catherine Callahan." She looked up in time to see that his expression had turned slightly dazed. "Never mind."

"Yes, well, in any event, you've left a good many of us red faced on this whole thing. Wilson would like to offer you a position. In his words, he would like someone *qualified* working the field on things like this."

"A position?" Her heart slammed.

"I understand you're due for a residency after you pass your exams. Wilson says that study time can be arranged into your schedule for the first six weeks or so, and he can have your Tufts credentials transferred to Atlanta. You can take the tests there. He'd like to meet with you next week, if that's possible."

"Where?" Now *she* was feeling dazed.

"Well, in Atlanta, of course."

"I can't afford the airfare." At least, not after buying the sheep and paying Eddie, she couldn't.

Weatherly smiled blandly. He reminded her for all the world of one of those FBI agents. "The CDC will take care of it. Just call Mr. Wilson."

"Of course," she whispered, and then he and his associates were gone.

Catherine carried the business card back to the desk. Well, she thought woodenly, you can't get more top-notch than the CDC.

So why wasn't she smiling?

She reached for the phone again, but she didn't call the number on the card. It was time to talk to Paddy, crow or no crow. The CDC could wait.

Calling Paddy was long overdue, after all.

Chapter 20

The plane taxied and its nose lifted. Catherine felt a familiar sinking sensation as she watched Atlanta fall away beneath her. She pressed closer to the window to watch the city's immense sprawl grow tiny and craved each breathless moment of ascent. It carried her closer and closer to...well, her spirit.

She thought of Paddy's clever manipulations and smiled softly. She wondered if he had been in cahoots with Uncle Ernie.

He had fully agreed with her that she had to go to Atlanta. She couldn't rush blindly into a choice this time. With Victor, she had caved in to an assault on her senses and judgment, and she had spent four years regretting it. Jericho deserved much more. This time she had had to be sure of her own heart. Because this time was forever.

Wasn't it?

He had never actually said as much. The realization that he hadn't left her panicked for a moment, but then her pulse settled. Because she knew, deep inside, that her choice would have been the same with or without him. *That* was what she'd had to find out, and she had done it.

With some none-too-subtle prods from Paddy.

The CDC had provided her with airfare, but Paddy had seen to it that she was greeted at the airport by a limo. He was dangerous with those savings of his, she thought, grinning. The limo had whisked her off to the finest hotel in Atlanta, where a bottle of very good champagne had been waiting in her room. An hour later room service had arrived with a virtual seafood feast—all her favorites. On the rare occasions when Paddy had been able to treat his girls to an evening out, Catherine had always ordered shrimps and oysters.

Now he was able to afford it on a limited basis, and he had provided her with all the wonderful things money could buy...all the things Victor had given her, only this time she knew that with a CDC salary she would soon be able to afford it on her own. It had been a very far cry from the dilapidated trailer on the Navajo reservation. The table in her room hadn't even wobbled.

And it had been a very empty and lonely experience.

She had met with Craig Wilson the next morning, and he had given her a proud tour of the facilities the CDC had to offer. The labs he had shown her were state-of-the-art, the equipment the best money could buy. Doctors and technicians had swarmed like bees around a hive, busy and productive—virtually bumping into each other.

Watching that, she had known her answer.

In the end, it hadn't had much to do with the beauty Jericho had offered her. It had had even less to do with Shadow's lecture or Paddy's machinations. It had been all that personnel, so many doctors. *Every* grad interested in epidemiology would kill to get there, would die for the offer Wilson was giving her. And nobody at all wanted to stuff bottlebrush into an alcoholic's skunk-bite wound.

In the end, it hadn't been a choice between Jericho and her career at all, and that was as it should have been. It had been a question of the goals that had taken her to med school in the first place. She had wanted to heal people, to wipe out every disease known to modern man. Lofty ambitions, certainly, but modern man was being well taken care of in Atlanta. Sooner or later she knew one of those doctors would have raised a brow at slightly mutated virion in a blood sample.

But who was going to battle Mrs. Nakai's cankerous toe?

She needed to *be* needed. And the Navajo needed a decent physician far more than the CDC did.

Catherine leaned her head back against the seat, closing her eyes, her throat tightening as she considered how painful each of *Dinetah*'s rugged sunsets would be if Jericho did not choose to share them with her after all. How would she practice in a land that shuddered with memories of him if all they really had between them was a flash of glory, like one of those sunsets that all too quickly faded away to darkness? She could transfer, she supposed. There was the Crownpoint clinic. She had never been there, and the place wouldn't ache with memories of him. Nerve-racking as it might prove to be, she knew she could only wait and see.

Finally, she dozed, as much at peace as she could hope to be. When turbulence jarred her awake somewhere over the Midwest, she looked sharply at the man sitting next to her.

It was the same man who had gotten on with her in Atlanta. He didn't speak to her. Catherine slept again.

Paddy's bounty had stretched back to Albuquerque. There was a rental car waiting for her, not behind a chain-link fence but right in the front of a line of shiny nondescript vehicles. Catherine wanted to be irritated with him for so smugly anticipating her decision, but Paddy was ... Paddy. She took the keys and headed for the Res. Not for anything would she have taken her foot off the gas in any of the washes. She would get Paddy to bring her Camaro west for her, but in the meantime she did not intend to be so stranded again. Even with her resident's salary, she doubted if she would be able to afford Eddie Begay's wages very often.

The parking area of the clinic was deserted except for Ellen's rusty Toyota. It was nearly closing time. Catherine left her car and went inside, the clump of her boots sounding unnaturally loud in the quiet.

She stood just inside the door, looking around, letting the familiarity of the place warm something inside her. Then Ellen came out from one of the exam rooms.

"Well, look what the wind blew back." If her voice wasn't exactly warm, then neither was it cutting.

"Sorry to disappoint you."

"You didn't. My money was on you turning up again."

"Sort of like a bad penny," Catherine responded dryly.

Ellen shrugged. "Even bad pennies spend."

The nurse went to the desk. A very small, very crooked artificial Christmas tree sat on its corner. A star perched on top, but other than that it was badly in need of adornment.

"I...uh...didn't think the Navajo celebrated Christmas," Catherine said finally. It was something she had fretted about on the trip here, wondering if she could perhaps take a few days off and go back to Boston, assuming Paddy's savings held out. Or maybe he would bring all the girls out soon.

"Everybody needs a Santa Claus," Ellen responded tightly.

The man of miracles. Catherine fought the urge to look over her shoulder at the mountain. She supposed it had had a few up its sleeve after all. Who knew how everything might have turned out if she hadn't given Louie those pills, if Mrs. Nakai had never mentioned those mice?

She wondered if the mountain was fresh out by now. Then her heart kicked and she thought maybe—*maybe*—it wasn't.

Ellen pulled an envelope out of the center drawer. "Jericho left this for you when we heard you were coming back."

Catherine opened it with trembling hands. His handwriting was starkly slanted, bold, filling up the notebook page without apology...even if he had written only eleven words.

I love you. I guess I never told you that either.

Tears sprang to her eyes hot and fast. She fumbled with the paper but couldn't get it back in the envelope.

"Didn't even have time to gather dust," Ellen muttered, slamming the drawer, standing again. "I'm supposed to send you to his house. Your trailer's temporarily indisposed."

Catherine gave a small, cracking laugh and surreptitiously wiped her eyes. "Don't tell me. The table collapsed through the floor."

"We had a freeze a couple of nights ago and the water pipes from the tank burst. Jack called somebody to fix them when you let him know you were going to stay here, but it'll take a few days. Navajo time, you know."

Which meant that the days would pass in a haze of sunshine and passion, and six weeks would be gone before she blinked. Catherine laughed again shakily. "I know."

"Anyway, if you go north on 666, you'll see a barrel cactus sitting all alone next to a wash about six miles from here. On the other side of the wash there's a trail heading west. It goes right up the mountain. You'll see Lance's windmill first. If he's there, stop and send him home. If he's not, keep going until the trail splits. Take the right fork."

Catherine nodded and took a single step backward, then she hesitated. "I'm sorry you got hurt," she said quietly.

Ellen met her eyes. Pain flared there briefly and Catherine felt as though she was trespassing. She had to look away.

But to her surprise, Ellen answered. "Look, there's a lot you don't know about me, and for the most part I'd like to leave it that way. But you should understand that I poured my heart into Jericho because I knew he was safe. I could never have him because he's clan. There was a certain protection in that that I needed."

She said it all as she tidied up the desk with a few heartfelt slaps and bangs, then she changed the subject bluntly and efficiently. "If he's not home, there's a key under a loose stone in the carport. Let yourself in and wait."

He was home.

Catherine turned onto the right fork and the house ap-

peared in front of her. Her hands went suddenly damp as
they clutched the wheel of her rental car and nerves fluttered in the pit of her stomach. She stopped behind the
Rover in the carport and walked around to the front, but for
a long time she only looked at the place.

She found without much surprise that it suited him perfectly, even if she also knew that it had to be the place he had
built for Anelle.

It was simple and rugged and of Anglo design, but it jutted dangerously out from the cliff face. More than that, it
seemed to grow from the mountain, an inherent part of it.
She could hear the essential generator humming someplace, but it was hidden so as not to blemish the land. The
water tank was barely visible in the dying light of the day,
tucked behind a stunted snarl of golden aspens. She had
learned that that meant there was also some groundwater
nearby.

There would be, she thought. He would have chosen a site
where the rugged land offered everything it could, and then
he had complemented it rather than assaulted it. The face of
the house was of red rock and raw weathered wood.

Her breath caught at the click of the door opening and she
looked that way again to see him silhouetted there. Behind
him, lights blazed in the twilight, beckoning, looking like
home.

Driving up here, she wondered what she would say when
she saw him again. On the flight back she had imagined a
thousand scenarios, all of them involving him thump-
thumping up the clinic steps again, taking her in his arms.
Now she knew that it hadn't happened like that because it
couldn't. She had come back, if not for him, then to him.
And so she said the only thing she could.

"I love you, too."

His smile was very slow and it made her heart leap. "No
doubt. You're here. So come on in where it's warm."

Catherine slipped past him, feeling the heat of him again,
reaching out, touching her. But suddenly her eyes were all

for the front room and the window there. It drew her and
she crossed to it and gasped.

It was huge and bayed, and Jericho's Navajo homeland
spread out below it, the distant lights of Shiprock twinkling, the shadows of the desert gathering and shifting. "So
this is where you come to sleep."

He was watching her hard. "I put the window in so she
could see the beauty. It only ended up terrifying her."

"It *is* terrifying," she whispered, placing her palm against
the glass. "It's so...*much.*"

"I wanted to give her privacy and seclusion. She felt isolation."

"I feel like God looking down on the world."

A corner of his mouth kicked up and he closed the distance between them. "Maybe a small forgotten part of it."

"Not so small, and I couldn't forget it."

She was still staring out the window. He put his hands to
her waist and turned her to face him. "Is that why you came
back, Cat Eyes?"

She traced her fingers carefully over his jawline, over the
hard, rugged lines of it, so like the land he loved. She could
tell him about the CDC later. Now there was only one thing
that was important.

"I came back because it gave me a miracle. It gave me *me,*
something I could do and feel good about, and it gave me
you in the very same place. I thought about it, and love
doesn't work when you compromise on the big things. Then
you each have to give up a piece of yourself. The giving
might be sweet, but by definition it has to leave an empti-
ness. So this was something I had to do for myself first."
She hesitated, but she saw in his eyes that that was exactly
what he'd needed to hear.

"It's not always twinkling lights and gathering shadows," he warned, pulling her closer.

"I know."

"Sometimes I look out and the horizon is cold and hard."

"And sometimes it rains."

"Not very often."

"Tell that to the old brown Ford."

She wasn't sure if he chuckled or not. His mouth came down slowly on hers and his tongue moved sinuously past her teeth, searching again. Then he made an odd sound that was half sigh, half groan.

"I'll believe it won't destroy you because I love you, and to love is to hope."

"I'll survive it because I love you and it's an integral part of you."

"Good enough."

This time his mouth came down hard over hers. For a long moment he only took her, tasting her, invading her. Then he tore himself away. "Hungry? Do you want something to eat?"

"No," she gasped, and he kissed her again.

"Tired?"

"No."

His lips gave that almost-smile. "Amorous?" he murmured finally.

"Now you're getting somewhere."

"I'd hoped so."

She caught his mouth fiercely with her own this time, savoring the dark, warm depths of him again. "For you." She sighed. "Just for you. It's so...*right*."

His arms tightened around her until she could barely breathe. Then he shifted her weight, easing her down to the floor with him without releasing her mouth. She gave a husky cry and moved against him until he covered her, the hard ridge of his flesh pressing intimately against her through their clothing, telling her better than words how much he had needed her to come back. And all the while he kept kissing her, hard and deep, relentlessly. Finally, he moved his mouth to her breasts, biting the tip of first one, then the other through the cotton of her T-shirt with shattering care.

No bra, he realized again, and this time he did chuckle, knowing that the land had touched her on some hidden level even before he had. He felt full with the sense of her, of this perfect woman he had stopped hoping to find. But he wouldn't hide her away and simply take her out at night to stroke her. He knew she would never allow that. She met his urgent hands on her body with smooth, hungry strokes of her own, pulling at his clothing, and he knew she would always be there, her temper sparking, stubbornly invading every corner of his soul, even the dark ones.

Without lifting his mouth from her breast he pushed her T-shirt up, releasing her tight nipple only at the last moment to slide the cloth up to her neck. She gave a low, broken moan as the warmth of him left her, but then his touch was back again, his hands this time, covering her, cupping the warm weight of her breasts in his palms.

She tried to hold them there with her own but they slid away anyway, pushing her jeans down, shaping her hips and her thighs with a caress that was no more gentle than the man. Catherine didn't object. When his fingers slid up between her legs, she opened for him with a gasp of hungry pleasure.

His fingertips slid through her soft tangle of firelit hair until she wept his name, begging for more. "This," he said quietly, "is how I remembered you most when you were gone, Cat Eyes. Naked and warm and wet, wanting me enough to shudder, all those times before I even succumbed to insanity and touched you."

His finger penetrated the waiting heat of her body hard and suddenly. He moved into her again and again, watching the gathering tension transform her face until the moment it began exploding within her. As her back arched and her hands clawed for him, trying to pull him closer, he wrestled fast out of his own jeans and plunged himself into her.

Her eyes flew open again in shock, but then her vision was filled with his own fathomless black eyes, penetrating her as deeply as his body. And impossibly she felt something quivering inside her again, coiling with each of his thrusts, winding tighter and tighter. The deep intimacy of his gaze stayed with her as her breath escaped her again on a shattered groan. She felt him stiffen as well, until he cried out hoarsely and eased weakly down on top of her.

His breath was warm and damp against her neck when he finally spoke. "A man could get used to this on an hourly basis."

He rolled over and she went halfway with him, bracing her head on her hand. He hooked an arm beneath her waist to rest his palm against the small of her back.

"Hourly?" she mused. "I think the Service might have a thing or two to say about that."

"No doubt." He yawned. "At least you won't have *Tah honeesgai* to contend with anymore."

She looked down at him curiously. "So you're finally conceding that it was organic?"

"No."

"*No?* What about the mice?"

"I'll go to my grave convinced that Becenti guy from Two Gray Hills blew some kind of corpse poison into them. They scurried out from that clan's country, all over *Dinetah....* Anyway, he's gone now. He packed up the day after you left for Atlanta. I guess he knew when he was beaten. You proved too much for him, Cat Eyes."

Catherine remembered the absurd thought she'd had when she'd been bending over her ravaged textbooks. She thought about mice that were shrewd enough and intelligent enough to fight back. And she thought about Richard Moss. She supposed it was entirely possible that he had read up on Navajo culture when he'd come out here to stalk her. He had certainly learned enough about medicine to successfully masquerade as a doctor. He *could* have known the native significance of that owl...but he couldn't have turned himself into a possum.

In spite of herself, she shuddered.

"Mmm, not quite yet," Jericho drawled.

She frowned at him, then she understood. "What happened to hourly?"

"It's only been sixteen minutes. And now *I'm* tired. I need the other forty-four." He looked at her more closely.

"It's been hell with you gone, Cat Eyes. It was hell staying away before you left. I wondered what was going to bring me back to myself this time, and I was pretty sure there was nothing that could. I wondered if I'd have to go after you."

Her heart skipped. "Would you have?"

"And dragged you back by the hair?" He looked out the window at the stars that were beginning to gather. "I don't know, Cat Eyes. I honestly don't know. It was the one thing I swore I'd never do again, but you could have driven me to it. And then I would have lived in terror all the rest of my days, that it was going to turn out the same."

"I'm stronger than that," she murmured.

"I know," he said simply. "You didn't force me to make the choice."

He caught a strand of her hair, tugging on it. There was a good inch of dark fire at the roots now. And he would be there to see the rest of it. Unless...

"Now's a fine time to mention it, but we haven't been using any sort of... protection. Have we?"

Catherine flushed. "Well, there's the pope..."

"How does he feel about Navajo kids?"

"You'd have to ask Paddy. He seems to have his doctrines down pretty well, even if he doesn't always abide by them."

Jericho's eyes narrowed. "You say that like I'll have the chance."

"I'm thinking of inviting them to come out for Christmas."

"Them? Your sisters too? In two weeks?"

"Sisters and nieces. There are twelve of them now. And yes, in two weeks." She grinned, then sobered. "Paddy and the pope don't matter, you know. You're asking the wrong person."

Something hard crossed his face again, something wary. "Okay," he said slowly. "So how do *you* feel about Navajo kids?"

"Do Navajo laws of excess apply to the Irish? How many can I have?"

His eyes cleared slowly. He reached to cup her face in his hard hands. "I love you, Cat Eyes. Will you marry me?"

She shuddered again and his arms tightened around her. "You let me go, so I came back," she whispered. "Now just try getting rid of me."

* * * * *

Get Ready to be Swept Away by
Silhouette's Spring Collection

Abduction *&* Seduction

These passion-filled stories explore both the dangerous
desires of men and the seductive powers of women.
Written by three of our most celebrated authors, they are
sure to capture your hearts.

Diana Palmer
Brings us a spin-off of her Long, Tall Texans series

Joan Johnston
Crafts a beguiling Western romance

Rebecca Brandewyne
New York Times bestselling author
makes a smashing contemporary debut

Available in March at your favorite retail outlet.

MILLION DOLLAR SWEEPSTAKES (III)

No purchase necessary. To enter, follow the directions published. Method of entry may vary. For eligibility, entries must be received no later than March 31, 1996. No liability is assumed for printing errors, lost, late or misdirected entries. Odds of winning are determined by the number of eligible entries distributed and received. Prizewinners will be determined no later than June 30, 1996.

Sweepstakes open to residents of the U.S. (except Puerto Rico), Canada, Europe and Taiwan who are 18 years of age or older. All applicable laws and regulations apply. Sweepstakes offer void wherever prohibited by law. Values of all prizes are in U.S. currency. This sweepstakes is presented by Torstar Corp., its subsidiaries and affiliates, in conjunction with book, merchandise and/or product offerings. For a copy of the Official Rules governing this sweepstakes offer, send a self-addressed, stamped envelope (WA residents need not affix return postage) to: MILLION DOLLAR SWEEPSTAKES (III) Rules, P.O. Box 4573, Blair, NE 68009, USA.

SWP-S395

HEARTBREAKERS

Hot on the heels of **American Heroes** comes
Silhouette Intimate Moments' latest and greatest
lineup of men: **Heartbreakers.** They know who
they are—and *who* they want. And they're out to
steal your heart.

RITA award-winning author Emilie Richards kicks off
the series in March 1995 with *Duncan's Lady,* IM #625.
Duncan Sinclair believed in hard facts, cold reality
and his daughter's love. Then sprightly Mara MacTavish
challenged his beliefs—and hardened heart—with
her magical allure.

In April *New York Times* bestseller Nora Roberts
sends hell-raiser Rafe MacKade home in
The Return of Rafe MacKade, IM #631. Rafe had
always gotten what he wanted—until Regan Bishop
came to town. She resisted his rugged charm and
seething sensuality, but it was only a matter of time....

Don't miss these first two **Heartbreakers,** from two
stellar authors, found only in—

INTIMATE MOMENTS®
Silhouette®

Patricia Coughlin

Graces the ROMANTIC TRADITIONS lineup
in April 1995 with *Love in the First Degree*,
IM #632, her sexy spin on the "wrongly
convicted" plot line.

Luke Cabrio needed a lawyer, but high-
powered attorney Claire Mackenzie was the
last person he wanted representing him. For
Claire alone was able to raise his pulse while
lowering his defenses...and discovering the
truth behind a vicious murder.

ROMANTIC TRADITIONS: *Classic tales, freshly
told. Let them touch your heart with the
power of love, only in—*

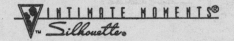